Give to local when withdrawn

D1588557

1960

Z 9757

THE NIGHT RIDERS

Novels by
NIGEL TRANTER

MAMMON'S DAUGHTER
HARSH HERITAGE
TRESPASS
EAGLE'S FEATHERS
WATERSHED
THE GILDED FLEECE
DELAYED ACTION
TINKER'S PRIDE
MAN'S ESTATE
FLIGHT OF DUTCHMEN
ISLAND TWILIGHT
ROOT AND BRANCH
COLOURS FLYING
THE CHOSEN COURSE
FAIR GAME
THE FREEBOOTERS
TIDEWRACK
FAST AND LOOSE
BRIDAL PATH
CHEVIOT CHASE
DUCKS AND DRAKES
THE QUEEN'S GRACE
RUM WEEK
THE NIGHT RIDERS

THE
NIGHT RIDERS

by

NIGEL TRANTER

LOCAL COLLECTION

WARD, LOCK & CO., LIMITED
LONDON AND MELBOURNE

First published 1954

MADE IN ENGLAND

Printed in Great Britain by
Wyman & Sons, Ltd., London, Fakenham and Reading

AUTHOR'S NOTE

In *Cheviot Chase* I got away with a lot, almost with murder. Thus encouraged, I plunge still deeper. What my good friends the Provosts, Mayors, Magistrates, and other blameless officials of the Border counties will think of this, I dare not consider. Safe only to say that none of them are likely to take me too seriously; their reputations are safe. No individual is pilloried herein, and the activities of my shameless characters, even when masquerading momentarily in the most respectable of offices, obviously would be quite unthinkable as coming from their true and responsible occupants. Though whether or not I shall ever dare set foot in Jedburgh or Hawick again, remains to be seen.

This is Fiction, with a capital F. And yet, and yet . . . there is a moral somewhere, I feel. Unrepentant and unblushing yet, I assert that it might be an excellent thing for all concerned if the good English Border communities would saddle-up and emulate and meet their Scottish counterparts at the annual Common Riding festivals.

Aberlady, 1954   NIGEL TRANTER

plantation there, sharp and black in all that verdancy, gave scale and perspective to a far-flung panorama under great skies—the East and Middle Marches of the Scottish Border, Rulewater, Jedwater, Kalewater, Teviotdale, Tweeddale, the Merse, lovely, legendary, bloodstained, where the cloud-shadows sped and a myriad waters sparkled in the sun. But not only waters sparkled and shadows sped; down there, over that first green ridge a mile away, horsemen had appeared, many horsemen, a great strung-out cavalcade, in ones and twos and groups and clusters, hundreds strong, lifting out of the farther valley, harness and stirrup-irons flashing like mirrors as they galloped, flat-out, headlong, into the afternoon sun. A colourful vital picture they made as they streamed southwards, upwards, for Carter Bar, for Redeswire, the Borderline, and the waiting company.

The buzz of excited comment and remark rose over that high thronged hillside, where Scotland sloped to one side and England to the other. Dead on time, they were. Joe Hastie was doing fine as Herald—did they see his red coat? How many empty saddles could they count? Wasn't that the lassie Douglas, her that had been Dacre, well up front? Looked like her piebald. Good riding for a lassie—and English at that . . .

The Convener turned to his left, to the group of prominent guests, County dignitaries, Provosts and representatives of neighbouring burghs, local lairds. "They'll be here in four minutes, gentlemen," he said. He glanced at his watch—unnecessarily, since he had been consulting it regularly all afternoon. "I calculate the Callant will be here exactly forty-five seconds before time. Not too bad for an eleven-miles ride over rough country!" This time pride was more than hinted.

A murmur of agreement and admiration rose from his hearers—as well it might. The distinguished General who was to make the Oration had a final and surreptitious glance at his notes. Was the confounded date 1575 or 1565 . . .?

The tension of the crowd mounted. All but the stragglers of the cavalcade had now disappeared down into the hidden

8

valley immediately in front, and in place of sight, sound came to thrill the waiting throng. Already many of the children, and not only the children, were down on their knees with their ears to the shaggy turf. To those upright it was barely a sound, as yet—a quivering rather, a pulsation that filled the air, a tingling that rose up through the soles of the feet. Then, quite suddenly, all could hear it, the hollow drumming of hundreds of hooves, the approaching thunder of a galloping host.

The crowd, brought there by car and bus and bicycle though it had been, responded notably, inevitably, to that sound. For moments, practically every man and woman and child was the more aware, more alive, more his or her essential self. Grown men swallowed constrictions in their throats, and women shivered even as they smiled. The folk of the Border Marches had had a long education in the significance of that sound.

Three riders came into view over the steep breast of the hill, cantering now, their mounts steaming and foam-spattered—the guides, the forerunners, who had opened gates, cleared stock out of the way, blazed the trail. They gained their own private cheer as they came up, and had earned it. In the middle, Robin Laing of Kersheugh waved a great hand, and jerked his bare head backwards.

"They just about had the tails off us!" he cried.

It was true. The forerunners were all but overrun. Already a single horseman had appeared in their wake, coming up in tremendous style, his tall black at full stretch with neck out-thrust and nostrils flaring. At sight of him, the crowd's voice rose in sheerest acclaim. It was the Callant, Jethart's Callant himself—Archie Scott!

It was right and proper that none should come in *before* the Callant, of course—but it was not often that the Callant so obviously and undeniably led the field himself. Jedburgh's standard-bearer had to be chosen for more than mere dash and horsemanship. As it was, his Right- and Left-hand Men, previously Callants, were a good two hundred yards behind, flogging their beasts to keep at that,

9

of Cosmos Pictures. Mr. Corson is from Hollywood, of course, but he's a Jethart man by birth. He left Jedburgh at six—wasn't it, Mr. Corson?—and this is his first time back to the Borders. Mr. Corson wants to make a film of all this . . ." and the Convener waved an all-embracing hand.

"Now, wait a bit," the American amended, carefully. "Sure, there's nothing I'd like better than to make a picture around here. But that's not to say I got *material* to make one, see. No, sir. You need a lotta material to make a motion-picture—a Cosmos picture, leastways. But I'm glad to know you, Mr. Scott. I reckon *you'd* go into a picture without a lotta trouble!"

"You do, sir? Do I take that as a compliment or not, I wonder?" Archie asked.

"I'd place you as a bit of an actor, sir—that's all," Mr. Corson said dryly. "Amongst most folks I meet up with, that'd be reckoned a compliment, I guess."

"M'mmm," the Callant said, and ran a hand along the jutting line of a long jaw. "I see. A bit of an actor . . .! So now we know!" There had been no trace of a smile there, but suddenly the fleering grin was back again. "Maybe you're right. Maybe I'll hold you to that, one of these days . . ."

The Convener coughed. "The Provost," he said. "The Provost of Jedburgh"—and he turned as a sturdy genial man in bowler and hacking-jacket trotted up on as sturdy a cob. "Jethart's here now, at any rate."

"Y'know, I don't think I just like the sound of that, Davie!" the Provost protested. "I'm not the last, anyway —there was a lassie behind me a couple of miles back . . . And hasn't somebody to see that the stragglers don't get lost? Well, gentlemen—I hope you haven't caught the cold up here, waiting for us . . .?"

"My beer . . ." Archie Scott mentioned, to no one in particular, and pushed his way on, through the throng.

★   ★   ★

12

Someone was keeping pace with him, at his elbow. He turned, to find a young woman, bare-headed, but workman-like in a black suit, with a pencil and open notebook in her hands.

"Mr. . . . Scott, isn't it?" she said. "Could you spare me a word. *Daily News*, Glasgow. I'd like . . ."

"Sorry. No words to spare. Not even to the *News*, ma'am. Nothing to say, anyway!" He sounded entirely decided. But, because she was a woman, and good-looking, he smiled. "I'm on important business. You see that hamper . . .?"

Because she was a woman and good-looking, she traded on his smile. "You owe me a few words at least, Mr. Scott. After all, you've barely finished covering me with mud and ruining my complexion! Look . . .!" And leaning forward and upward, she not so much exhibited as paraded her comeliness under his very nose—a shameful and un-scrupulous performance. Thus unfairly constrained, the man suffered a fatal hesitation. He saw precious little that was ruined, by mud or anything else, but plenty that would be ruinous to any man's integrity—a blue-eyed, ashen-haired, scarlet-mouthed, warm-complexioned charmer, about his own age, fair as he was dark, and wickedly assured. He saw, perceived the pit—and notwithstanding, fell therein inevitably, even smirking.

"Maybe I owe you *something*," he conceded. "A drink, for instance. D'you like beer, by any chance—out of a bottle?"

"For lack of anything better—yes," she nodded. "We can talk as we drink."

"We can drink," the man amended, but not hopefully. And side by side they made their way to the hampers.

"You had a good ride, Mr. Scott?" she asked, as they waited for their beer.

"Yes."

"It would be a stiff course?"

"No stiffer than usual."

"It was a big turn-out. Better than last year?"

13

"I dare say."

"The riders, I gather, are not all from Jedburgh? There are representatives from all along the Border?"

"That's so." Archie handed her her drink. "Look, Miss—the *Daily News* does not usually concern itself with our humble doings. You didn't come all the way from Glasgow to hear such as myself answer questions like that. Whatever you're here for, I suggest you've come to the wrong man."

She looked him up and down, a telling glance. "You scarcely sound as gallant as you seem, Mr. Scott!" she said.

He took her at her own measure. "It is too crowded, for that!" he asserted, that fleering eyebrow still farther upraised.

The young woman dropped her eyes—but that might have been deliberate, too. She permitted herself a flicker of a smile, anyway, when the other stooped to clink the neck of his bottle against the tumbler that somebody had found for her.

"Cheer up, Glasgow," he said. "Here's *more* mud in your eye!"

Perhaps it was the drink that did it, for of a sudden she was all disarming frankness. "The fact of the matter is that my editor is interested in the question of Cosmos Pictures making a film in this country," she revealed. "It's an open secret that Mr. Corson's looking about for a subject and a location. Cosmos Pictures, as I expect you know, have a controlling interest in our British-Plaza cinema chain. They can't take all their profits from that out of the country, so every now and then they have to plough some of it back into the business by making a film over here. They do things in a big way, once they start—make a big impact on the district they choose. So I'm detailed to keep an eye on Mr. Corson."

"I see." Archie nodded. "And why is the *News* so interested?"

"We like to be first with a story—that's all."

14

The man looked sceptically from his bottle to the girl, and back again. "Is that a fact?" he said.

"Yes." She did not appear to notice his disbelief. "Do you think Mr. Corson is going to make a film about all this, Mr. Scott?" And she made a wide gesture with her arm.

"I've no idea. Why don't you ask him?"

"Mr. Corson is not very forthcoming to the Press," she admitted. "Didn't he say to you something about *you* getting a part in a picture . . .?"

"I'm afraid that was not just what he meant, ma'am! No—I'm afraid not."

"I wish you wouldn't keep referring to me as ma'am—as though I was my grandmother's Sunday-school teacher!" the girl exclaimed. "The name's Hepburn—Barbara Hepburn. Didn't he say something about you——"

She was interrupted by a high flourish of the Herald's horn.

"That'll be the Provost going to speak. I'll have to get over," the man said. He gulped down the last of his beer, considering her from under his bottle. "Hepburn, eh? I never yet heard of a Hepburn doing any good to the Borders!" he declared, wiping his lips. "Afraid I've got to go."

Frowning a little, she watched him stalk long-strided over towards the official party.

Beside the great weatherworn block of red sandstone the Provost of Jedburgh was speaking into a microphone. He was saying that it had been a grand ride-out, if a wee thing hasty for douce and sober citizens. He doubted if even his famous predecessor of four hundred years ago had made as good time of it, even with the spur of a real free-for-all at the end of it to urge them on. He was afraid that they had nothing as exciting as that to come for, today—but at least they would have the pleasure and honour of listening to that gallant soldier of these days, General Sir Aylmer Campbell, who would now address them on the significance of the Redeswire Ride.

The General was no orator, but what he had to say to

15

them, though an old story, soon had the great company listening attentively, next to tensely. Speaking in brief staccato sentences, he took them back to that summer's day in 1575, with Scotland's Queen Mary in an English jail and the unscrupulous Regent Morton ruling in the name of the boy King Jamie Sixth. On such a day, each year, a truce was called to the bitter and incessant strife that seared the Border, and the Wardens of the Marches, English and Scots, met in at least a semblance of peace, their companies only armed in token, to discuss outstanding grievances, adjust causes, and arrange the exchange of hostages. On this occasion, the meeting was here at Redeswire where the Borderline crossed the high watershed of the Rede at fourteen hundred feet. Here came Sir John Carmichael of Fenton Tower, the Scots Warden of the Middle March, and Sir John Forster, Governor of the English castle of Bamburgh, with their retinues. Wary greetings were exchanged and discussions began. Merchants actually set up their booths, pedlars hawked their wares, and with these grassy slopes beginning to resemble a fairground, men relaxed for once— on the Scots side, at any rate. All went well enough until the English failed to produce a notorious freebooter, whose guilt had been indicted on the one side and accepted on the other. He could not be found, said Forster—he had fled. But the matter was of small import. The Scots Warden thought otherwise, and exhorted his opposite number to play fair. The proud Englishman, gorge rising, snapped that Carmichael should speak thus only to his equals. In a moment or two, the cheerful bustle of the scene was quelled. Smiles faded. A Scot, glimpsing stealthy movement at the back of the Southron assembly, loosed the cry of treachery. But too late. A shower of arrows soared, to fall amongst the Scots, and to the slogan of "To it, Tynedale!" the English charged. Sir John Carmichael was one of the first to go down. Unprepared, outnumbered, and in confusion, the Scots were pressed back, fighting fiercely, desperately. But hopelessly; there could be but one end to the unequal struggle. And would have been, had not a party of Jedburgh

16

men, led by their Provost and coming late to the tryst, perceived the onset from down on yonder hillock, and spurred to the aid of their fellows. They were only a relatively small company, but, as today the cavalcade had appeared in ones and twos up over the swell of the hillside, so then; there was no knowing how many the valley concealed. To the ringing cry of "Jethart's here!" the Provost and his gallant townsmen had galloped into the fray, swords swinging. And the tide turned. Fearing large-scale reinforcements, and possibly with bad consciences the English turned and forsook the field, leaving many slain, and Forster and numerous men of rank prisoners in the Scots' hands. So ended the Raid of the Redeswire, one of the last battles to be fought on the Border.

The General paused, and once again the lonely wheepling of the curlews prevailed. That was history, he said at length, dead and gone . . . and better forgotten, some might say. But was that so? Forget the rancour and the bitterness, yes—but not the gallantry, the love of freedom, the sturdy independence of their forefathers. Each year they celebrated the occasion when Jedburgh saved the day for Scotland, during the Callant's Festival. Why? What message had that ancient struggle for them today? A fine, a notable message, Sir Aylmer asserted. It kept alight the flame of local patriotism—surely a very worthwhile thing in these couldn't-care-less days. It encouraged independence of spirit, pride in their past and determination for the future. It encouraged Jedburgh, though small, to consider itself no mean city—just as their own traditions, founded on many not dissimilar pages of history, encouraged, perhaps wrongly, other Border burghs—Hawick, Kelso, Selkirk, Galashiels and the rest—to an almost equal sense of their own worth, and therefore a healthy rivalry . . .

The General had to stop here, tugging his moustache in simulated surprise, while the laughter resounded—good laughter, and necessary, as elbows were dug in the ribs of the Hawick Cornet, the Selkirk Standard-bearer, the Gala Braw Lad and so on, with their sundry supporters.

And so, General Campbell concluded, he was all for this Redeswire Day and all similar occasions. The more the merrier. They made a splash of colour in a drab world. They brought out the individuality in men—individuality that our present mass-production age was trying so successfully to iron out. They were the answer to dull uniformity— even though he was a dull soldier that said it! He just wished that many more towns would take a bit more interest in their history and traditions—and thereby save their souls. Jethart's here! Up, Jedburgh!

Loud and long came the applause—as much for the sentiments as for the speaker. It was a while before the Provost could get in his request for three cheers for the General.

John W. Corson had listened keenly to the oration and the reactions. The Convener had not failed to note the fact, and was gratified. Now, the American nodded. "Uh-huh. Very nice," he said.

"The historical background," the Convener mentioned. "More material, eh? What you needed?"

"Look." The other turned on him, crisply. "That's not material. Background, yes—like you said. But background's not material, see—not for a motion-picture. You gotta have drama, a conflict of wills—a clash. All this is very nice, sure—but no clash, no drama. Where's the English?" That last was snapped out.

"Eh . . .?"

"Where are the English, man? There were two sides to this Redeswire Raid, weren't there? This is only half a story, as I see it. Where's the other side?"

The Convener shrugged. "There'll be English folk in the crowd, I've no doubt. There's always invitations go out to one or two on that side . . ."

"That's not what I'm aiming at. You got your Provost and your Callant and your riders from along the Scotch side. They represent this Carmichael, and the Jedburgh outfit. But what about this other guy, Forster, and all his folks? If there was a big bunch of riders coming up from the other

18

side, to meet you here, with their big-shots and so on—then you've got something like it. Shaking hands, see. Old scores settled up. Tomahawks buried. Symbolic. There's a story in that. It would mean something. This means . . . well, I guess it means you got long memories, that's all."

"M'mmm. Well . . ." The Convener, not unnaturally, looked somewhat crestfallen. "I see what you mean, of course. But . . . well, we can hardly help it if the English don't see fit to join in! Oh, Provost—Mr. Corson is just a little bit disappointed with our celebration. He feels, I think, that it was just slightly inadequate."

All around those near enough to hear were listening intently, not to say askance. Miss Hepburn was writing rapidly in her notebook.

"I'm sorry to hear that, Mr. Corson," Jedburgh's Provost began, when the film magnate stopped him.

"Now, don't get me wrong, Mr. Provost," he declared, with upraised hand. "I'm saying nothing against your celebration. Nossir. It's mighty a fine show, I reckon. Very nice. It sure makes me proud of being born in Jedburgh, and I'm grateful to you for bringing me here today. But that's not to say there's a motion-picture in it. It's one-sided, see. This is the Scotch giving themselves a cheer—but where's the English? A story's gotta have two sides, an ending as well as a beginning. Right now, there isn't the germ of a motion-picture in this—just the trimmings. That's all I said."

Into the local silence in which this statement was digested, it was the young woman's voice that spoke, clear and explicit. "Then Cosmos Pictures is not likely to make a film on this march-riding theme, Mr. Corson?"

"That is so. And I'd remind you folks that nobody ever said it *was* likely. The idea was put to me, and I came along. Nothing I'd have liked better, of course, than to make a picture around my old home town. But..." He shrugged.

"But you *would* have considered making a film if the English had been represented?" That was Archie Scott.

19

"I might, young man—I might."

"But what's the difficulty, then, sir?" the Callant went on. "It would be the easiest thing in the world to arrange, for the purposes of the film, for a party to ride up from the English side there, to meet our cavalcade here. Nothing simpler."

"Sure. But it would be phoney."

"Yes—but what does that matter . . . for a picture?"

"Plenty—if it's a Cosmos picture, made by John W.! Look, gentlemen—the whole idea about making a picture around all this would have to be that it was genuine. The real thing. I'm not looking for some ordinary feature show, some slick studio piece, nor yet some star-spangled epic production. I got plenty. Nossir. What I'm looking for in Scotland is some genuine piece of tradition, straight outa life, see. Living history. Something we run kinda short of back home in the States. Something I can make into a forty-minute—one of a series we're running. They all gotta be one hundred per cent the real McCoy—or ninety-nine per cent, anyhow. I'm sure not making one on my calf-country a phoney!"

That seemed to be final.

General Campbell cleared a military throat. "H'rr'mm. Quite right too, sir!" he said. "No faking. If the English don't want to commemorate the Raid of the Redeswire, I don't know that I altogether blame them! Anyway, all this is much too good to start messing it up for the sake of any celluloid raree-show."

If there was a murmur of agreement with these sentiments, it was not a loud one. Obviously there were very mixed feelings on the subject, and a deal of disappointment.

Big Joe Hastie, the Herald, had pushed his way through to the Provost and the Convener, and was waving his watch at them both. The Provost nodded, and raised his voice.

"This is all very interesting, gentlemen—but it's time we were on our way. We have to run this programme as near

20

to the minute as we can. Will those who are not riding kindly get back to their cars, and drive down to Riccalton, for the Races. The cavalcade will proceed by Arks Edge, Fawhope, and Browndean Laws. We'll meet again at the farm of Riccalton in approximately forty-five minutes."

The company broke up. Archie Scott, recovering his horse from its youthful and admiring escort, mounted, and sidled over to where the Provost was climbing just a little less agilely into the saddle.

"A pity, that, Archie," the older man said, sighing. "I had real hopes. Man, Jethart could have done with that film. It would have set us up, just fine. Brought tourists to the town from all over the world. Just what we need."

"You thought it was in the bag, eh, Provost?"

"Well, I must admit I did—after last night. I put in some good hard work on the man—and a dram or two, forbye! After the way he was talking . . . and this being his birthplace . . ."

"Maybe it was just the drams that were talking, Provost?" Archie Scott half-turned, to find the young woman journalist still there, watching them thoughtfully. He raised that eyebrow at her. "Satisfied, Miss Hepburn?" he asked.

"Satisfied . . .? What do you mean, Mr. Scott?"

"Just that I imagine you'll be quite pleased—and your editor with you—that the film doesn't look like coming to the Borders."

"I . . . I don't know what makes you say that . . ."

"No? Just put it down to me being a bit of a newspaper-man myself . . . though on nothing so magnificent as the Glasgow *Daily News*, of course . . . and with different axes to grind!" He adjusted his stock, and tipped his blue bonnet with a single finger. "See you at the races, ma'am . . . or shall I? I think not." And bowing mockingly, he pulled his fretting beast's head around.

A little mystified, the Provost raised his bowler, and

21

turned to follow the Callant towards the head of the great waiting cavalcade of riders. Biting a red lip, the girl watched them go.

The Herald's horn blew, and in a few minutes that high moorland had returned to the green solitude that it enjoyed for three-hundred-and-sixty-four days of the year.

2

The races had been won and lost, the dash to Oxnam made, with its brief breather and stirrup-cup hospitality; back in Jedburgh once again badges had been presented by the Provost's lady to those riders who had completed the gruelling course for the first time, and now, pleasantly relaxed, many of the day's principals leaned and lounged and sprawled in the big comfortable smoke-room of the Ker Arms Hotel, stocks loosened, waistcoats unbuttoned, glasses and tumblers charged. The atmosphere was agreeably thick with the compound scents of man, horse, leather, spirituous liquors, and tobacco smoke, and an aura of easy masculinity prevailed. Now and then men belched gently in a decent appreciation of a dinner worthy of the day.

By mutual but unspoken agreement the unfortunate subject of the film had been allowed to lie. Desultory mention had been made of it, of course—but it had been accepted that it would be a pity to spoil the proper ending to a proper day by any emphasis of what undoubtedly had been a grievous disappointment to many of those present. And not only Jedburgh men; all the Scots Border was involved in this, in some measure, for though rivals, the Border burghs were closely linked and all were deeply concerned to increase the tourist trade as a counter-balance to their too great dependence on the fluctuating textile industry. But John W. Corson had departed long since for Edinburgh in his great Cadillac, and now the Provost of Hawick and others were glancing at their watches. Archie Scott, who was not noted as a comfortable man, at all, spoke up.

"Are we going to accept what was said today as the final

23

word on this film business?" he demanded, in a momentary hush, of the room at large. Deliberately, he looked round them all, over his tumbler. "I think it's a pretty poor show."

There was something almost like a sigh, a clinking as spurred boots were shuffled, and a murmur of agreement.

"You're damned right, Archie," a young voice asserted.

"It sounded pretty final, up at Redeswire, Archie," the Jedburgh Provost pointed out. "The man knows what he wants. The pity is that we just haven't got it to give to him."

"Aye, the pity of it!" The Provost of Hawick, largest of the Border towns, a big man, like a gentle lion with a twinkling eye, shook his head. "If only your Mr. Corson had had the sense to be born say a dozen miles to the west, now. In a place like Hawick, for instance. Man, we could have given him something worth making a film about! Nae bother at all . . ."

That was the right line. Chuckles greeted it. The old easy familiar badinage and banter was more like it, tonight, after a hard day in the saddle and a good meal. Charge and counter-charge were tossed about the low-ceilinged room. The Kelso Laddie poured the slops of his drink into the Hawick Cornet's glass.

"Drink to the saga in glorious technicolour—*Under Two Flags*, or . . . or *A Banner with a Stained Device!*" he cried.

Archie Scott laughed with the rest, but briefly. And he was no sobersides. "The situation is black—but not so desperately black as all that!" he claimed. His voice changed, deepened. "For my part, I think we should accept Corson's challenge!"

"Challenge . . .?" the Jedburgh Provost echoed. "Did he make a challenge, then?"

"I think he did. I think he was right in making it, too. He said that this show of ours was very nice. But it was only half a story—one-sided. He said it only meant that we'd got long memories, on the Border. Maybe he's right, gentlemen."

He had their attention now. Every eye was on him. No one spoke.

24

"Corson asked, where were the English," the Callant went on. "I say that we should take that as a challenge. Not only in connection with this film idea, but to the whole validity of our celebration. He said we were just giving ourselves a cheer. It seems to me that our American friend's got something there. It was maybe a bit hard-hitting—but if our show was to have its fullest meaning, the English *would* be there to shake hands with us at the Redeswire Stone. And at other Common Ridings, too. Then we'd really be getting somewhere. And if they won't come themselves . . . then I'd say it's up to us to go and fetch them!"

"Fetch them . . .?"

"How?"

"What d'you mean, Archie—fetch them?"

"Whae wants to fetch the bluidy English, onywey? . . ."

"*We* do. Look—if we were to ask the Northumbrian towns, our opposite numbers on the other side of the Cheviots, to send parties. Ask them officially—not just individuals, but as burghs, municipalities—to send mounted representatives. Point out the historical significance, and all that. Places like Wooler, and Rothbury, and Corbridge, and Hexham. Even Morpeth. Some of them might play. After all, it was their history, just as much as ours—*their* ancestors we fought with."

"We tried something like that, at Coldstream. To meet at Flodden Field, on the anniversary of the battle," the Coldstreamer pointed out. "It's difficult, because they're not organised for this sort of thing on the English side, like we are."

"That's just it," Hawick's Provost put in. "They don't seem to go in for Common Ridings and March-trooping and Border festivals over there. I've often wondered why. They've got precisely the same sort of background as we have. The Border warfare was as much theirs as ours. I expect they suffered just as much at our hands as we did at theirs. It seems strange . . ."

"It's just because they're the poor damned English . . .!"

25

"Och, there's decent enough folk amongst them, Wattie . . ."

"They *ought* to be celebrating their history, same as we do," Archie contended.

"So's Jethart can get a film made, to boost its tourist trade . . .!"

"Not at all. At least, not only that. For their self-respect's sake. Do them a lot of good. Stir folk up. Bring people around. Look at the good it does us—all of us. There isn't a single Scots Border burgh doesn't run a Border festival of some sort, is there? And it's always the high spot of the year. Damn it—we'd be giving these places a new lease of life!"

"I've said the same myself, more than once," Hawick's chief magistrate agreed. "I suggested something of the sort to our friends at Hexham. But it didn't seem to cotton on . . ."

"Och, they're half-dead, over there!" his Cornet, Dand Fairgrieve snorted.

"No, Dand—I wouldn't just say that. It's just that they look at things differently from us, somehow."

"They could do with a waking up, anyway," Archie Scott insisted. "And now's the time."

"But we can't just impose Common Ridings on these places, man," the Jedburgh Provost objected. "And even if we could, it would be years before they got really going, into their stride. It's *now* that we want this film. . . ."

"Not exactly now, Provost. I had a word with Mr. Corson, just before dinner, and he said that he was not likely to make his final decision as to where his film was to take place for a month or two, and anyway, the actual work on it—shooting, he called it—wouldn't start until next spring or early summer, at the earliest. They need strong sunlight for outdoor photography, and they'd have to bring technicians over from Hollywood. So it's next year's Festival that would be involved. That gives us some time."

"Yes . . . but even then . . . "

"I know. I know. We couldn't get anything very

26

permanent fixed up by then," Archie conceded. "But even if we could get agreement in principle that some sort of annual ceremonies should be held, and a promise to send mounted parties to the next Redeswire Day, then that surely would be enough for Corson. That wouldn't be phoney. In fact, I believe he'd be greatly bucked, to think he'd brought this about. The sort of thing that would go down well, back in the States. 'Cosmos Pictures chief brings about Border reconciliation, after four hundred years!' That sort of thing. Gets him personally involved. Wouldn't that line be apt to predispose him strongly to make this film?"

"By Gemini—I do believe he's got something there, Charlie!" the Hawick Provost cried, slapping his knee. "There's possibilities in this—for all of us, not only Jethart. Maybe this is just the lever we want to get something started over there. After all, this film presumably would do the Northumbrians a bit of good, too. It's a bait, anyway. . . ."

"I'm inclined to agree, you know," the Festival Convener said, a fine-featured thoughtful man, who was also Jedburgh's Dean of Guild. "My reading of Mr. Corson's character is that such a thing, even the attempt, would have a big effect on him. I'd say it's worth a trial."

"Hear, hear!"

"Have a go! Why not?"

"Well, we might write a letter or two——" the Provost of Jedburgh began—to be interrupted, not very courteously, by his Callant.

"Letter, my foot!" Archie exclaimed. "What we want is a delegation, an embassy, a demonstration. And in force, too. Something to make them sit up. What attention d'you think they'd pay to a letter, Provost? No— what's required is for a party of us, as representative and high-sounding as possible—Provosts, Councillors, Cornets, Callants, Marshals, the whole boiling—to make a sort of visit-in-state to three or four of the principal places, warning them we were coming, of course. All dressed up. Give them the whole treatment—shake them up into doing something."

27

"Mercy on us—we couldn't do a thing like that!" the Provost declared.

"Why not? What's to stop us? Not the Northumbrians!"

"Och, they mightn't like it. . . ."

"Damn that! Our forefathers wouldn't have let that worry them! And, anyway—why shouldn't they? We're honouring them, aren't we—going out of our way to give them a place in our celebrations? And, for that matter, maybe a little feeling aroused wouldn't be altogether a bad thing, either. We might get them moving, then."

A general clatter of tongues broke out, as men savoured the idea. And that the over-all picture had its appeal for them was obvious; it appealed to the tradition in which they all had been brought up. The opportunity to waken up the Auld Enemy, to make a demonstration over the Border, to show the flag again, was something that could not fail to stir them. Did not every song they sang strike the same note . . .?

"Archie's right, you know—it's worth a try."

"It would make a real ploy, all right . . ."

"And the newspapers would lap it up! Even if nothing came of it, we'd get a lot of good publicity for the Borders."

"Aye—trust Archie, and him a newspaperman himself! Is this a boost for the *Journal*, Archie?"

But the Callant was watching the Provost of Hawick, as the individual most likely to influence his own Provost. That man caught his eye, and nodded.

"I'd be game to have a go at this, Charlie," he said. "So long as this young man doesn't try to get me on a horse! I draw the line at that. . . ."

"Good for you, Provost!"

"Teri-bus . . .!" the ancient Hawick rallying-cry rang out.

"This would have to be a car-borne invasion, Archie . . .?"

"Both cars and horses, I'd say. All you Provosts and magnificoes would be best in cars, I think, with your robes and chains of office and so on. But the rest of us should

28

be mounted, to produce the right effect—at least for our entry into the towns. In between, we'd have to have horse-boxes behind cars, of course, for there'll be a lot of ground to cover."

"And how long would it all take?" the quiet Provost of Kelso wanted to know. "I don't see that we can afford any prolonged affair. . . ."

"Och, it shouldn't take long, unless we *make* it long, ourselves. A single Saturday should do the job," Archie declared. "A little organisation's all that's required."

"But, look . . ." somebody objected. "This is all very well—but is it going to be any use? I mean, even if some of these English burghs listen sympathetically, have they got the folk to make up these mounted parties? We've been doing this sort of thing for centuries—but over there, quite likely, they wouldn't be able to scrape together the necessary horsemen, apart from anything else."

"There speaks an ignorant Lauder loon, from the depths of the Lammermuirs!" he was mocked. "What did Lauder ever know of the English? They've got plenty of horsemen over there. It's a prosperous countryside, full of farms, and mighty keen on fox-hunting. . . ."

"They've got nine packs of hounds, in Northumberland!"

"Oh, well . . ."

Archie turned to his own Provost. "What about it, then, sir? Is it a go? Do we accept the challenge?"

That genial man shook his head—but quite failed to look in any way distressed. "You're an awful man, Archie! Heaven knows what for we voted you in as Callant this year! But . . . all right. I'm willing to consider it, at any rate. The Council will have to take the decision, of course . . ."

"Most of the Council's here."

"Aye, maybe. But I think we'd have to have a pretty good indication that Mr. Corson would be prepared to look kindly on this effort . . . to make it worth our while."

"I agree with you there, Charlie."

"All right. Will the man be back in Edinburgh yet?

29

He's been gone more than a couple of hours, hasn't he?" Archie demanded. "In that car . . . The Caledonian Hotel, didn't you say? I'll go and try to get him on the phone, now."

The young man strode from a room loud with discussion. It was still louder when he came back, after five or six minutes. He had to beat a riding-crop on a table for silence.

"That's okay," he called. "Corson's all for it. He said he was tickled pink—though I can't just imagine him! He can't just promise us the film, mind—but he said that it's a good show, and he'll certainly reconsider the matter if we're successful. I don't see that he could have said much more."

"Good work, Archie."

"No. That sounds fair enough."

"When will it be, then? When will we cross the Border?"

"It'll take a bit of organising. We want most of the Border burghs represented, if not all. It'll take a month."

"All of that, Archie."

"Can you make it in a month, Provost?"

"Well—we'll see . . ."

The Jethart Callant drew a long breath. "This calls for one last drink, I think," he said. "Blue bonnets over the Border . . . and damn the Glasgow *News*!"

"Eh . . .? What about the *News*?"

"Three times within the last week or two, the *News* has said that it's high time that there was a film made about the story of Loch Lomond! The Bonnie Banks in Song and Story—from Rob Roy to the Hydro Board! J. S. Graham, the editor, comes from Balloch. And they're running Corson in every issue. We've got strong competition, gentlemen. Loch Lomond's a trump card with the Tourist Board—and we're not!"

"Well . . . can you beat that!"

"With a little luck, I think we can."

30

3

By five minutes before noon on the first Saturday of August, the grey and hilly Market Place of Jedburgh was very much astir. Already the lines of cars and horse-boxes extended, from the Provost's car flying the tall Jethart Flag at the foot of the Town Steeple, in three directions—down the High Street, up Castlegate, and along towards the Abbey. This last column, unofficial cars and the Press, was much the longest; it was astonishing where they all had come from—and since public roads *were* public, there was no means by which they could be prevented from tailing along. The Chief Constable of the county was even now arranging for two extra police-cars for the escort. The Provost of Duns and his Reiver had already arrived, as had Lauder's Chief Magistrate and Cornet. With Jedburgh's own official party, eight-man strong, they stood around the Mercat Cross waiting, part in red robes and chains of office, part booted and spurred, while about them Pressmen circulated, a great crowd eddied, through traffic crept and sidled, and a convoy of five huge yellow charabancs from Scarborough on a tour to farthest Scotland, edged and inched, bewildered, like be-shoaled leviathans, panting and honking their protest. Jedburgh folk, of course, paid but little heed; their narrow streets and strategically-placed bridges had been a bulwark and bottleneck to more potent manifestations of the Southron flood than this.

Archie Scott, hands in breeches' pockets and alean against the tall cross, was watching with derisive eye his fellow seekers after truth endeavouring to trap his Provost into some indiscretion in the interests of their respective publics.

31

"What sort of replies have you had from the English towns, Mr. Provost?"

"Would you say that they are encouraging over there, or not?"

"Did you read the article in the *Newcastle Journal*, sir? Have you any comment to make?"

"Which towns are you actually visiting today, sir? Have any towns refused to receive you?"

The Provost cleared his throat. He had to shout to make himself heard above the hooting of horns, the revving of engines, and the general clamour. "I have had letters of acknowledgment from each of the burghs to which we wrote—except one, that is. No, we're not going to Newcastle. They were all . . . quite friendly. No—I wouldn't say any of them have committed themselves. We intend to go to Hexham first, and then by Corbridge to Morpeth. Then up to Rothbury, and possibly on to Alnwick if we've time. Yes, we'll probably come back through Wooler, on the way home . . . ."

"Have you any message for the nation, Mr. Provost?"

"Good lord—no!"

Archie grinned. His glance lifted, as he perceived a young woman inserting her way skilfully and determinedly through the throng. The grin persisted. "I wondered where the *Daily News* had got to!" he said. "How's Loch Lomond, Miss Hepburn?"

Perhaps she did not catch all that—though he had a penetrating voice, and the swift look she shot at him in the passing was not without expression. At any rate, she did not answer him, but slipped and insinuated herself to the forefront of her own colleagues, with brief but charming apologies, until she was right under the Provost's nose. There she smiled at him, at them all, entirely winsomely, and her voice took up where that of another representative's tailed away.

"I'm so glad I got you before you started, Provost," she mentioned. "I've just been on the phone to Mayor Stannard, of Hexham. It *will* be Hexham that you will

32

come to first, won't it—going by Carter Bar? He didn't sound to me at all sure as to what all this is about. In fact, I think he imagines it's some sort of nationalist demonstration! And he hopes it won't take too long—for he's due to make up a golf foursome, at three o'clock!"

To a general raising of eyebrows and hasty scratching of pencils, the Provost frowned. "Tsst-tsst," he said. "My letter was perfectly clear. I couldn't go into full details, of course —but there should have been no misunderstanding. . . ."

"Would you suggest, Provost, that this misunderstanding might arise possibly through a lack of sympathy with your aims . . .?"

"I would suggest nothing, young woman! We are going in person to see these people, just so that there shall *be* no misunderstanding as to our intentions."

"But, Provost . . ."

Just as her further words were lost in the echoing clang of the first stroke of twelve from the Town Clock in the Steeple above them, a cheering, a new braying of horns, and a commotion in the crowd down in the narrow neck of the High Street, drew all eyes. Another string of cars was surging slowly up through the press, and from the leading vehicle a flagstaff projected from which a silken standard fluttered proudly. Farther down, a second banner could be descried.

"Kelso and Coldstream, dead on time!" Archie cried. "Give them a cheer!"

The cheering, the stir, and the striking of the clock ruled out any more difficult Press questioning meantime—and the official party did not appear to grieve therefor. The Provost hurried forward to shake hands with his fellow-magistrates, and the Callant went to greet his opposite numbers from the eastern burghs. Sundry photographs were taken and pleas for ritual posing were made by the Press. The Jedburgh Town Officer, in top-hat and uniform, produced a tray with bottle and glasses for a stirrup-cup for the road, which was well received. But with the reporters gathering round again, pencils poised, Archie

N.R.—C   33

Scott jerked his head in the direction of the Chief Constable, and his Provost nodded.

"Time we were on our way," he declared. "This business has got to stick to the clock, or it could get right out of hand. Besides, I hear Mayor Stannard's got an important appointment for three o'clock! To your cars, gentlemen."

There was a prompt dispersal, the police sought to clear a way, and the crowd seethed and split. The Town Band struck up the opening bars of "Blue Bonnets Over the Border", and to its rousing refrain the cars were filled up. Into the first big black limousine flying the Jethart Flag, the Provost, the Festival Convener, a Bailie, and a Councillor climbed, Archie Scott's own more modest equipage was next, towing its horse-box, with his Right- and Left-hand Men behind with the Herald. The Chief Constable in a sleek patrol-car moved out, not without difficulty, from behind the Sheriff Court-house, to act as forerunner. An exchange of signals, and the entire procession started into motion, to the prolonged cheers of the crowd, southwards, under the magnificent ruins of the great Abbey, down to the Abbey Bridge, and on up the green valley of the Jed Water. Behind the leading cars there was some jockeying for position in the narrow streets. The Kelso group, by a bold spurt across the packed Market Place, headed off the Lauder Provosts' car by inches, and clinging nose to tail got in directly behind Jedburgh. Seeing what was happening to Lauder, Duns manoeuvred slickly out from Castlegate and managed to insert all three cars in front of Coldstream, whose Provosts' vehicle stalled at the hasty application of brakes. Taking grateful advantage of this, Lauder made up for a hesitant start, nipping in with redeeming agility behind Duns. In this order, then, and with the Town Band stopping in the middle of the stirring third verse and bundling into a large bus, the official cavalcade set off for England, shepherded by two more police-cars and followed by a motley collection of private vehicles, Press and sightseers, legitimate road-users and delayed and

34

grumbling heavy transport, jostling, jinking, jerking, amidst a storm of hooting and a cloud of exhaust smoke. It was as spirited an exodus as the old grey town in the hollow had witnessed for quite some time.

Due south, following the sylvan windings of the Jed, the long strung-out, seemingly endless procession, sped. At his own road-end, Robin Laing of Kersheugh was awaiting them, to represent the Marshals—and had some momentary difficulty in convincing Kelso that his place was before and not after them. And soon they were lifting up, out of the constriction of the valley, on to the great swelling breasts of the green Cheviots. Smaller they became, forthwith, less impressive and consequential—merely an attenuated ribbon, like a busy column of ants, snaking up and up over the vast uncaring hillsides. Above the tree-level, Archie Scott looked back, and was astonished to perceive the extent of their following. He had visualised a score or so of cars, no more—but there seemed to be hundreds. He hoped that they might shake a good proportion of them off, presently. Just beyond a hairpin bend in the climbing road, a small open car painted a chaste shade of aquamarine swept past them all, a young woman driving alone, her ashen hair streaming in the breeze. Archie did not congratulate himself that at least they had got rid of one of the hangers-on.

Up at the summit, at Carter Bar itself, where the kingdoms met, a side-road slanted in, contouring the ample flank of Catcleuch Shin on the right. Along it was drawn up another impressive row of cars and horse-boxes, their flags gallantly spread to the wind of the high places. In front was a magnificent Rolls, under the famous blue-and-gold Hornshole Banner of Hawick, and behind, at intervals, the standards of Selkirk, Galashiels, Melrose, Peebles, and Langholm danced and fluttered. Mocking eye or none, the Jethart Callant had to swallow something at sight of them. All the East and Middle March was there; the balefires had flamed this time to good purpose.

There was a pause, for the Roxburghshire police were

35

careful to provide an escort no farther. The Chief Constable, who was coming along hereafter only as a passenger, transferred into a private car; apparently he had rather expected to hand over here to a representative of the Northumberland Constabulary, but none such materialised. The civic chiefs from the westerly burghs took the opportunity to greet their compeers from the east. All commented upon the length of a tail that they seemed to have acquired. Hawick's jovial Provost opined that it would be the militia and the Home Guard that England would be having out to meet them, at least. The expressions of occasional astonished motorists going in the opposite direction seemed to bear out this impression.

The black police-cars turned off into the side-road, and the augmented cavalcade moved off again, over the watershed into England. The Hawick Rolls, by its sheer complacent splendour so overawed the foremost Kelso driver that he gave way before it—and was lost. With only inches between their bumpers the western convoy moved in, in front, behind only Jedburgh, the county town. Civic pride was one of the admirable things the Scots had to urge upon the feckless Northumbrians.

Down the infant Rede to the great sheet of Catcleuch Reservoir they bowled, through hills that were sombre now and empty, and on down the long straight valley of Redesdale, mile after mile, to Elishaw where the road forked, left to Otterburn and Newcastle, right to Hexham. There the Provost of Jedburgh glanced at his watch. It was ten past one, and they had eighteen miles to go. They were doing nicely.

Chollerton, the first English village, was passed half an hour later. People stared from windows and doorways and dogs barked, as well they might. The line of the Roman Wall was crossed, and they ran down the Vale of Tyne. On its hill ahead, Hexham rose, a town ancient and grey as Jedburgh, and likewise dominated by its Priory. In every car men stirred themselves and sat up.

* * *

36

Over the broad Tyne bridge they came to the open area around the railway station, in the haughland below the climbing medieval town. Here a halt was made; indeed, the Scots took over the entire wide station-yard and transformed it promptly into something between a marshalling-ground, a paddock, and a car-park. All the riders' cars and horse-boxes were drawn up in rows and the steeds led out and attended to. The Provosts' limousines, all eleven of them, were lined up in order on the road outside, their radiators pointing towards the town hill. The Pressmen were a law unto themselves, but were not allowed to clutter up the proceedings, and the great line of sightseers' cars was sternly herded away in the direction of the goods yard and coal depot. Archie Scott, the Convener, Robin Laing, and the Herald, took firm charge, with the Chief Constable giving moral if not official support. The bandsmen's bus was manœuvred in, and disgorged its load amidst a great buttoning-up of tunics and depositing of beer-bottles. Two or three round-eyed employees of British Railways watched, nonplussed.

In exactly seven minutes all was ready. Joe Hastie, the Herald, resplendent in scarlet coat and blue bonnet, mounted his great white charger, and motioned the Band forward to take up position in front of the Jedburgh Provost's car, himself at their head. The Cornets and Standard-bearers took their towns' banners from the vehicles, and with the other horsemen, climbed into the saddle. Two or three semi-official cars brought up the rear, with behind them the concourse of onlookers, to which a porter and a couple of engine-cleaners had become attached—and at the last moment three small boys with glass jam-jars and minnows joined them from the river. Joe Hastie glanced at his watch, nodded, blew a blast on his horn, and to the Band's resumed rendering of "Blue Bonnets", the entire entourage moved forward at a marching pace.

It was a steep hill up, trying to wind instrumentalists. But Jedburgh Town Band had to be used to hills, and took this one nobly. The brae narrowed and became a tapering

37

cobbled street, almost a wynd, which the cavalcade completely filled. Window-sashes were thrown up and heads thrust out. Children appeared in close-mouths, shouting shrilly. A young policeman materialised in the throat of this climbing street where it opened on to the Market Place, stared doubtfully down at the approaching procession, decided that there was more urgent business elsewhere, and disappeared down an entry. Two o'clock chimed from the tower of the Priory, as Joe Hastie led the way into the square. Timed to a minute.

If there was distinct similarity to Jedburgh's town centre here, in ancient buildings, tall stone houses with narrow pends, Market Cross in mid-square, all under the shadow of the noble cathedral-like Priory, the similarity did not extend to the crowds. Not more than a score of people were to be counted, in the pleasant Market Place, and most of these were congregated up at the top end beside a charming pillared street-market under the soaring Priory buttresses. It was early Saturday afternoon, of course, and the roast beef of Old England still in process of digestion, no doubt. Parked near the waiting group was the small sea-green open car.

The Herald reined up his horse a few yards from the arcade, the Band blew itself to the end of a verse, and there was a great drawing up of cars and climbing out of robed and be-chained figures. The mounted men came forward, but remained in their saddles. Colour certainly had come to that grey place.

From the little watching group, dull-seeming in ordinary suits and caps, a stocky iron-grey military-looking man, dressed in boldly-checked plus-fours and a regimental tie, stepped forward briskly after an eloquent glance at his companions.

"Name is Stannard," he barked. "Mayor. Welcome to Hexham—all the lot of you!" It was for the Provost of Hawick that he made, thrusting out his hand. "Well, Provost—we meet again! No hard feelings? Got that fellow Douglas with you, this time?"

38

"No, Mr. Mayor. Mark Douglas is a reformed character, I'm afraid, since your Miss Dacre married him! But I'm glad to see you again, and to be in Hexham. A bonny town. This is the Provost of Jedburgh, who wrote to you. And the Provost of Kelso . . ."

There followed a deal of necessary hand-shaking, but no unnecessary chatter. The selection of Hexham Councillors and presumably leading citizens looked just a little out of their depth—as who would blame them? The Press photographers had to be quick. Something in the expression of Mayor Stannard discouraged them from making their usual suggestions.

"Well—we hardly expected anything like this, gentlemen!" he declared, the introductions over. "More just a call in passing. You must be going somewhere mighty important?"

"Nowhere more important than the ancient and historic town of Hexham!" Jedburgh's Provost declared handsomely. "And we consider our mission important, too."

"Oh? You mean, about some contribution from us to this Pageant you intend to hold?"

A certain amount of swallowing might have been perceptible to the keen-eared. The Scots spokesman enunciated carefully.

"That is not quite the idea, sir. The Redeswire Ride is held annually, to celebrate the battle, or Raid, of that name, that took place in 1575—an occasion in which your town, Mr. Mayor, was involved equally with mine, as well as many others along the Border. We feel, all of us, that it would be an excellent thing, a happy gesture, if Hexham was to be represented, in future . . ."

"You mean, by a deputation of some sort—not just a contribution?"

"We are not seeking financial assistance, Mr. Mayor. A deputation, yes—but what is really wanted is a mounted contingent to ride up from the south to meet our people at the Redeswire Stone, at Carter Bar."

"From *us*? From Hexham-on-Tyne Town Council?

39

Good lord, sir—what for? We're a Local Authority, Mr. Provost—not a riding academy, nor yet an antiquarian society! Seems to me you've come to the wrong people. We don't go in for much horse-riding on our Town Council!"

The Jedburgh Provost looked at his Hawick colleague for assistance, and that leonine figure responded with imperturbable good-humour. "Come now, Captain Stannard—I seem to recollect certain highly efficient equestrians coming from Hexham a year or two ago! Your own family not unrepresented! But we're not suggesting that Hexham Town Council should hoist itself on to horseback to come to Redeswire—only that it should be officially represented. I'm no horseman myself, I should say. We hope that you, and some of your Council, will attend by car, but that a few riders may represent this ancient burgh at this annual ceremony—and maybe others like it held elsewhere—to symbolise the happy relationship that now exists along this bloodstained Border, the burying of ancient feuds and bitter memories——"

"Bitter memories!" the Mayor broke in, strongly. "That's just it! That's just what I say about all these Common Ridings and carry-ons of yours—to my mind they're nothing *but* a digging out and keeping alive of bitter memories and hatreds much better kept buried! Damn it— that's the spirit that was behind all that trouble we had over those two flags! It was that spirit that inflamed all those irresponsible youths to their utterly deplorable actions. No, gentlemen—I'm afraid I'm all against Common Ridings, on principle!"—and His vehement Worship cast a comprehensive and disapproving glance over the ranked and rosetted horsemen.

There was a shaken pause, in which the champing of bits and the scrape of hooves on cobbles sounded noticeably. The galaxy of Provosts caught each other's eyes, and cleared throats. Hawick's representative, who knew his man, recovered first.

"We're sorry to hear that, Mr. Mayor," he said. "Know-

40

ing your strong sense of civic pride, we were hopeful that you might be prepared to start some sort of March Riding, or Border Festival here in Hexham. It is a wonderful spur to local patriotism and citizenship, we can all vouch. And——"

"And to xenophobia and out-dated nationalism, too, sir! No—that is a suggestion that quite frankly will receive no encouragement from me. I'm sorry. However, as to this specific Jedburgh celebration, we wouldn't wish to appear unhelpful. I put your letter before my Council, and by a, h'm, majority vote it was decided to make a subscription of five pounds towards your expenses, from our Common-weal Fund. That, I'm afraid, is as far as we can go. Perhaps, as regards the odd horseman, you might get in touch with the North Northumberland and Percy Hunts. Some of their members might be persuaded to do a bit of exercising in the off-season, by riding over your way. And now, if all you gentlemen would care to slip round with me to the Council Chamber, I think we might find enough sherry to give us all at least a thimbleful. . . ."

Hawick coughed. "You are very kind, Mr. Mayor. But there are a great many of us. All things considered . . ." And he looked at Jedburgh.

"No. I think we must regretfully decline your hospitality, sir. We have a big programme to get through. If there is nothing more to be said, on the subject of co-operation——"

"Always ready to co-operate in anything *constructive*, Mr. Provost—anything *forward*-looking. I've no use for looking back over my shoulder, myself—at long-dead history, or anything else. I'd forget it, if I were you. Much more healthy."

"Er, thank you for your advice at any rate, sir. I don't think there is anything more, gentlemen, is there?" The Provost of Jedburgh's voice quivered just a little, in the grip of his self-control.

From the saddle of his restless black, Archie Scott spoke, in a last effort to save something from the wreck. "Your son, Mr. Mayor—wasn't *he* rather more interested in bringing

41

history up to date? Something of a horseman, too—at least, I gather my Hawick friends thought so! Wouldn't he, perhaps, consider making an appearance, with one or two of his friends . . .?" A flicker of a smile. "On this occasion, he'd be most welcome, I assure you!"

"My son, young man, is *usefully* serving his country with Her Majesty's Forces in the Middle East!"

"Oh . . ."

"Well—I think there only remains for us to say good afternoon, sir." Archie's Provost bowed stiffly, formally. "Oh, and to gratefully decline your five pounds, which no doubt you can put to a more needy cause!"

"As you will. Good day to you, gentlemen. Delighted to see each and all of you any time you happen to be near our town."

A non-magisterial comment on that from one of the Provosts as they turned away, fortunately failed to carry clearly.

Mayor Stannard watched them go, with just the glimmer of a wintry smile.

Despite its identical composition it was astonishing how much less dignified and impressive was the procession that went back down that hill towards the station than that which had come up. The marshalling was at fault, undoubtedly perhaps those responsible did not have their minds fully on the job. The Provosts, once they got back into their cars, seemed unanimous in desiring to get away from the scene as quickly as possible, with some consequent competition at the narrow entrance to the steep wynd. The horsemen split up into groups, heads together, brows black. The Press kept up a running commentary with anyone who would speak to them. The Band, left more or less to its own devices, hung about for a few moments, and then, evidently deciding that nobody appeared to desire stirring music, broke up and started to stroll back whence it had so conspicuously come, instruments under arms, to the loud-voiced disappointment of much of Hexham's youth that had now put in its appearance. At varying speeds,

42

but much hampered by the constriction of the street, the whole company streamed downhill towards the river. At the tail-end of it all, Archie Scott, Joe Hastie the Herald, and Dand Fairgrieve the Hawick Cornet, exchanging sour impressions, found an open green car creeping along at their horses' heels.

"The Rout of Hexham!" Barbara Hepburn called out to them cheerfully. "Any comments, Mr. Scott?"

4

Down at the station-yard quite an effort was required to sort everybody out, get the horses boxed, wind up the fierce discussions, re-arrange the order of route, and see everyone embarked. Archie and his helpers were glad of the Chief Constable's undeniably authoritative aid. It was two-forty when they moved off, due eastwards down the Tyne valley—every car loud with dissertation.

Not unnaturally, the talk had little abated when, crossing the river by a handsome seven-arched ancient bridge, they found themselves in the middle of Corbridge, a mere three miles along the road. It was an easy place to come upon the middle of, being small, little more than a village, a pleasant sleepy spot with a fine old church and a peel-tower actually in its churchyard, all adoze in the afternoon sun. While it would be inaccurate to suggest that there was any reluctance to disturb this idyllic peace, the general concensus of opinion was rather that it would be a waste of time to make any representations here. It seemed that the place was not a burgh, had no administration of its own, and was unlikely anyway to be able to support any sort of Common Riding . . . though somebody unkindly pointed out that with a population of two thousand it was double the size of Lauder. But it could be expected to be under the thumb of Hexham, being so close. It was with some relief, then, that everybody settled themselves back in their seats, and the half-mile-long cavalcade started forward again, to take the left fork, due north for Morpeth.

Sundry bemused inhabitants peered after them, heads ashake. It was over-early in the season for the circus . . .

44

It was a run of more than twenty-five miles, much of it over high moorland, through sparsely populated country, with the great rampart of the Cheviots ever on their left front, until at Scots Gap they turned eastwards, seawards, down the fertile valley of the Wansbeck. The Provost of Jedburgh, leading, did not hurry; they were not scheduled to reach Morpeth until four o'clock, and, owing to circumstances, had ample time in hand.

There were hopes that here at least they would find some trace of that fighting Border spirit of old, for Morpeth was reputed to have suffered more than most at the hands of raiding Scots. Indeed it was said that at one time they rode in and out to it for plunder as they would to market. Such soil ought to be fruitful. And, next to the Newcastle-Tynemouth industrial area, it was the largest burgh in the county.

The cavalcade approached the town from the north-west, and they were encouraged to find a police-patrol awaiting them. Though the Inspector obviously was surprised at the size of the embassage, and unprepared for its transmogrification into a brass-band-led and partly mounted procession, he kept his comments entirely courteous, waited patiently while the change-over was effected, and eventually escorted the company down the gentle winding hill into the streets of Morpeth, sitting poker-faced in his crawling car a few yards ahead of Joe Hastie's white charger. This time the Band played "The Campbells are Coming".

There was no lack of people about here, to gaze and comment, for this was the centre for a wide agricultural and semi-industrial area, and the streets were full of Saturday afternoon shoppers. Morpeth had little of the appearance of the medieval town about it, for it had been largely burned down towards the close of the seventeenth century, and the Queen Anne period that followed was a good one for building. The place, if lacking Hexham's air of antiquity, had an aspect at once bustling and gracious—and undeniably English. The clock on the old square tower at the end of Oldgate showed a quarter to four.

45

They entered the town centre by Newgate Street, and despite being thus previous, the Mayor and what looked like most of his Corporation were drawn up at the door of the turreted Town Hall on the west side of the wide Market Place, to receive them, with chains, Town Officer, and all. A smiling dapper man, in black jacket and pin-stripe trousers, if he was at all put out by what he saw, he did not show it. When the Band allowed him, he made a brief and felicitous speech of welcome, shook a selection of hands, and turned to lead the way inside through the covered butter-market, and upstairs to the Council Chamber—a move which entailed a certain amount of commotion amongst the horsemen, the Press, and the hangers-on generally. But everyone who could get inside seemed to be welcome, and some proportion of all categories achieved an entry. At a word from Archie Scott, the Band remained outside, beside the horse-holders, and regaled the populace to a selection of patriotic airs, even going the length of "Blaydon Races" and "John Peel".

Within, tea and refreshments were set out—admittedly for less than the total number present, but the Morpeth Councillors and their ladies gallantly held back, and most of the visitors obtained something. It was all very pleasant and encouraging—but Archie and the Convener kept their eyes on their watches, and as time went on, grew restive. At last, after some fairly pronounced pulling at Provosts' sleeves, the matter in hand was brought to the fore—almost with some reluctance, it might have seemed, by most of those concerned.

Jedburgh's civic chief, however, once started, did nobly—with the speech that he had had no opportunity to deliver at Hexham. He spoke, and eloquently, of the past, glorious and not so glorious, of the wars and feuds and reiving of the Borderland, the battles, the balefires, and the balladry. He pointed out their respective districts' mutual concern in all of this, and emphasised the satisfactory good-neighbourliness of the present day. But also he urged the value of keeping alive of ancient traditions and pride of

46

ace, in these duller and humdrum times, stressing the wonderful effect on local patriotism and civic pride of Common Ridings and so on. Then he came right down to the Redeswire Ride, and declared that they were here formally to invite the ancient town of Morpeth to send a delegation to Redeswire next July, as well as to other Scots burgh's ride-outs, and to urge on them their participation in at least some sort of ceremony that would prove that the spirit of Percy and Heron and Fenwick and Dacre was not dead, in the valiant North . . .

He had to stop, for the volume of applause that filled the chamber, and maintained.

Amidst it all, the Mayor stepped forward and shook the speaker by the hand warmly. And the acclaim rang out anew.

Then it was Morpeth's turn. The Mayor made a model speech—in fact, it might have been modelled upon the Provost's, so consistently did it echo the sentiments therein, underlining the value of tradition etcetera, dwelling on the romantic past and battles long ago, expressing admiration of the Scots Common Ridings, and declaring that so long as there were Douglases, Scotts, Kers, and Turnbulls and the rest in the Border hills, Scotland need never fear the future. This was the cue for renewed applause. Englishmen shook Scots by the hand. Amity was complete. The Mayor had merely to add how happy they were to see their friends from over the Border, and now that they had found their way, he hoped that they would visit them more often.

The "hear hears" were generous.

Surprisingly, this phase of the meeting thereupon showed every sign of breaking up, with talk of viewing the town's treasures, its portraits, ancient charter, the mace presented by Belted Will in 1604, and the like. Urgently, Archie Scott jogged the Hawick Provost's arm, and that man spoke up.

"The Redeswire Ride, Mr. Mayor," he reminded.

"Ah, yes—of course," His Worship conceded. "That is a very kind invitation, which I am sure is much appreciated. It is rather a long way from here, of course, and we are all very busy people in Morpeth. An industrious and progressive

47

community, I think I may say, in all modesty. But, should any of us happen to be in the vicinity of Jedburgh about that time, I'm sure we'd be delighted to look you up. Delighted, gentlemen."

Morpeth clapped, even if Scotland did not.

"That is not quite what we visualised," it was pointed out. "What we would like is an official deputation to meet us at Redeswire, as your forefathers met ours, to symbolise the healing of old sores and scores. We suggest a small mounted party, as well. If Morpeth could be represented by her own Ensign or Standard-bearer . . ."

The Mayor coughed, and there was some shuffling of feet. "I'm afraid that is rather more than we could consider, gentlemen—at this stage, at any rate," he said. "You will realise, of course, being Local Government men yourselves, that any such development would have to take place as on the direct desire of the people of Morpeth—the ratepayers, whom we only represent. And I must admit that they never have as yet indicated a wish for anything of the sort. I'm sorry—but there it is. Perhaps, while appreciative of the past, gentlemen, we are not quite so steeped in it as you are! A pity, may be . . . or again, perhaps not! Ha, ha!" And he beamed on them all.

Outside, the Band was playing "The Flowers of the Forest", and all within seemed to listen to it for three or four bars.

"Do we take that as final, then, Mr. Mayor?" Jedburgh's Provost asked, heavily, at length.

The other raised another hearty laugh. "Well—nothing's final in this world, is it, Provost? Certainly not in Morpeth, where we're great believers in progress. Who knows what time might bring forth . . .?"

"But you won't personally recommend it to your people, sir?"

"Well—no. I'm afraid I can hardly see my way to doing that. My term of office will be up by then, any-way . . . And it hardly seems to fall within my sphere, at all. We do ride our own bounds, occasionally—not every

48

year, you know, but intermittently. We did it in 1950. But that's done in April, on the Thursday nearest St. Mark's Day. . . ."

"And could that idea not be extended a bit? Developed into a mounted festival, and held annually? At least a party delegated to come north and meet our people . . .?"

"No, no—I'm afraid that's out of the question. Quite beyond our powers, as a Town Council. I'm sorry, gentlemen . . ."

"Then we're bluidy well wastin' oor time—an' yours, tae!" a realist near the door growled, but loud enough for all to hear. "Let's get the hell oot o' this . . .!"

Despite the blinkings and frowns and throat-clearings, there seemed to be a certain general sympathy with this point of view. Anyway, a drift along the corridor and downstairs set in—and no one was at any great pains to stem it. Determinedly affable, the hosts accompanied their preoccupied guests down to the street, to the car doors if not to the horses' heads—the Scots tending to live up to their national reputation for dourness, and rather cutting short the leave-taking.

The Band was striking up the opening bars of "Cock of the North", when Archie Scott, stalking over, curtly suggested something a trifle less triumphant. To the nostalgic strains of "The Land o' the Leal" then, car doors slammed, steeds were mounted, the Herald blew his horn, and, the Inspector leading again, the procession turned in the Market Place and made off up Newgate Street with a quite remarkable celerity that but ill-matched the music, and indeed almost threatened to overrun the puffing instrumentalists. Hospitable Morpeth waved, and even raised a cheer. It got scant encouragement.

*   *   *

Back at the assembly-point, just outside the town, heated discussions broke out by the score, to coalesce presently into one great and outspoken council-of-war. A sizeable and vociferous proportion of the company urged that they call the whole thing off, and get back home forthwith. These English were beyond hope or persuasion, they claimed —dull, spiritless, who could only be appealed to through their pockets or their bellies. This was a waste of time.

If all did not assert their feelings quite so strongly, there was little real enthusiasm for further attempts. It was not a very dignified business, this getting shown the door, courteously or otherwise—and dignity is a matter of some moment to civic fathers. It was Archie Scott who urged most strongly that they should not give up, yet, reminding them that the film was at stake—and more than that, a really worthwhile cause. If even one English community would lead the way . . .

It was eventually agreed, without much in the way of acclamation, that one more attempt should be made, at Rothbury. If they were unsuccessful there, then they would skip Alnwick—which had only been notified of a *possible* call, anyway, owing to the time factor, and which had not acknowledged the communication. As for Wooler —well, they had to pass through it on their way home anyway. But it was a small place. They'd see . . .

Their time-table had set their arrival at Rothbury for five-fifteen, and now, thanks to all the talking, public and private, they had to cover the fifteen northward miles at speed. Through steadily rising pastoral country they raced, up the River Font, by Nether Witton and Brinkburn, an unlikely entourage for such sequestered roads, till the abrupt descent into the steep Vale of Coquet brought them suddenly right on top of the little grey town nestling under its crags. In full view, it seemed quite ridiculous to retire back over the hill in order to get out the horses and the Band and so on; moreover, nobody was feeling very like making further great efforts to impress. So down the brae and over the arched bridge of the Coquet the wheeled cavalcade proceeded, into the unexpectedly wide streets of hill-bound Rothbury.

And not only into the streets. It *filled* the streets, spacious as they were—even though the assembly of cars was barely

50

so large as when it left Scotland. All but choking the place with its concourse of vehicles, it was as though an army of occupation had descended upon the tight little town. Such would not have been the first, either. Scots armies were no new thing to Rothbury—nor English ones for that matter. Here the tide of Border warfare had ebbed and flowed; here King John had camped, and Edward, Hammer of the Scots, signed one of his many and ill-kept truces.

Whether Rothbury greatly heeded these others, it heeded the present invasion little enough. Despite the stir they made, the manœuvring of cars, the opening and slamming of doors, the disgorging of robed and horsy men on to pavements and grassy greens, and the clamour of jaded Pressmen and others on the subject of licensing hours and bona-fide travellers, the little grey town went about such business as it might have at tea-time of a Saturday afternoon with placid unconcern.

Like Corbridge, it appeared that Rothbury, though larger than many of the Scots burghs, was not a municipality, and therefore possessed no Town Council nor Mayor. And by the same token, no Town Hall. So the visitors' immediate objective was not very obvious. There was a Rothbury District Council office, amongst the shops, but being Saturday afternoon, it was shut. There was a stone cross on a triangle of green, but it was a monument to a modern benefactor, not a Market Cross. While groups of vaguely disgruntled dignitaries and representatives stood about, then, smoking cigarettes and looking either bored or critical, Archie, the Convener, and the Herald, were despatched to try to find authority.

Enquiries at shops on both sides of the grassy tree-lined bank that pleasantly divided higher and lower Front Street elicited little substantial save that a Dr. White was Chairman of the Rural District Council. A sergeant of police who was run to earth at the top of the town, pointed out reasonably that this was no time to expect Councils to be in session. If it was something really important, they should try Morpeth, or even County Buildings, Newcastle.

51

Thus far only enquiries had advanced, when a clergyman on a lady's bicycle came pedalling amongst the drawn-up cars, to wobble to a halt in the vicinity of the band of Provosts, most of whom had now discarded their scarlet robes but who still managed to retain some air of consequence. With somewhat breathless apology he explained that he had been waiting for them at the north end of the town—coming from Scotland, he had expected them to arrive from that direction. No, he hadn't realised that they had been at Morpeth. He really knew very little about it all . . . Perhaps Dr. White had known—but the doctor had been called away, unfortunately, at the last moment—the divine lowered his voice, suitably—a, h'm, confinement. Unfortunate, but most, er, necessary. He himself—Jobson was the name—was Dr. White's deputy. On the District Council, that was. The doctor had hurried round to his house, just half an hour ago, asking him to meet them, and to give them this hasty note.

The Provost of Jedburgh, in tight-lipped silence, took the folded scrap of paper—the back of a National Health Service prescription form, actually—and scanned it. After a moment, he cleared his throat, and read aloud:

DEAR SIRS,

Sorry I have to rush away, but Mr. Jobson will explain. I would have liked to have met you—my wife's mother came from Jedburgh. Afraid we're not very knowledgable or interested in Common Ridings and that sort of thing here—though we've an excellent Common. We rather prefer fox-hunting, to riding round Commons, actually. More exciting. Arrange a joint meet, with the Duke of Buccleuch's, and we're with you every time. How about a Joint Hunt Ball, at Berwick-on-Tweed next winter?

Hope you have a nice run through our county.

Yrs,

JOSIAH WHITE

Chairman, R.D.C.

The Reverend Jobson beamed. "That's right," he said. "The doctor's a great hunting man—he farms too, of course, as well as being a medico. So are a lot of the farming members. Of the Council, I mean. Hunting men, that is. I'm not much of a follower, myself. Not that I've anything against the sport on *principle*, you know. I must make that clear. I do think the antifield-sports people are just a little ill-advised in this matter——"

The clerical voice was rudely interrupted by the slam of a car door. And then another, and another. Surprised, he glanced around, to perceive that the company of listeners had most evidently diminished in numbers, with the process still going on.

Jedburgh's Provost took a long breath. "You discussed this matter, sir, before your Council? Not fox-hunting—I mean the Common Riding proposals and the Redeswire ceremony?"

"Yes. Oh, yes. Last Thursday evening. At least, the letter from, from . . . Jedburgh, was it? The letter was read out."

"And discussed?"

"Well . . . more or less. We had a rather long agenda. . . ."

"I see. Well—thank you, sir. I'm sorry your afternoon was interrupted. I'm sure we all are!" He looked around, to find that only the Provost of Hawick, Archie Scott, and the Convener remained to support him, grim-visaged or expressionless.

"Not at all. Don't mention it. No, no—it's been a pleasure. I just wish I'd been at the right end of the town to welcome you. . . ."

In silence the four Scots bowed to him.

"Good afternoon, gentlemen. A pleasant journey . . ."

Archie followed his Provost to the Jedburgh car. "Wooler . . .?" he began, as the other climbed in.

"Tae hell wi' Wooler!" somebody from inside declared succinctly.

"It's on our way. We've got to pass through it. . . ."

53

"Through it—precisely!" the Provost said, sharply for that kindly man. "I'm sorry, Archie." And he closed the door firmly.

In somewhat ragged order, without any undue regard for precedence or anything else, the cars poured out of Rothbury, on the road for Scotland.

5

Archie Scott glowered at the *Daily News* propped up before him on the desk, while he held the telephone handset to ear and mouth. "That Hawick 3909?" he asked. "Could I speak to Mr. A. Fairgrieve, please? Yes—Andrew Fairgrieve." The Hawick Cornet was son of a small hosiery manufacturer. While he waited, Archie's pencil point jabbed holes in the pile of Monday morning's newspapers under his hand, contentiously.

"That you, Dand?" he said, presently. "This is Archie Scott, Jedburgh. You'll have seen the papers? Yes. And the *News*? That female's certainly rubbed our noses in it! Trust a Hepburn! Yes, that's her name. You've not read her piece? Oh, well—you should! It's headed 'FIASCO ON THE BORDER. BLUE BONNETS AND RED FACES'. Here are some excerpts. 'Seldom can the Scots have taken such a beating at the hands of the Sassenach. . . . In pomp and circumstance a pride of Provosts and a canter of Callants set out over Carter Bar on Saturday, to coax the poor feckless English into patronising the Border Common Ridings, for the greater glory of Jedburgh—and, may it be whispered, perhaps to impress a certain film magnate from America.' Yes—and listen to this: 'Their ermine tails between their legs, they all scuttled back home. . . . Said the Mayor of Morpeth, we are busy folk! The Mayor of Hexham wanted to play golf. The Chairman at Rothbury preferred fox-hunting. . . . The English will not cross the Border, at any price . . . and the Scots are not likely to again, either!' She closes: 'So ended the Rout of the Redeswire. Shades of the Moss-troopers!'

55

And so on. What? Yes. Some of the other papers are bad enough—but this takes the biscuit. I agree. Exactly. Look, Dand—how d'you feel about all this? The whole business, I mean—not just the Press reports?"

Archie drew the ear-piece back a little, at the vehemence of the reply, and a flicker of a grin lightened his features. "You do? That's the way I feel myself . . . but man, you should watch yourself—there may be a telephone-lassie listening! Uh-huh. Quite, quite. Well, see here, Dand —I've got one or two ideas on the subject. I say we can't just leave it this way. No—*they* won't do any more, I know that well enough. The Provosts and respectable folk have taken a beating. But some of us who are not quite so respectable as all that . . .! Yes—the younger folk. I agree. We've got to *discuss* it, anyway—even if we do nothing more about it. How about a meeting, then? Somewhere sort of private, I suggest—I mean, where we're not all too well known. And central. Surely, anywhere'd suit me—but I'm thinking of the boys from Coldstream and Duns and Lauder. Yes—I'll sound them all. The ones that were there on Saturday. I know the Kelso Laddie was mad enough. Yes, of course—bring your Right and Left, and anybody else you think would be interested. But, Dand—I wouldn't bring anybody unco guid and respectable . . . or that would be liable to talk! You get me? By the way, what's the Langholm Cornet's name? Oh, yes—of course; the butcher. Well, shall we make it the Buccleuch Arms at St. Boswells? That should suit Gala and Melrose, and Peebles too. When? As soon as possible. No—I agree. Better avoid the week-end. Wednesday next? Well, Thursday then? Right. Thursday at eight. Uh-huh. I'll let you know if that doesn't suit the majority. Right, Dand—up the Teries!"

Archie laid down the instrument, his face set into rather more cheerful lines—that yet boded no good for somebody. He picked the telephone up again, almost at once.

"Kelso, please," he requested. "Kelso 2913."

*   *   *

56

The gathering of young men that assembled in the smoking-room of the Buccleuch Arms at St. Boswells that Thursday evening, looked in no way out of the ordinary. In tweeds, sports jackets and flannels, and in one or two cases, working clothes, of all aspects and all classes, they might have been the supporters of one or other of the Border rugby clubs—as indeed most of them were. There were no colourful rosettes, no distinguishing marks, no gallant trappings. But the company consisted, nevertheless, of the cream of the younger Common Riding personalities of all the East and Middle Marches, and the chosen standard-bearers of a dozen burghs whose names read like a fanfare of trumpets. The Duns Reiver could not be present, but he had sent his predecessor, and the Melrosian was to arrive later, on returning from Edinburgh; but otherwise there was full representation, even to as far west as Langholm. Thirty-two young men were present, nearly half of whom had been on the ill-fated expedition to Northumberland twelve days before.

The temper of the company was uneven, as was not to be wondered at. Opinions differed on many aspects of the situation, and there was criticism of more than the English. But the common factor of ire and resentment in greater or lesser degree, born of injured pride, affected them all. Over the preliminary chatter and the charging of glasses and tumblers, there was only the one subject of conversation, whatever its tenor.

Archie Scott took up his position at the empty fireplace, his elbow on the mantel, and waited for quiet. "I've asked you fellows to get together here, because it seems to me that the last word on the business of two Saturdays ago has still to be spoken," he declared, presently, in conversational tone. "At least, I hope so!"

There was a somewhat ragged chorus of general agreement, but with sundry scurrilous and cynical additions.

"I don't know how it strikes you all—though I had some small conversations with most of you over the 'phone," the Callant went on. "But personally, I feel pretty hot

57

about the whole affair. Of course, it was my idea to start with, and naturally I feel some responsibility for the outcome. Maybe we went about it the wrong way—it certainly looks like it, from here! But I still think it was a good idea—and is."

"It had one fatal weakness, from the start, Archie," Wat Hogarth, from Selkirk announced. "It depended on the bluidy English!"

"Hear, hear!"

"You've said it, Wattie. Up the Souters!"

"I see Wattie's point, of course," Archie admitted, smiling faintly. "But since the whole object was to bring the English in on this, the observation doesn't take us a long way!"

"Then dam'-well leave them oot, I say! They're nae use, onywey. Never have been . . ."

"That's right, Sandy. They're a gutless, gormless, god-forsaken crew, just! Hell—let them be!"

"You got no option, Jings. It's them that's letting *us* be. They'll no' budge, cooper them! Yon geyser wi' the plus-fowers . . .!"

"Aye, an' the parson-guy wi' his auld wife's bike . . .!"

"Wait a bit," Archie called, slapping the mantelpiece. "Maybe I haven't got as poor an opinion of the English as some of you. I think they're pretty good, taken all over. Can be, anyway. They've given us a pretty fair run for our money, in the past, haven't they? It's the getting *at* them, somehow. . . ."

"Archie's right," Sanny Elliot, the Coldstreamer, averred. "They're all right, the English, once you get them moving. But they're lazy, easy-going, compared with us. You've got to rouse them, somehow . . ."

"Exactly!" Scott took him up. "That's the thing in a nutshell. You've got to rouse them—and we didn't rouse them, that Saturday."

"By Jings, we didna . . .!"

"An' you needna reckon on another dollop, Archie man!" Dod Wilson, the Kelso Laddie asserted. "No' from *my*

58

Provost, anyway. Damn't, you should've heard him, yon night. Och, he's a decent-like wee man enough, but yon had him right scunnered!"

"Losh—you should have heard *mine*!" Peebles cried. "He's got a sight mair weight to him than yours, Dod—and was he laying it about! You'll no' get *him* having another go . . ."

Archie held up his hand. "I'm not suggesting anything of the sort," he assured. "I know the Provosts and the official folk have had it. I don't blame them, either. They've got their dignity and their positions to consider, and the ratepayers, and heaven knows what besides. But there's more than Provosts and Councillors in the Borders. There's us, and hundreds more like us! All I say is—are *we* going to lie down under this? Are we going to take the raspberry we got the other day, for our answer, and say no more? Are we content to leave the matter where it is—and any hope of getting this film, with it? Are we going to let that woman on the *Daily News*, and the rest of the Press, get away with the things they said? Or aren't we?"

"No! No!"

"Tae hell wi' them a'!"

"No' likely!"

"But what can we do, man?"

"That's right, Archie," the Hawick Cornet agreed. "Let's hear your proposals first—if you've got any."

"I want to know the general feeling of the meeting before I get down to details, Dand," the Callant said. "What I've got to suggest will only appeal to those who want to go the whole hog, I imagine. If there's not many feel that way—then I'm keeping quiet."

He had them now, of course—every man-jack of them. There was not a soul in the room who was not sitting forward eagerly, eyes on the face of the man at the fireplace.

"Go on, Archie—out with it," Fairgrieve urged. "We're all with you. Aren't we, boys?"

59

Words of a sort did not fail the company in general. A pandemonium of exclamation, admiration, question and comment broke out. There was no one present unmoved by excitement. Reaction seemed to be fairly equally divided between the long view and the short—the ultimate effect on the Common Riding spirit, and the opportunity to give the Auld Enemy the hiding which all were convinced he needed for his own good. Out of the commotion, one or two more cautious voices made themselves heard, presently.

"What about the after effects, Archie?" somebody asked. "It'd be an illegal act, mind."

"Aye—who gets the jile oot o' this ploy, eh?"

"None of us, I hope," Scott claimed. "First of all, it'll have to be properly organised—done in the dark, and all of us out of the way before there's any hue and cry. The beasts should be discovered long before there can be any identification of who did it—even if there are suspicions. And anyway—what could we be charged with? Scores, maybe a hundred, of us? For it's going to take a lot of us to do the job. We won't have *stolen* the cattle—only removed them from one place to another. What offence does that come under? We'll have to be careful there's no injury done to any of the brutes—that could cause trouble. But if it was made clear that we'd never had any intention of doing more than move the beasts, I don't know what charge they could get us on. Nothing serious, at any rate. Acts liable to cause a breach of the peace would be about the worst of it—if they could get witnesses to testify to anything definite. And if they could pin it on any individual, for that matter, ten bob, or a pound, for a first offence, would be about the size of it. . . ."

"Put me down for a quid's worth, any day!" Jock Murray, the Hawick Right-hand Man and former Cornet cried. "I wouldna miss this for a fortune!"

"Me, too . . . !"

"Hell, aye — it's the best thing since Hopalong Cassidy!"

62

"Round 'em up, boys. Run alawng, l'il dogies, run alawng!"

"Yippeee!"

The tide of acclamation and enthusiasm ran high, amidst heartening clamour. But Archie Scott paid little heed to it all. His eyes were on one or two of the more responsible and influential—Dand Fairgrieve, Elliot the Coldstreamer, his own Right-hand Man and predecessor Rab Pringle, and a scattering of the slightly older men. They would decide the issue.

"I think it's a magnificent idea, Archie—if it'll work," Dand declared, when he could make himself heard. "It's going to take a lot of doing, a lot of organising. I accept that. But what I want to be sure about is—what effect it's going to have on the English? Is it going to make them any more interested in the Common Riding idea, and come to the Redeswire, or is it not? Unless we're pretty sure that it is, however good a ploy it may be, it's not worth either the trouble or the risk, in my opinion."

"That's good sense," the Coldstreamer supported him, though there was a certain amount of demur from the enthusiasts.

"I agree," the Callant nodded. "That was the main question I had to ask myself. Look at it this way. Suppose the boot was on the other foot. Suppose you were an English Border farmer, and somebody came down from Scotland one night and drove away some of your cattle, and you had to go scouring the hills for them, and when you'd found them, sort them out from a herd of hundreds of others? What would your reaction be?"

"Oh, I'd want to hit back just as hard as I could, of course."

"Just that. At first, though, you'd probably talk about having the law on those responsible. But when it became clear that this was going to be mighty difficult, you'd want some other means of expressing your feelings. But what could you do? Faced with direct action, in these law-abiding days, what *can* one do? Precious little, that has any satisfaction about it. Either you can take direct action

63

yourself, in retaliation—which is not very likely, but which would be an excellent thing, just the spirit that's wanted—or else you'd hold protest meetings, pass resolutions, get your M.P. to ask a question in Parliament, or something equally inadequate like that. Then, when you were thoroughly frustrated, and we've given you the idea that it might all happen again, you'd probably begin to get organised, locally, wouldn't you? And isn't that what we want? If we can get even the hint of an organisation going over there, to counter our efforts, then the battle's half-won. The Common Riding spirit is reborn. If we issue a challenge or two—say to the Races at Riccalton for next year, or to your own ones up at Hawick Moor, Dand—then I think the game will be ours."

"Fair enough," the Cornet admitted. "There may be flaws in your reasoning, Archie—but I must admit I don't see them at the moment. Okay—I'm with you."

"Yippee. Teri-bus ye Teri Odin!" his Right-hand cried, and was shouted down with salvoes of rival slogans.

"I've got ... I say, I've got a question," the Coldstreamer put in, with some difficulty. "At least, I've got plenty, on the organisational side. But they can wait. It's more on the principle of the thing. How are our Common Riding Committees going to look on this? I mean, most of us here are official representatives one way or another. Cornets, Standard-bearers, Rights and Lefts, and so on. Isn't this going to run our Committees into a deal of trouble? In fact, I don't suppose many of them will agree to it."

"I didn't suppose they would, Sanny. But I'm not proposing that they should be told or involved. We won't do this as Cornets or Callants or Coldstreamers—just as individuals. Then there'll be nobody to worry us. No reason why we shouldn't, is there?"

"No-o-o. I suppose not. D'you think we can keep the thing a secret from them—from everybody—when there's going to be so many of us in it?"

"We've got to. Secrecy is vital, of course. But that's

64

a matter of organisation. We'll attend to that once we've decided on the policy of the thing. Are we going to do it, or are we not?"

A great shout of assent and acclaim, and a stamping of feet, shook the smoking-room and set the tumblers dancing. It was much more than an answer to a question—it was an ovation. And it continued for fully half a minute.

Archie raised his hand, smiling. "That's one hell of a noise!" he declared. "The management will be wanting to know what it's all about—and what will we tell them? And maybe some still small voice was lost in the din? Somebody not so keen as all that. Any objections? It's now or never."

No one spoke. Then Archie's own Rab Pringle, the Jethart Right-hand Man, cleared his throat. "I wouldna like to be a wet-blanket, mind," he said earnestly. "But I'm no' awfu' keen on a' this."

"Never mind, Rab—there's no need for anybody to come along that doesn't want to."

"Och, I'll come along, a'right. But I'm no' jist throwin' my bunnit up into the air an' skirlin', see."

"Why? What's the trouble?"

"Man Archie—I was aye dreadfu' feart o' coos," he said.

That settled it.

*   *   *

There was an enormous amount of detail to be discussed and decided upon, of course—not all of which could be dealt with there and then. Moreover, the mood of the company was on the elevated side for due, sober, and effective solution of organisational problems. But many essential decisions were made, nevertheless, before the meeting disintegrated.

It was agreed that the project would have to be carried out on a Saturday night, to give them the time they needed and the advantage of early Sunday morning lethargy.

N.R.—E

65

Also, that since they needed a fairly long period of darkness, and there was a lot of arranging to be done, it would do no harm to wait till mid-September. There would be nine hours of darkness, then, and the harvest ought to be in, too—which was important in view of the large numbers of farming folk involved. It was recognised that to be really effective, the thing should be done on as broad a basis as possible—a combined operation, working on at least four fronts, but with some centralised control and synchronisation, if possible. Geography and sheer distance was going to create difficulties to this, but fast cars, spare horses, and good map-work ought to get over much of that. The main assault would have to be in the east, in the valleys of the Till, and Aln, the Coquet, and the Wansbeck, with secondary thrusts down Redesdale and North Tynedale; and it was resolved that a deputation should visit Dumfries and Annan, to try to bring the Scots West March into the scheme. Obviously a detailed reconnaissance of the whole area was essential, to spy out suitable farms, map communications, and search for beef-tubs. Two week-ends hence was selected for this, and three or four small parties briefed for the task. On the subject of man-power generally, area leaders were appointed to recruit suitable types from amongst their followers and supporters. There would be no lack of personnel, for even the most modest of the burghs' standard-bearers could call on forty or fifty mounted supporters. The problem would lie in gaining volunteers sufficiently adventurous yet reliable, discreet and able to hold their tongues yet willing to risk possible repercussions and prosecution—and at the same time, reasonably useful as cowboys. However, this was likely to be the least of their difficulties. It was stressed that nobody was to be told of the venture without first being sworn to secrecy, whether or not he eventually participated. Herein lay the greatest danger, it was acknowledged, and all must be on their guard. Finally, a small Executive Committee was appointed, to tie things up and generally supervise, with Archie Scott as Chairman, and Dand Fairgrieve, Dod Wilson, Sanny Elliot,

66

Rab Pringle, and Dougie Armstrong the Langholm Cornet, as members.

The meeting broke up amid considerable hilarity. Fortunately the bar had been closed for half an hour. The sleepy village of St. Boswells, around its green, was undoubtedly relieved to hear the last of them.

6

The three young men sat their horses, and frowned. Across
their knees open maps were spread, and in their hands were
field-glasses. It was no vista to frown over. Their mounts
stood high on the steepish flank of Cochrane's Pike, on the
site of a Roman Camp, and on all sides save north-west-
wards, at their backs, the land dropped away in great sweeps
and folds, by the verdant dales of Breamish and Aln and
Coquet, to the rich rolling farmlands of Northern Northumbria, the level coastal plain, and the distant sea. Below
them, to the left, the hamlet of Ingram nestled in its green
valley, and over to the right Alnham and its church could
be seen backed by the trees of the Collingwood demesne.
From the sheep-strewn foothills at their feet the fair land
spread out, scattered with farmsteads, dotted with cattle,
patched with yellow cornfields, a noble prospect under the
flooding golden sunlight of a late-August afternoon. But
it was not the sun in their eyes that set the trio frowning,
nor yet any resentment at the fairness of the scene. Rather
it was the message that their maps were impressing upon
them, and the grievous tale of miles.

Since early forenoon, when colleagues had deposited them
from cars and horse-boxes on a quiet side-road just over the
hilly Border from Yetholm of the gypsies, they had been
riding round the wide-flung skirts of the eastern end of the
Cheviot range, around the hub of great Cheviot itself, indeed,
on an eight or ten miles radius, keeping to the foothills, by
tracks and bridle-paths and no-paths. They had contoured
and rounded and shouldered innumerable hills, whose
names sang a stirring song of ancient days—Paston Hill,

68

Tom Tallon's Crag, Yeavering Bell, Homildon Hill, skirting the frequented areas of Kirknewton, Wooler, Ilderton, and Ingram. Farms by the score they had noted, and surveyed their accessibility from the hills and their distance from the Borderline. And now, with thirty-odd miles of rough going behind them, they were faced, not so much with all this promised land, but with the stern realities of geography and mileage.

"I must admit, I hadn't realised the distances involved," Archie Scott declared, at length. "We'll have to scale down our ideas a bit, I'm afraid. Either that, or relax some of the conditions we made. Both, maybe. You're a farmer, Dod —how far d'you reckon it's a practical proposition to herd stirks and beef-cattle? In the dark, over rough ground, mind. And how fast?"

"Depends on who's doing the herding, whether it's close or open country, and so on," Wilson told him. "Och, an' the numbers in each batch is important, too. You'd be right lucky to average three miles an hour, I'd say."

"Even with mounted herders?"

"Sure. Sometimes you'll dae twice that, but jist as often you'll be chasing your tails—or even going back the way. An' the farther you drive them, the harder it gets, mind. Hoo long d'you reckon the average bunch will have, for this driving?"

"Well—we've got to make our approaches in the dark. And we want folk in their beds, as much as possible. Fortunately, farm-servants aren't the type that keep late hours. We won't have to start driving much before midnight—say eleven-thirty at the earliest. Sunrise will be about six o'clock —by which time we want the brutes safely corraled in their beef-tubs."

"Uh-huh. Man, wi' the kind o' herding we're likely to have, and the darkness, and the sort o' country the last laps'll be over—it'll be sheer bluidy mountaineering, mind, and these'll be field-reared beasts—hell, we'll be lucky if we average a dozen miles. Damned lucky . . ."

"M'mmm. Only a dozen? What d'you think, Sanny?"

69

The Coldstreamer shrugged. "I'm no farmer—but I can see we're going to have our work cut out. I wouldn't like to guarantee to drive unruly cattle twelve miles over this sort of country, between midnight and dawn."

"It certainly would be interesting to know how far our forefathers covered with their booty, of a night," Archie mentioned. "But if Dod's right—and I've been fearing something of the sort this while back—then this Rothbury area's as far south as we can operate. Morpeth's right out, and so is Hexham and Corbridge. And, hang it—I wanted to have a smack at that Hexham! That Mayor Stannard asked for it, if anybody did! But, according to my map, it's all of twenty-five miles from the nearest point on the Border-line. Morpeth's more. Even Rothbury, down there on the Coquet, is about fourteen, I'd say. All this area here, of course, is part of the Rothbury district, which is good enough . . ."

"Can the Hawick fowk no' get at Hexham?" Dod asked. "Ower the Note o' the Gate? Instead o' doing it frae Redesdale?"

The Callant, his eyes on his map, shook his head. "Even that way—by the North Tyne Valley—it seems to be nearly twenty-five miles to the Border at Deadwater. I'm afraid Hawick will have to be content with raiding the Bellingham district, and my own folk from Jedburgh with lower Redesdale and the Otterburn area. It's a pity, but . . ." He shrugged. "I'm afraid we've got to lower our sights."

"We could use cattle-trucks, of course," Dod Wilson pointed out.

Archie shook his head. "It would complicate things too much. It would mean we'd be largely dependent on roads. There would be the noise. The trucks could be identified. We'd have to borrow them, anyway, involving the owners . . . and one or two might get bogged down. No. . . ."

"I suppose the beef-tubs *must* be on our side of the Border?" Sanny Elliot put in. "I dare say we could find plenty good enough places, near enough to Hexham and Morpeth, amongst these English hills . . .?"

70

"But that wouldn't be the same thing, at all," Archie claimed. "The whole point is that the cattle must be driven off over the Border. Just to remove them from one bit of English soil to another, wouldn't ring any bells . . ."

"No, no—I see that. I was just meaning, as a sort of temporary measure. I was thinking, if the far-away cattle could be brought north in two laps, as it were. So far on Saturday night, lie up somewhere, and finish the trip on Sunday night. But that would lengthen the whole proceedings, of course. You were thinking of us all being away, safely home, by Sunday forenoon?"

"Surely. That's the whole idea. Let the English spend Sunday looking for their beasts—we'll all be back home, or at the kirk maybe! Anyhow, the entire countryside will be roused by Sunday night, this side, and any herd that had lain up during the day wouldn't stand a chance moving up to the Border at night—even if it hadn't been found already."

"I guess you're right, Archie. Forget it. It was just that I don't like to see Hexham getting off . . ."

"Nor I. But your notion's given me just half an idea, Sanny. There's a great lot of mighty empty country north-west of Hexham, all the way to the Border, utterly unpopulated. The area between Redesdale and North Tynedale. Look—here on the map. Kielderhead Moor, East Kielder Moor, West Kielder, and so on. Between these two roads—damn it, there's ten by twelve . . . there's over a hundred square miles of trackless watershed. That's the area where Mark Douglas of Ashiebank got lost, the time the Hawick flag was stolen—you remember? Where he got himself landed with the girl Dacre, now the Honourable Mrs. Douglas. Well, now—couldn't a token bunch of cattle be lifted from near Hexham somewhere, and driven right up through that stuff, cross-country, night *and* day? Nothing short of aircraft's likely to find them on the Kielder Moors. It would be a tough bit of herding—but worth it, maybe?"

71

"*You* do it, Archie," Dod Wilson declared urgently. "Me, I'm just a farmer body, an' real fond o' a quiet life . . . !"

"You mean, it's impossible?"

"Hell, no! Nothing's impossible. But it'll be a gey long miserable job. Think o' it—a' night an' a' day, trailing tired stirks over god-forsaken moss-hags and bog. . . ."

"If I thought they were Mayor Stannard's cattle, I'd do it myself, on my two feet!" Archie asserted strongly. "But leave it, just now. We can decide about Hexham later. Do we want to go any farther south just now, on these foothills, before we strike over to Redesdale to meet Dand?"

"See here," Sanny Elliot said. "It seems that where we draw the cattle from is not so important as where we're going to drive them *to*. You get me? The important thing seems to be to find the beef-tubs first, and then decide where, within a radius of ten or twelve miles, we can get the cattle. Right? Well—don't you think that's what we ought to be doing? Looking for beef-tubs?"

"Sanny—you couldn't be righter," Archie agreed. "It's back into the hills for us. I've got one or two places that look possible on the map. And an old shepherd I know, who used to work these hills, told me about a couple more. Let's go."

* * *

They rode west by north, through a jumble of ever-heightening hills, until they struck a bridle-path which followed the upper waters of the river Breamish, which rises out of the great green womb of Cheviot itself, whose mighty bulk now dominated all the landscape before them. The track, obviously an old drove-road, was marked only as a faint dotted line on the map, and led right up over the watershed by a ridge called Butt's Roads, and down to the head of Bowmont Water, on the Scots side, reaching Yetholm eventually, after some twenty-five lonely miles. It was joined presently, moreover, by other tracks coming up from the headwaters of the Aln, and from upper Coquetdale, making an ideal assembly-lane for droves from four different

72

dales. Archie had had high hopes for this route, from his map-reading, and now, on the spot, it turned out to be even better than visualised. The two marked houses thereon, which might have proved a problem to get past, with herds of cattle, without difficult explanations and identifications, both proved to be deserted, one ruinous and the other no more than a grass-grown site. In addition, higher, where their track ran through a narrow valley right under Cheviot they found a fine cleuch, a steep grass-floored cul-de-sac into the hillside of Shielcleuch Edge, which would serve to pen the first-arriving cattle until the whole herd from this area was assembled to make the final lap across into Scotland. A good enough beef-tub on its own, but on the wrong side of the Borderline.

Thereafter, their bridle-path swung away sharply at right-angles westwards, and began to climb somewhat dauntingly towards the first high ridge of Lintlands Hill. But cattle undoubtedly had been driven this way at one time —even if it was a long time since the last ox-hoof had scored the green veining that was all that the track amounted to now. Sheep used it, and rabbits, but no other imprints were visible. Mounting steadily, the horsemen eyed its contours and gradients a trifle anxiously.

However, apart from one or two patches of boggy ground, which could be serious in wet weather, and a landslide of bare red earth and stones that would have to be circumnavigated, they reached the first ridge, at some sixteen hundred feet, reasonably satisfied. They had not once had to dismount.

There was a slight drop ahead of them, now, across a mile-wide moss, where the Davidson's Burn was born, one of the headstreams of the Coquet. This looked unpleasant, and the track was only discernible in brief patches. But by keeping carefully to the line of it, they found the going better than it appeared, and though soft, the ground nowhere degenerated into deep bog. Obviously there was stone near the surface, and the tussocky growth gave an added firmness. All the same, it was apparent that the cattle drovers

73

would have to keep their herd very closely under control and cling strictly to the line of the old track, indistinct as it was even in daylight, for there were numerous patches of treacherous emerald-green and black all around, whose warning was not to be ignored. Archie added one more entry to the growing list in his notebook.

The ground firmed as it began to rise again to the ultimate spine of the Cheviots range, along which ran the Borderline. The riders crossed it at about seventeen hundred feet, to stare out over the welter of summits and hogs' backs and ridges that stretched for a further fifteen miles into Scotland. Directly below them, a system of burns, patterned like the veining of a leaf, drained the land mass, to run together eventually into the long valley of the Bowmont Water, down towards which their bridle-path continued.

"Over there, to the left, a mile or two west, old Gib Turnbull says there's a place that should do," Archie told them. "He called it a hole. He said, if we kept along the ridge here, we'd see it. . . ."

"I see it now," Sanny Elliot declared, pointing. "Look—the third dip along from here, just under that big summit. That'll be Windygate, won't it? Yes. Well, half-way down. See that deep shadow . . ."

Obviously, where he pointed, was a sharp-lipped and sudden hollow in the broad flank of the hill, the mouth of which the levelling late-afternoon sun was picking out in pronounced shadow, different from all the other depressions and corries and burn-channels. Towards it the horsemen spurred.

The old shepherd had not misled them. Within a mile, they were at the edge of a great basin, gouged out of the broad breast of Windygate Hill, presumably by glacial action, two hundred feet perhaps in depth, with steep smooth sides plunging down to a floor of four or five acres, the only entrance a wedge in a shallow lip to the north, out of which a small burn spilled. And across the mouth of this wedge, plainly visible from above, were the traces of a bank, grass-grown and broken but obviously man-made, blocking the

74

entrance save for a gap a few feet wide. Undoubtedly, the trio were not the first to perceive the usefulness of this handiwork of nature.

Delighted, they rode round and down, to assure themselves of the accessibility for cattle. They were not disappointed in this, either. The place entirely suited their purpose. They reckoned it to be no more than eleven or twelve miles from where they had stood on Cochrane's Pike, surveying the land to be despoiled.

From here they rode north along the high ridges, to seek for another hollow to serve the raiders coming from the Wooler and Flodden area. On the west face of great Cheviot itself they found a fine cleuch, marked on their maps as Hen Hole, but reluctantly decided that it was still too far south for their requirements. The massive round hills of The Schel and The Curr drew them on, but seemed deplorably smooth for hole-hunters. Quartering the southern flanks of both, they found nothing that would hide even a couple of calves. Up on the connecting ridge, however, on the very line of the Border itself, they stumbled on the unmistakable traces of another old drove-road that had come up out of the College Valley on the English side, and ran north-eastwards down into Scotland. It led them to the head of the Curr Burn. This stream quite quickly scored a deep ravine for itself in the north face of the hill, and right down into this, presently, the traces of their track plunged. And since it rose right out again, only a hundred or so yards farther down, and on the same side, a reason for the descent was called for—and apparent. This section of the ravine also had been used as a penning-place for cattle. The steep scree-like nature of the banks below and the chaos of tumbled rock blocking the linn-like burn-channel above, meant that the track itself was the only access and exit for the place for four-footed beasts—and that could be barred readily enough. Their Scots forebears had been industrious and enterprising surveyors.

Content, the three young men turned their faces southwards.

75

Nearly three hours and twenty long rough miles later, they paced their weary mounts down the straight-striding reaches of the old Roman Road of Dere Street into Redesdale. With the sun setting behind them and drawing great shadows from every fold and eminence and hollow, they rode along that lonely causeway of the past, broken and overgrown and breached, but still distinguishably and indefatigably a road. Only the moorfowl called in their sorrow and the shaggy blackfaced sheep flounced off into the deeper heather and moss, but if, sometimes, the encroaching shadows seemed to the horsemen to take on the shapes of men, Roman legionaires or Border reivers, and march along that green road with them, honest weariness could account for such folly. Dropping, by the high camp at Chew Green, down past the great fort of Bremenium, they came to the tarmacadam of the Queen's highway in the long long valley of the Rede, and saw, in an occasional car, the first of humanity that they had observed since the forenoon.

Two miles farther northwards, they turned off the road and down towards a small hazel-wood by the riverside. The cheerful red glimmer of a fire greeted them, before the whinny of horses from within the trees issued to welcome their own tired steeds. Out of the hazels Dand Fairgrieve and his Hawick Right and Left stepped.

"You're late," Dand declared. "Only the burnt sausages are left, see. Come you and get them."

*   *   *

The Hawick trio had arrived in the haugh an hour-and-a-half earlier, and had a small tent pitched. Apparently they had had a satisfactory day, spying out the wide pasturelands of lower Redesdale, Otterburn, and Bellingham, and checking up on tracks and drove-roads. They had early come to the conclusion that Hexham and Corbridge were much too far distant for their purposes. But they had been fortunate indeed over their beef-tub. Their map had shown them a spot called The Scrathy Holes, under a most aptly

76

named hill, Dand's Pike, not far from the head of Jed Water, and readily reached from the Borderline at Deadwater on the North Tyne by the ancient Roman Road known as the Wheel Causeway. Inspection had proved this to be a group of glacial hollows, ideal for holding cattle, placed conveniently midway between the parallel roads of Rede and Tyne, with moreover a distinct hill-track leading up quite close to it, via the Kielder Burn from Tynedale. As well that there was this track, for the Kielder hills were largely covered with the new-planted spruces of the Forestry Commission, which could complicate droving. They had not sought out any further cleuchs, for there was room enough in the Scrathy Holes for all the beasts likely to be reived in the whole venture, and more. So they had devoted most of their day to surveying routes and farms on the low ground—for which they had found no lack of material.

Inevitably there were some comments on some people's luck, the dropping of windfalls into undeserving laps, and the easy notions some folk had of their responsibilities.

But it was on the whole a contented party that sat round the cheerful crackling fire and drank somewhat gritty cocoa, as the night settled on the bare hills of Redesdale. That is, until Archie Scott began to expound his latest proposition with regard to the due chastening of Hexham-on-Tyne. As has been indicated, the Jethart Callant was not a comfortable man, at all. He did not get a lot of encouragement for his project, Mayor Stannard or none.

On a grey Sunday morning, not too early, the six young men rode out of their little wood, across the shallows of Rede, and into the dew-drenched hills to the south-west, to seek out an operational area just over the Cumbrian border for the Langholm people to raid. Annan had agreed to come with them, though Dumfries, while proffering moral support and promising a few riders to assist Annan, had pointed out reasonably that the Solway Firth and the distances involved precluded any direct assault on England.

On their way over to Liddesdale, the reconnaissance party had perforce to cross that same vast watershed of the

77

Kielders through which Archie proposed to bring his Hexham cattle. Though they did it by a mapped bridle-path for most of the way, it took them nearly four bog-bound hours. The first two of these were very largely enlivened by a succession of head-shaking assertions as to the folly of thinking that cattle could be herded across this waterlogged wilderness, by five-sixths of the company, a catalogue of expostulation and indeed scorn which had the effect of forcing Archie Scott's long chin farther and farther forward. When the obviousness of it all was sufficiently established, and besides, everyone's attention fully occupied with coping with thoroughly hostile geography, it might have been noticed that the Scott chin did not recede any. He was that sort of man. And his silence was ominous. As, at last, they won out of it all, down to the road and railway and river at Kielder Station, he volunteered his one and only comment for a considerable time—that that tract was meant to be crossed north and south, not east and west as they had done it. The reception accorded this statement was as might have been expected.

Thereafter they threaded the remote Larriston and Bewcastle Fells, settled on a penning site to recommend to the Langholme Cornet, at the head of the Kershope Burn, and then rode thankfully and ploddingly north again, up Liddesdale. At the village of Newcastleton they telephoned their respective lieutenants, assembled waiting at Hawick, to fetch the horse-boxes and cars, and settled back to relax in the comfortable hotel until they arrived an hour or so later.

Though the others accepted their well-earned ease unconditionally, it was to be observed that Archie Scott continued to pore over his map. And over that ominously brown portion of the map where the rivers of Tyne and Rede and Tarset and Turret were born amid moss-hag and peat-bog, in particular. He was capable of a wicked obstinacy, to add to all his other faults.

78

7

Archie pushed back his chair, and at the same time the lists of names and places, times, map-references, carbon-copies of plans, and typed instructions that littered his desk. All was settled, save for one or two last-minute details—though it is to be feared that editorially, the *Jedburgh Journal* had suffered somewhat in the process. The printing-house office down the narrow pend off the High Street had, this first week of September, tended to resemble a military operations-room. As well that Archibald Scott, senior, otherwise Auld Baldie to much of the Borders, was more inclined to farming than journalism these days, with a brand-new scarlet-painted combine-harvester his pride and play-thing—or he would have had something to say about it all, in the straightforward and unmistakable language for which he was noted. His son was fully appreciative.

He had just completed his final preparations—the arrange-ments for the sham ride-out, the diversionary ceremonial progress to Morebattle and Kale Water, that was to cloak the assembling of his expeditionary force the following Saturday afternoon. This Morebattle ride-out, normally ridden during the first week of July in the Jethart Festival, had that year had to be cancelled owing to a thunderstorm and cloudburst. Now, Archie perceived the best of reasons for reviving it, out of due season though it was—but for invited riders only. It would give the necessary excuse for the eighty-odd horsemen to leave their respective and widely scattered home areas openly on Saturday early afternoon . . . whenever they might quietly and unobtrusively return. Moreover, Morebattle and the upland valley of the Kale Water was

79

ideally and centrally situated for dispersal for all four main thrusts over the Border—and little populated. The Langholm contingent, of course, would only make a token gesture of riding east for this gathering, and as soon as they were safely free from observation, would turn south on their own affairs.

The man was rising to his feet when the spring-hung outer door bell jangled, and a few seconds later the head of the office-boy-cum-printer's-devil-cum-junior-reporter appeared round the inner office door-jamb.

"Lady to see you, Archie," he announced, and volunteered a judicious click-click out of the side of his mouth for added significance—significance, because Jedburgh was not too large a town for practically everyone who called at the *Journal* office to be known and introduced by name.

Nevertheless, despite this prior warning, Archie was unprepared for the advent of Miss Barbara Hepburn of the *Daily News*, from far-away Glasgow. She was dressed this time in suitably autumnal tweeds, rural in implication if far from rural in cut. She smiled with entire friendliness and equal frankness.

"Good afternoon, Mr. Scott," she greeted him. "Glad I caught you in. I happened to be in Jedburgh again—so, of course, I felt I shouldn't go without looking in on you."

"No?" the man commented cautiously. "How do you do."

She laughed. "You don't sound just overjoyed to see me, I must say! Perhaps I've come at a vital moment in the production of the *Jedburgh Journal*, with the presses panting for the editorial epic?"

He ignored that. "You will soon be knowing the road from Glasgow to these parts, Miss Hepburn," he observed heavily. "I wonder what the draw was, this time?" He cleared his throat. "I admire your courage, anyway!"

"Courage? I'm glad you admire something about me, Mr. Scott. But why my courage?"

"After the report you wrote for the *News* on the North-

80

umbrian trip, I wonder you dare show your nose in Jedburgh again!"

"Oh? You didn't like it, then? I'm sorry to hear that. I thought it was rather good, myself. And so very factual, you know. As a newspaperman yourself, I'd have thought that you'd have appreciated the objectivity of it all!" The young woman opened her hand-bag, to produce a slim gold cigarette-case. "Is it permitted that one smokes in your sanctum, Mr. Scott?"

Too late he fumbled in his own pockets. She waited, patiently uncritical, for him to provide her with a light however, meanwhile resting one tweed-encased hip upon the edge of his desk, and swinging a shapely nylon-clad leg. It was all an act, of course—but wasn't *he* supposed to be the actor?

"Do sit down," he invited sardonically. "There's *one* thing I do appreciate about your piece, Miss Hepburn— and that is that it won't increase your paper's reputation or circulation in the Borders! However much you may have raked in from the North English papers for second rights!"

She tipped her red lips with a pink tongue at that shrewd thrusting. "My . . . my editor hasn't said so, Mr. Scott," she answered, a little less assuredly.

"It wasn't your editor I was thinking of," he gave back. "I rather gather that he equates Scotland with the bonnie bonnie banks somewhere! It was the circulation manager —the man the owners listen to!"

Barbara Hepburn rose from her desk-corner and stepped over to the window that looked out on to a narrow yard, crow-stepped gables, and the quickly-rising hillsides of the Jed Valley. "Perhaps the forthcoming excitements will enable the *News* to regain all this lost ground in the Borders that you are so concerned about, Mr. Scott?" she suggested.

"Eh . . .? What . . . do you . . . mean?"

"Just that I gather that you *are* planning some sort of a demonstration? A return match, as it were, to North-umberland? I thought I might come along."

The man swallowed, audibly enough for his visitor to

hear. She turned to face him, blowing a thin jet of tobacco smoke. There was no doubt who held the cards, now. Archie gripped the back of his chair. "To what are you referring, Miss Hepburn?" he asked, but in a voice which but inadequately disguised a sinking heart.

"You know very well," she told him. "Some sort of raid, isn't it? Next Saturday. Something to do with cattle."

Carefully the Callant walked round his chair, and sat down. He fingered one of the typewritten papers on his desk. "Just how do you come to know anything about this?" he asked, as though from quite a distance.

"The *News* has its sources of information. Reliable sources," she said. "We have every reason to trust this one." The girl looked at him thoughtfully. "I gather, from your attitude, that this was meant to be entirely hush-hush? A close secret?"

"It was." Grimly he said it. "I'll admit you've shaken me."

Barbara Hepburn took a step forward, her woman-of-the-world pose forgotten for the moment. "I'm sorry, if this . . . hurts," she told him, coming to the far side of his littered desk.

He jerked his head, as though to shake off any of her sympathy. "How much d'you know?" he demanded.

"Not a great deal perhaps—more than I have told you. I know that some kind of widespread raid on Northumberland has been planned to take place next Saturday. In retaliation for the reception you got from the English, that time. And that *you* are organising it."

"And who else knows this, as well as you? As well as the Glasgow *News*?" he rapped out.

"Not many, I should think. No other papers, anyway. We keep our information to ourselves. The *News* likes to get exclusive stories!"

"You mean, you don't think the rest of the Press will have got it from the same source?"

"I'm sure they haven't—or I'd have heard. Things get round, in the Press Club, you know."

82

"And this one hasn't got round?"

"Not yet!"

He looked up from the list of map-references that he was holding, directly into her eyes. "I should very much like to know where this, er, information came from."

She smiled faintly. "I dare say you would. But from what I've seen of your methods, it's possibly just as well that I can't tell you—couldn't, even if I would. The news came from an agent that we have in these parts, who said that it was reliable but he was not at liberty to divulge the origin. But, Mr. Scott—I understand that there are lots of young men involved in this thing. Isn't it almost impossible to keep a secret that so many people know?"

"Perhaps. But I'd have thought we could trust these people. The whole affair depends entirely on secrecy. If any details leak out beforehand, it will just have to be called off, completely."

"And that would be a pity, wouldn't it! For I gather there's quite a story in it."

"But not for the News!" Archie almost snarled.

"I wonder?" she said, and held her peace.

Angrily the man pushed himself back in his chair. "Look —this could ruin everything," he declared. "If it gets out before Saturday, the whole business will be stopped. Not only by ourselves. Or even by the English being ready for us. But by our own authorities. The Provosts and magistrates and so on, will clamp down on it—bound to. They have no option, once they get to hear of it."

"Quite. I recognise that." She nodded. "As well that it's me that's been let into the secret!"

His glance was less than complimentary perhaps. Then he shook his head.

"But even accepting that—the man who let this out to you can do the same to others."

"No—I think not. The News has its methods of keeping its exclusive stories exclusive!"

"You mean, whoever squealed will be paid to keep his mouth shut?"

83

"I wouldn't put it quite as crudely as that, of course . . ."

"I see." Archie stroked his chin pensively. "I suppose that's something, at any rate."

"A great deal, believe me." She sounded entirely bright and cheerful. "So now you've only me to deal with!" There might have been some slight emphasis on that word "deal".

"M'mmm." The man eyed her, wary again.

"Yes," she nodded. "I come along, the *News* gets the full, inside, and exclusive story . . . and nobody else gets to hear anything about it until the Monday morning!"

"No," Archie said baldly. "Impossible."

"Yes," she insisted gently. "Like the Provosts and magistrates, you have no option, Mr. Scott. And, though I say it myself, I'm really much the lesser of two evils."

"You mean, if you don't get what you want, you will let the story out before Saturday? Blackmail me into it?"

"What a horrid way of putting it! Say, I might bring a little legitimate pressure to bear."

He tapped finger-nails on desk-top. "But you don't know any details. You've practically no story to publish!"

"We could make some awfully intelligent guesses . . . which you would find rather difficult to correct or deny, Mr. Scott! I've heard about these cattle. And horses. And if my colleagues on the rest of the Press got to hear about this, their methods of gaining information might not be so straightforward and sympathetic as mine!"

"Sympathetic . . .!" the Callant snorted. But he saw the need to shift his stance. "Anyway, you couldn't come with us," he declared. "The trip will certainly be no ploy for a woman."

"If by that you mean, as I suppose, that it will all be done on horseback and over rough country, let me reassure you, Mr. Scott. I've ridden quite a lot in my day. I've even had a go at that pony-trekking into the Cairngorms, from Newtonmore. You provide the horse, and I'll do the rest . . . and be no trouble to you, at all."

84

He glowered at her, nibbling his lip. "You are a . . . a damned nuisance!" he asserted, with complete sincerity.

Quite unabashed, she smiled at him, apparently with equal sincerity. "I'm not, you know—really," she assured, prepared to be placatory now that she had made her unassailable position quite clear. "I should think I might be very useful to you. Judging from what I've heard, the right kind of Press explanation and treatment could make a lot of difference to the way this exploit of yours is received, after it's all over. Don't you agree?"

"The *right* treatment, perhaps . . . !" That was no concession, but sheerest disparagement.

Her response held a touching humility, nevertheless. "Yes. Isn't this the ideal opportunity for me to redeem myself? To undo all the harm I seem to have done to the Borders by my previous effort?"

The other did not commit himself, being rather more suspicious than ever when she took this line. "Ummm," he said.

"Anyway, I'm coming," she added, with a sudden change of tone—and sounding distinctly more like herself. Her hearer almost grinned. Business-like, she stubbed out her cigarette, and reached into her bag for her notebook. "Now for some details," she said briskly. "You'd want me to have the background right, wouldn't you . . . ?"

Archie Scott sighed, and ran fingers through his dark curly hair. "Heaven save us from inquisitive women!" he requested. "What would be the female of a newshound. . . ?"

85

8

It was four-thirty of a golden September Saturday afternoon as the great cavalcade of riders trotted southwards out of the village of Morebattle amongst its green foothills, along the by-road that climbed towards the lonely ruin of Whitton Tower. So far, the company had kept to the time-honoured programme of the Morebattle ride-out. Now they were passing out of populated country, and a new spirit and tension very quickly was becoming evident amongst the party. The irksome play-acting was over; now they were getting down to serious business. As a consequence, spurs and riding-crops were by general consent brought into play, and the rising ground towards Whitton was covered somewhat faster than was usual—indeed, at a rousing gallop. And there were no stragglers.

But then, this was not a gathering in which stragglers might be looked for. Young men all, carefully chosen and well mounted, here was the cream of an ancient and hard-riding tradition. With one exception—the hatless, jacketed and breeched, fair-haired girl who rode a mettlesome grey just behind Archie Scott. And rode in such fashion as to stay in that position, hard as that man might lead the way. However conspicuous Barbara Hepburn might seem, for various reasons, in that otherwise all-male company, she was not so on account of inferior horsemanship.

They did not continue all the three miles up to Whitton Tower. Whenever the green shoulder of Morebattle Hill intervened between them and observation from the village, they swung off left-handed, to climb more steeply to the

86

ridge that separated them from the deep valley of the Kale Water. At the col in the crest of it, Archie drew rein, holding up his hand to halt the rest. When all were clustered together in a tight group, the Callant trotted out in front, to turn and face them.

There were eighty or ninety riders present on that hill-top, with two or three spare horses—rather more than he had expected, for the Langholm and Annan people, of course, were absent. Also elsewhere were the couriers with fast cars and motor-cycles, whose duties would be to maintain communications by such roads and by-ways as the terrain so grudgingly conceded. Looking at the assembly, stirring as was the sight, Archie could not help reflecting that amongst them presumably was the man or men who had given away their secret to the Glasgow *News*. He quelled the impulse to mention this fact, however, on the recognition that such would be definitely the wrong note on which to start their adventure.

He cleared his throat. "I'm not going to make a speech. We get plenty of that at the more orthodox ride-outs," he declared, and gained a cheer. "We're at the parting of the ways, now. Though it's been impossible to have a general get-together and pow-wow beforehand, I've no doubt you all know pretty well what we're going to try to do—what we're going to *do*!" he corrected himself. "And the leaders of each section are well briefed in their own part of the over-all picture. Briefly, the broad scheme is for a selection of Northumbrian cattle to be drawn off by means of four main thrusts, at this end—that is, in the East and Middle Marches. The east-most will be on to the area of Flodden, Wooler, and Kirknewton. This will be a joint effort of Kelso and Coldstream, led by Dod Wilson the Kelso Laddie. They'll drive their beasts up the College Water, and pen them in a beef-tub that you can almost see from here—up there on The Curr." And he pointed south by east into the jumble of great hills before them.

An excited buzz of comment broke out, and Archie had to raise his hand again for quiet.

87

"That thrust shouldn't take so very long, and most of those involved ought to be home in their beds by daylight tomorrow. Next will be the group tackling the valleys of the Breamish, Aln, and Coquet—that is, the Whittingham and Rothbury areas. This will be Jethart's job, supported by Duns and Lauder. They'll herd up the headwaters of the Breamish, below Cheviot itself, to Kelsocleuch, a hole up there on Windygate Hill, right ahead of us now. This lot will have one of the trickiest pieces of droving to do, of the whole show. Incidentally, Headquarters will be up on the summit of Windygate. Each group will send somebody to report there when their job's done, before dispersal—or if they need help. Got that?"

A chorus of assent and some raillery on the subject of staff-wallahs followed.

"Sure. Sure. The next assault will be down Redesdale, to the Otterburn—Elsdon district, and will be run by the Teries, with Melrose and Peebles assisting. Dand Fairgrieve in charge. Their herding-place will be a group of hollows called the Scrathy Holes to the west of Carter Fell. They'll share this place with the last group, that's raiding the Upper Tyne valley and Bellingham area—Selkirk and Gala are doing this, Wat Hogarth in command. Those are the four thrusts. Each of these groups will work in maybe four sections of four or five men to a section, and each section will be responsible for four or five farms. The idea is to make the impact of all this felt as widely as possible. Up to half a dozen beasts from each farm is what's wanted. If twenty farms in an area are raided, losing an average of five cattle each—that ought to give the English something to think about. That means about a hundred cattle from each thrust to be driven up into the hills—a total of four hundred or so. That's the general scheme. All right?"

Apparently that *was* all right—though one or two improvements and refinements were shouted out.

"Fair enough. You can keep your good advice for your own leaders—maybe they'll thank you!" Archie called back. "There are two side-shows, as well. The Langholm and

88

Annan people are staging a similar performance in the west. And there's going to be a small long-range thrust right down as far as Hexham. This is only a sort of token gesture, and the few cattle taken will have to be driven back all of twenty-five miles to cross the Border. That'll take a lot of tomorrow as well as tonight, and will be the riskiest part of the venture. Now—for generalities. Don't get involved in any trouble with the people. If you're disturbed taking beasts, leave them—there's plenty more to choose from. And be careful, droving. We don't want injured beasts, with broken legs and so on, that would have to be slaughtered —and replaced! So don't rush it. Naturally, make as little noise as you can. And I don't suppose I have to point out that it's beef-cattle we want, not dairy-stock! When you get your cattle safely penned, and have sent word to H.Q., don't hang about, but get quietly back home. We don't want anybody about these hills in the morning when the English farmers start following trails looking for their stock. That would just lead to violence. Okay? Any questions?"

"Aye. Whae gets the dame, Archie? Is she a mascot, or what?"

"Och, she's to milk the coos you bring in by mistake, Pe'er, man!"

"Hell—d'you no' ken she's the prize, for the boys wi' the best bunch o' stirks . . .?"

Archie glanced over at the object of these enquiries. She was smiling easily, evidently not in the least put out.

"That's the Press," he said shortly. "To make sure that we get a good write-up *this* time. And it had better be— or some of us will be taking appropriate steps!"

"You've said it!"

"Hear, hear!"

On that note the party broke up. All descended into the valley of the Kale Water, but at different angles, Dod Wilson leading his score of riders eastwards towards the Yetholm hills, the two groups for Redesdale and Tynedale slanting

89

westwards to pick up the Roman road of Dere Street, and Archie Scott with his Jedburgh, Lauder and Duns contingent heading straight downhill, for the confluence of the Hounam Burn with Kale.

In only a few minutes the welter of the Cheviots had swallowed them, without trace.

* * *

Up past the lonely farm of Hounam Mains, nestling in the green lap of the hills, they rode. The farmer here was a friend of Archie's, and would ask no awkward questions. And now this party at least was finished with all roads and houses and the haunts of men. Winding amongst steep bracken-clad braes, climbing over high green shoulders, sheep-strewn, they presently reached the upper Bowmont, and turned along the sketchy traces of its ancient drove-road. Thereafter it was just steady mounting, mile after mile into the broad breast of Windygate Hill, with the sinking sun and all Scotland dwindling behind them, and the evening silence of the hills around them. The Kelsocleuch Burn, lusty tributary of Bowmont, took them right up to their chosen beef-tub, now a bowl of purple shadows, brimming over. Here all were made familiar with its dimensions and immediate approaches. The sun had set by the time that they reached the ultimate summit ridge, and the Borderline, at two thousand feet, and the shadowy half-light brooded on all those far-flung uplands. And now Rab Pringle, Archie's poker-faced Right-hand Man peeled off with three Jedburgh volunteers, for the long, long ride to Hexham, leading a spare horse. The Callant led the remaining two dozen of his party down across the treacherous little watershed of the Davidson Burn, grimly adjuring them well to watch their steps—not so much for present comfort as for future safety. Every step from now on must be considered as one over which reluctant cattle were to be driven, and in the darkness. He succeeded in sobering his companions quite notably. Barbara Hepburn rode closely in his tracks, watched and wondered—and wisely held her tongue.

90

By nine-thirty the Cheviots were a blackly-looming mass behind them, and darkness settled on the fair land of Northumbria. Ahead, occasional pin-points of yellow light stirred them strangely. The company split up beside one of the deserted cottages in the valley, two groups of six following the Breamish down towards Ingram and the farms around Hedgeley and Brandon, the other two taking a passably-marked path over higher ground that led to the little village of Alnham. In half an hour they were heedfully skirting to the west of its few houses and church. Here Archie dropped his third section to cope with farms in this neighbourhood, advising them to wait at least an hour before actually commencing operations. And with five remaining stalwarts, including Johnny Hume the Duns Reiver, plus the persistent Miss Hepburn, he rode on southwards through the night, towards Rothbury.

It was ten miles still to Rothbury town itself, which unfortunately put it out of effective range. However, Archie's diligent researches had revealed that the Chairman of the District Council, the sportingly-inclined Dr. Josiah White, farmed at a curiously-named spot called Snitter, that was a good four miles nearer them than the town. Moreover, another of the Councillors was still closer, a squireen at Netherton. Archie was determined to get as far as Snitter.

By narrow back-roads and field-tracks they trotted, avoiding all lights like the plague. Not that there were many of them, for it was still but sparsely populated country, semi-moorland and rough pasture—cattle country indeed. And there was plenty of cattle about—shadowy beasts plunged away from them beyond every other hedge and drystone dyke. It was tempting just to take a selection of these and be gone. But Snitter called.

They circumnavigated the farm-place of Netherton, noting two fields containing cattle sufficiently distant from the house to make raiding easy. Already the farm-cottage lights were going out.

Following the haugh-lined banks of the Wreigh Burn, a

91

well-doing tributary stream of Coquet that ran roughly parallel with the road, they pressed southwards, Archie consulting a one-inch ordnance map frequently with the aid of a carefully shaded electric torch. Down through the meadows flanking the stream they picked up ridiculously a string of inquisitive bullocks, which insisted on accompanying them in high-tailed good spirits, and actually and embarassingly mooed their lusty protest when shut out behind a gate at the side-road eventually reached and crossed beside the darkened cot-houses of Low Trewhitt. Clinging to the burn beyond, the horsemen let its grassy links and chuckling reaches bring them right down to Snitter itself. It was ten-fifty of a star-lit, not too dark, and distinctly chilly autumn night, with a heavy dew drenching the grass. Two lights only shone in the neighbourhood.

Dismounting at the stream's edge, beside a group of hazels, Archie sent out two scouts to spy out the immediate vicinity, on foot. The rest of them stretched their legs, munched sandwiches, and, following Barbara Hepburn's example, lit a discreet cigarette or two. Archie almost stopped them, but relented.

"Tired?" he asked of her.

"No. Just a little stiff, perhaps—and sore, where one gets sore, you know."

"You will be stiffer and sorer!" he prophesied succinctly, with what sounded suspiciously like a certain satisfaction.

One of the scouts was back very promptly, to report that there was a farm just up on their right, with a group of cottages beyond. In a field bordering this haugh only a hundred or two yards away there were at least a dozen bullocks. Also there was a gap in the hawthorn hedge, filled in with a rickety bit of wooden fencing. They could have what beasts they wanted down through there as easy as winking, in five minutes.

So far so good—but when the second scout returned, some few minutes later, it was rather to complicate the pleasing picture. It appeared that there was more to

92

Snitter than they had envisaged. There was quite a little village in fact, over to the left, eastwards of this burn, around a road junction—one or two shops, an inn, and at least two more farms, probably three . . . though the last might be more like a mill.

Archie Scott frowned. Owing to the very long road back from here, it was essential that they did not burden themselves with too many beasts, or they'd never get them back. The bulk of their herd they must pick up much nearer to the hills. He had intended only to collect five or six here, from Dr. White. But which were Dr. White's cattle? When he had ascertained that the doctor farmed at Snitter, he had assumed that to be the name of the farm— and now it seemed that there were at least three farms. It would be ridiculous if they took away beasts from some other farmer, and left the doctor's untouched. But how to find out which was White's farm . . .?

He did not require to underline the problem to his companions—it was apparent to all. Heads were scratched over it, and Johnny Hume suggested that the only thing to do was to take maybe two beasts from each farm, to be sure of including Dr. White's. But that this would add enormously to both the work and the risks was equally evident. Also, not knowing the field boundaries of each farm, they could not be sure that each place was mulcted.

It was Barbara Hepburn who voiced the obvious alternative. "Someone will have to go and enquire which is the doctor's place," she pointed out reasonably.

"Quite. And waken up the village, arouse suspicions at this time of night, and generally give ourselves away!" Archie Scott added, sarcastically.

"Not necessarily," the girl disclaimed. "There are two houses with lights still lit, at least. And, after all, he *is* the doctor. It's quite reasonable for people to come, even late at night, asking for a doctor's house. There might have been an accident. There need be no suspicions . . . especially if it is a woman who does the asking."

All eyes turned on her. "You mean—*you'd* be willing

93

to do this?" the Callant wondered. "Wouldn't the *News* be rather taking sides? The wrong side, too . . .?"

She shrugged. "Say that it's to help out the story," she told him. "The *News* likes a good story, you know. That's why I'm here."

"Well . . . if you're willing. But wouldn't even a woman, dressed in riding-breeches and high boots, be likely to arouse some comment at this hour?"

"M'mmm. Yes, I suppose so. It's dark, of course. If I didn't show myself too much . . ."

"If whoever came brought a light to the door with them, as they well might . . ." Archie shook his head. "What you need is a skirt of some sort. Then you'd just look as though you'd got Wellingtons on."

"Try a potato-sack!" somebody suggested, less than respectfully. "Sure to find old ones lying around any farm."

There was a laugh. But the young woman took the proposition seriously. "Why not?" she said. "In the dark, I dare say it would pass. I'd stand well back."

"Sackcloth strikes me as most suitable!" Archie commented, but less sourly than he had addressed her hitherto. "Come on, then. I'll come with you, so far at least. Before those lights go out."

So, led by the scout, a Lauder youth apparently named Wally, they moved down to the burn's edge, searching for a place to cross. It was shallow enough, in spots, but apt to be a good ten feet in width. Wally previously had just splashed across, it seemed.

"Sensible man," Archie declared stoutly, and stepping forward, stooped. One arm encircled the girl's back, one scooped up behind her knees, and staggering only slightly, straight into the water he strode, all in the same rhythm of movement.

Barbara Hepburn gasped, stiffened in his arms for a moment, and then relaxed. "Quite a . . . a masterful man!" she said, a trifle breathlessly, and when, in reply, he only grunted—"for heaven's sake, don't fall or drop

94

ne now—or all Snitter will know about this, I promise you!"

He did not answer this either—for she was a fair specimen of adequate and curvelineal womanhood and no mere armful of thistledown. While her respiration was evident and with its own attractions, he was not anxious for *his* to be too apparent. He was thankful that the stones under his feet seemed to be little more than pebbles, at any rate, and that he chuckling waters flowed over-swiftly for slippery weeds o grow.

As he set her down on the farther bank, just a little less deliberately than he would have planned, she asked, "Was hat chivalry, Mr. Scott—or just tentative wolfery, I wonder?"

"Take your choice!" he jerked, less than graciously, and talked on.

The ground sloped up towards the road. One of the lights shone from a cottage at this side of the road, quite nearby. They found a gate in the hedging to their haughland, and stepped out on to the tarmacadam.

"There's a ferm aboot a hunnerd yerds doon this bit roadie opposite," Wally informed.

"Let's hope there's no dogs," Archie said, and they moved across the road junction.

The side-road had more cottages on either side. The second light came from somewhere down on the left.

"That's the ferm," Wally whispered, as they walked, as quietly as they might, down between the darkened houses.

Sure enough, the light shone from the bulk of a two-storied house surrounded by bushes and a tree or two, and to which a short drive and a white-painted gate gave access. To the side was the loom of black barns and farm-buildings. A little farther on they found a roadway leading in to these latter.

"No need for us all to go in," Archie directed. "Wait here, in the shadow of the bushes."

He crept down and into the huddle of the buildings. It was darker here. With a range of what smelt like byres

95

coming between him and the house, he risked a carefully shaded light from his torch. No sacks were actually lying about, that he could see. He approached a half-door to the byre, listened, but heard no movement within, and cautiously unhooked the latch. There were no beasts inside—the milkers would still be out at grass of nights, of course. But there seemed to be no sacks either. A door at the far end of the long spick-and-span modern byre had something written on it which caught the man's eye in the roving beam of his torch. Closer inspection revealed the words KEEP CLOSED. Inevitably opening it, he peered in. It was a meticulously-kept and whitewashed dairy. Stepping inside, his spurred heel caught on something soft on the floor. Shining his light down, he found a sack spread on the concrete, to wipe byre-soiled feet on. Thankfully stooping to pick it up, he jerked upright as there was a rustle of quick movement behind him, and a soft thud. He swung round, to find a pair of green basilisk eyes regarding him out of the darkness of the byre. Hastily his torch stabbed thither—to reveal a thin black farm cat, which stepped forward, tail upright and purring, to rub round the ankles of his mud-spattered boots. Swallowing, Archie gathered up his sack, closed the dairy door carefully, and hastened back whence he had come, thanking his Creator that He hadn't made cats to bark.

Out at the roadway, he took out his penknife and slit open the bottom of a somewhat unsavoury sack, and handed it to the girl.

She sniffed, audibly.

"Best I could do," he declared defensively. "Good essential rural smell. Make you seem much less suspicious to country folk."

"D'you think so . . .?" She sounded unconvinced. But holding the thing by somewhat fastidious finger-tips, she stepped into the slit end of the sack, and pulled it up round her waist. It was considerably too long, and she had to bunch up quite a lot of it under her jacket. "Afraid there's too much of this," she decided.

96

"Nothing of the sort. All the better," Archie maintained. "You'll look like a maternity case. Shut up, Wally!" And to discourage further unnecessary comment, he promptly led the way back between the houses.

At the road junction they were relieved to see the cottage window still lit up. Taking up their position at the opposite side of the road, in the shadow of a gable-end, the men shooed the young woman over.

"You look grand," Archie assured. "Try and talk like a country wench, though probably the less you say the better."

They watched her cross the street, less than jauntily, to be lost against the loom of the cottage. They heard her rap on the door, saw a shadow come between the yellow light and the window, and then the light itself move—an oil-lamp, obviously. The door opened, and a man in his shirt-sleeves was revealed therein, holding a flickering glass-chimneyed lamp in his hand. The girl was standing well back and to the side, so that he had to peer out.

They heard the murmur of voices, saw the man point. Unfortunately, thereafter, he remained standing in the doorway, as though to see that his enquirer took the right direction. Whether he was in any way suspicious could not be guessed from his attitude. Silhouetted in the not very powerful glow of the lamp, the girl backed away from the vicinity, expressing thanks and apologies in a not notably Northumbrian or countrified tone. Archie was relieved to see her walk past their hiding-place, and along the road whence they had just come—thankful also that she had no spurs attached to her riding-boots, as he had, which would rather have spoiled the effect from the rear.

When, presently, the door was closed, the two young men hastened after her, coming up with her at the corner of the side-road. She was divesting herself of her skirt.

"The other house with the light showing is Dr. White's farm!" she informed. "I think you ought to give him back his property, don't you?" And she handed Archie the sacking. "Unless, that is, your chivalrous inclinations impel you to keep it as a romantic souvenir!"

"Well, I'm damned!" that man said, and strode off farmwards again.

*   *   *

Avoiding the farm-buildings this time, they went farther down the road and into the field beyond, to circle back. This field was permanent pasture, and contained cattle; but as Archie had expected, it was the milk cows from the byre. Also, a pair of fine hunters. Dark shadows in the field beyond proved to be stooks in oat stubble. Wally said, however, that farther over to the east a bit, the land sloped down towards another fair-sized burn, and that was almost certain to be grassland. They moved back in that direction, and sure enough, beyond a tall hedge, was sloping rough pasture, dotted with stocky bullocks. Working down the hedge, they found a gate in the bottom corner, leading into the cornfield. Archie leant on it. "I think we can do this ourselves," he decided. "No need to go back for the others. Ever herded cattle, Miss Hepburn?"

"No-o-o," she admitted. "But I'll try anything—once. They won't . . .?"

"Not them. They're much less dangerous than men, actually! They'll be much more frightened of you than you of them—and with reason! Just shoo them—only quietly, you understand. The thing is, we don't want too many—and they'll all be apt to come, or most of them. Wally—you'd better stay by the gate here. We'll round them up, and you let only the first half-dozen through. Only, we don't want very young stirkies. I think I saw one or two young beasts there. If they come with the others, you'll just have to let them through along with five or six decent beasts, and we'll weed them out later. Okay? You'll have to be pretty smart with that gate, or you'll have them all through."

"Sure. Fine, that."

Archie, who had been feeling about in the hedge for the

98

last few moments, cursed as he jagged fingers on thorns, but managed to detach a green wand to give to the girl. "There you are—hit them over the nose with that, and they'll respect you," he told her. "Come on."

Dr. White kept fairly good gates and gate-fastenings, and there was less wire-disentangling than there might have been. Wally stood guard in the half-open entrance, and his two companions moved inside, to make a wideish circuit, clockwise.

It was soon evident that there were a fair number of cattle in the place. Far from having to round them up, the brutes came along at a stiff-legged trot from all quarters, intrigued by this nocturnal visitation. Archie found the young woman keeping ever closer to him, as the bullocks came lumbering up on all sides, shadowy and huge-seeming. He permitted himself to squeeze her elbow reassuringly.

"Just stewing-steak in bulk," he mentioned. "Excellent with dumplings and sage." He glanced around them. "How many d'you say we've got here? Grown beasts?"

"Oh, hundreds! Too many. And, and overgrown, I'd say!"

"Fully a dozen, anyway. You know, I think we hardly need to drive these over. He jabbed a fist into a thrusting puffing inquisitive large snout—and the subsequent rearing commotion drew a quick gasp from his assistant. "If we just walk towards the gate, I believe they'll follow us."

"You mean . . . turn our backs on them?"

"Surely. They won't mind! See, take my arm, if you want. Or better still, walk in front of me—and then you've only got to worry about getting shunted at second-hand!" Turning, he spoke confidentially. "Really, of course, I'm much more of a menace to be alone with in the dark than these critturs, you know!"

"Don't flatter yourself!" she answered brave-voiced. And more bravely still, turned to walk at his side, rigidly but without availing herself of either of his kind offers. For the first three or four yards, that is. But with great lumbering shapes jostling at her very elbow and hot steaming

99

snuffling breath blowing down her neck, she was forced to edge up against the man, tuck in the small of her back, and eventually slip her hand within his arm.

He pressed it to his side, encouragingly. "There's a lot to be said for bullocks," he observed. "I always say . . . Hey!" he exclaimed as she was cannoned against him by a too-closely affectionate steer. "Don't let them do that. Hit them over the nose with that stick I gave you, when they get too matey."

"No . . . oh, no. That would just offend them . . ."

He laughed, and patted her hand in avuncular fashion, almost stroked it indeed. "Not them. They're thick-skinned brutes, but good-hearted. Just English stirks, and mannerless!"

"Is that the gate . . .?" she began, and then swallowed her words. Behind them somewhere arose a hollow sound, like distant thunder, and the very ground began to tremble beneath their feet. "Quick! Quick!" she cried, and, still clutching his arm, started to run.

"It's all right! Just more coming over. Don't flap . . .!" Archie urged. But willy-nilly, he was forced to hasten also, by her tugging and by the promptly increased pace of the creatures so closely encompassing them. In the interests of self-respect he tried very hard to keep it to something that might still rank as a very fast walk. But it was no good. Barbara's dragging was too vehement, and the pressure all round too great. Also, the noise of what sounded remarkably like a stampede behind, and rapidly approaching, was not reassuring and without some small effect. In a few moments the man was running too.

Thus, in impressive career, the whole assembly bore down on the gate—and it would be hard to say who or what was the foremost.

"Here we come!" Archie shouted, perhaps rather unnecessarily. "Open wide." He did not want them to be crushed against a half-shut gate by some tons of solid meat. "Get it shut behind us—quick!" Whether Wally would hear all that was doubtful, with the noise the cattle made,

100

but he had the gate swung wide, anyway, and they pounded through like a charge of cavalry. Straight into the cornfield they hurtled, wherein rows of stooks loomed up in front of them, and slap into one of these man and girl plunged, and fell headlong. The enthusiastic bullocks swung left and right around them, wheeled by general consent, and so stood, in almost martial array, blowing lustily and waiting happily for the next round. With commendable calmness and presence of mind Wally swung the gate shut on their very heels, in face of a solid advancing phalanx of beef from the far side of the field—and the day was saved.

Archie picked himself up from the oat-stook, dark-browed, dusting himself down. "That was quite ridiculous!" he averred, tight-lipped. He let the young woman get up on her own, too. A man's dignity makes its due demands.

"My Goad!" Wally exclaimed. "Yon's a hell o' a way o' herding stirks! Wis it a race, or what? An' whit aboot the five or six beasts I wis to let through?"

"We'll sort them out at the next gate," he was told stiffly. "D'you think . . .?" The Callant coughed. "D'you think they'd hear all that noise up at the farm-house?"

"No' if they're deaf or blin' drunk!" the Lauder youth asserted cheerfully.

Archie rubbed his chin. "It's a good four or five hundred yards. They'd probably hear the cattle, all right—but so long as they didn't hear *us*, voices. I dare say they'll be used to these brutes getting skittish. There's no lights showing this side of the house, at any rate." He had so far recovered himself as to half-turn to the girl. "You all right?" he enquired.

"Yes—oh, yes. Except for a couple of horns still left in the small of my back . . .!"

"These beasts have no horns," she was assured, starchily. "They appear to be a Shorthorn-Angus cross. Come on, then—we'd better get them driven across to the road."

But that was not so easy, either. Whether it was that current excitements had got the creatures worked up, or

101

that, like the British Army, they preferred to be led rather than driven, or even that the cornfield had a distracting influence, was debatable. But whatever the cause, their beeves deliberately or otherwise displayed a distinctly frivolous disinclination to proceed in a body to the far side of that field, to proceed in a body anywhere, indeed. Individuality was as strongly evidenced now as the herd instinct had been previously. No sooner was an attempt made to herd a brute forward, than it circled in heel-kicking frolic round the nearest stook, and came in from behind, its unattached fellows abetting. Others set off on a high-spirited stook-butting progress in all directions. Three fine specimens attached themselves closely to Miss Hepburn, with the apparent intention of herding her back to their own haughland, and she had to be rescued. Altogether there was a lack of coherence about the operation, which so mortified Archie Scott that he decided to leave the brutes where they were, and go for reinforcements and horses. Ordering a general disengagement, he set off westwards at a brisk pace.

And then, of course, the cattle came too—on a very broad front, at varying speeds, and not forgetting to deal with the stooks *en route*. Setting the girl between them, the two men each took an arm, and with their free hands grasping sticks with which they lashed about them intermittently, they covered Dr. White's hilly stubble across to the hedge flanking the Netherton road. Turning left-handed along it, they sought for a gate, discovered none, and had to go back on their tracks, northwards. At the far end they found their exit, opened it narrowly and slipped through—to the manifest disappointment of their escort.

Here, after a brief debate, Archie left Wally, who volunteered to keep the brutes amused for a little longer. Barbara Hepburn, also, apparently feeling twice the woman this side of the gate that she had felt the other side, offered to wait with Wally; perhaps she preferred to let the Callant ford the Wreigh Burn on his own, this time. He crossed the road, squeezed through a gap in the hedge, and slanted down over the grassy slopes towards the stream and their waiting companions.

Deciding that it was good to feel a lot of substantial horse between his knees again, Archie led his four colleagues and the two riderless mounts over the water, up to the first gate, and on to the road. The hooves seemed to make an almighty clippity-clop on the macadam, even though they tried to keep to the inadequate grass verge—but probably the sound would barely carry to the houses. More serious would be any benighted traffic using the road—though there, car headlights at least should give them some warning.

They quietly walked their steeds along the few hundred yards to the other gate, where Barbara and Wally greeted them relievedly—even if the gambolsome bullocks seemed less gratified over the arrival of all the horseflesh.

With three of the riders blocking the road to the south, Wally half-opened the gate. But would the cattle come out? Not one. They stood about, backing and puffing, and lowering suddenly sulky heads. Archie and Johnny Hume then rode into the field, and though the bovines thereupon set off at speed back towards their own haughland, the riders found it extraordinarily easy, on horseback, to overtake, head them off, and bring them running back in considerably chastened mood. Wally, at the gate, let through the first six, which unfortunately included a young half-grown beast, and then shut the door on the rest.

"Can you catch that youngster? Get it by the tail," Archie instructed. "That's it—now twist it. That's right —it'll come like a lamb. Well—sort of, anyway. Get the others on up the road, the rest of you. Now—open the gate, Wally. Good enough. Look—Johnny and I will drive these brutes we're not taking, back to their own pasture. They could do a deal of damage if we left them in this corn. It's easy, with the horses. We'll make up on you. Keep on up the road, to the first side-road on the left—nearly a mile. Turn along there, and into the haugh of this Wreigh Burn again, higher up. But we'll be up with you, by then.

103

Keep your eyes skinned for cars. If you see the lights of one, just leave the cattle, and scram. Get the horses hidden, if you can, behind the nearest hedge, or away into a field. Stray bullocks can get on to any road—but *we* don't want to be seen. Okay? Right—off you go. And I hope that darned brute stops belly-aching . . . !"

announced. "We've just to get round a farm called Hazel-tonrig, then it's hill-paths onwards, and empty country."

*　　　*　　　*

"Astonishing to think, really, that all along the line of these hills, right down to Cumberland, young men are doing what we're doing here at this moment!" It was Barbara Hepburn who spoke. She sat her horse beside Archie Scott, as their parcel of now considerably sobered, not to say sulky, beeves was driven through the last of the gates before the open Cheviots. The great mass of the hills loomed black and featureless before them. "Think of all the cursing and swearing, the hurrying and sweating, the gates being negotiated, houses avoided, beasts being whacked and badgered. . . ." She shook her head. "And all for what? All just to make a demonstration!"

"It's a bit of a thought, I admit," her companion conceded, looking just a little bit uncomfortable.

"And is it worth it all?"

He frowned. "It would be a wee thing late to ask that —even if there were any doubts on the matter!" the man declared. "This demonstration, as you call it, is much needed. And a lot of good could come out of it."

She looked at him, curiously. "You really believe that —don't you? I mean, you're not doing all this just out of spite, to get your own back on the Northumbrian municipal types. At the back of it all, you look on this as a constructive gesture?"

He bowed from his saddle, ironically. "Strange as it may seem . . . !"

"Not everyone may see it as you people do, you know."

"Then that is where the *Daily News* is going to put them right—isn't it?"

"M'mmm . . ."

They rode on, after the others, with the ground rising steeply ahead, the first of many bracken-clad and heathery slopes that would eventually bring them up on to the high ridge of Windygate itself, seven miles and seven hundred

109

feet above—they hoped. But cattle had done it before—and English cattle at that.

Archie was going to see how the beasts took this immediate hillside, a sharp rise of perhaps one-hundred-and-fifty feet, before leaving them all for a quick tour of sundry other attempts.

They had come this way, earlier in the night, surveying the way, and now they put their little herd slantwise at the brae. After some abortive turning this way and that, but finding horsemen close and inexorable all around them except upwards, the bullocks took the slope reluctantly. Archie then rode ahead, picking out a route for them, over the fading bracken, the tussocks, and the wet patches. It occurred to him, half-way up, that he had almost forgotten that it was night-time, that he was picking this way for them in the dark. He was not aware of peering, or of any particular eye-strain. It was surprising how the sight adjusted itself to relative darkness, when the light had faded gradually. He could make out small natural features, such as a gorse-bush or a burn-channel, at more than a hundred yards—though sizes and distances in themselves tended to be misleading—and large features such as woods and hill-shoulders were visible possibly up to half a mile, and more if there was a skyline to silhouette them. It was not a really dark night, of course—though from a lit house or city streets it would seem pitchy enough.

Unfortunately, this satisfactory line of reflection was rudely shattered. The ground immediately at his feet was, strangely enough, considerably less distinct—evidently to his mount, also. For just then, the horse either put its off forefoot in a rabbit-hole, or the surface was undermined and collapsed under it. Without warning, the animal lurched over, went down on one knee, scrabbling with its other hooves, and the rider was pitched headlong over its shoulder, to land heavily, jarringly, on his own, and roll over and over down the hill.

Fortunately or otherwise, the slope here was honeycombed with burrows, and offered a softer landing than might have been the case. Fetching up on a levelish patch of bracken, Archie picked himself up, shakily. He spat some Northumbrian soil out of his mouth, and felt himself over gingerly, deciding that nothing was broken—though his groin hurt damnably, where the electric torch in his pocket had no doubt bruised him. He set out, a little unsteadily, to climb up to his horse again, afraid for what he might find.

But his steed was standing still, upright, and even trying to crop the already rabbit-cropped turf. Taking the bridle, the man led it a few paces. There seemed to be no sign of a limp. Stooping, to run a hand over hocks and fetlocks, dizziness overtook him, and he got down on his knees to the task. All seemed to be well with the horse—though he felt distinctly queasy himself.

"Ferreting, or something?" Johnny Hume enquired, interestedly, from just above him. In the interval, the cattle and herders had come up, slightly higher on the hill, with Johnny riding this lowermost flank.

"Watch out for rabbit-holes," Archie exclaimed. "Just come a cropper, myself . . ."

"Oh—are you hurt?" That was the girl's voice, as she reined up, and jumped down from her mount. Archie was uncertain whether to be flattered or annoyed by the evident anxiety in her tone. But it was safer to sound the latter, at any rate—as well as more consonant with his feelings at Jethart's Callant being the first to fall off his horse.

"Nothing of the sort," he jerked. "Nothing to get into a flap about."

"Are you *sure* you're all right, Mr. Scott?"

"Of course I am. I just slid off, that's all. And, dammit —fancy calling me Mister at this stage!" he added ungraciously. "You're not on the Social and Personal Column, tonight!" He was mounting again, a little clumsily, and raised his voice. "Watch those cattle!" he called, authoritatively if not too steadily. "They could break their legs in these holes."

But fortunately, it seemed that the beasts were passing

111

just high enough to avoid this warren, and there were no further casualties.

"I'm glad to hear that you appear to have broken nothing more than your temper . . . Archibald!" the young woman declared, winningly.

"*Archi*bald . . . oh, Archi*bald*!" Johnny Hume carolled joyously, as he spurred on up the braeside. "Oh, why did they call me Archibald . . .?"

Tight-mouthed Archie Scott followed them up, very content not to make up on the others meantime. It would be quite tragic if he was to be sick, to cap all.

Thus preoccupied, it was not until the entire party was slanting down the gentle declivity beyond, that Archie realised that the cattle had indeed safely and fairly expeditiously surmounted their first hill. Surely he might confidently leave this lot, now. Admittedly the ground was now on the wet side, tending towards bogginess, and it could be argued that he ought to stay with them to see them over this hurdle too. But he had much wider responsibilities, this night, than merely to this little group—and the thought was beginning to prey on his mind. Moreover, this appeared to him to be a desirable moment to be off on his own; he felt like getting behind a convenient outcrop somewhere, and being quietly ill. There are times when even the most congenial human companionship palls.

He rode up to Johnny Hume. "I'm leaving you, now," he told him. "Got to go and see how the others are getting on. You know your route, from now on?"

"Sure—the way we came," Duns's Reiver affirmed. "Ower twa mair bits o' hills, and doon to the Breamish. Then up to yon big cleuch, an' turn left."

"That's right. The real test will follow after that, when you start climbing to really high ground. But with any luck you'll find quite a bunch of the others, with their cattle, waiting for you at this cleuch below Lintlands Hill. We've had the farthest to go, of this area, so the others should be there first. I told them to wait for us at Lintlands Cleuch. We'll all do the last bit together."

112

"Okay. Hoo far's it?"

"You've got four miles to go yet, I'd say."

"Aye. Gie's an oor-an'-a-hauf. See you later."

"Right. Good luck."

"Bye-bye," Barbara Hepburn called out cheerfully.

"Yes. You'll be all right with Johnny," Archie nodded, as he pulled away.

"Oh, no, I won't!" Her denial came from close at his own side. "It's him I'm saying bye-bye to. I'm coming with you."

"No, no. You're far better here. I've got a lot of ground to cover—ranging all over the place . . ."

"Then I'll range with you. That's what I came to do. I want an over-all picture of the operation, you know—not just of one little group. That's what you want too, isn't it?"

If it was, the man did not admit it with any fervour. But that did not seem to worry his companion. She came along anyway, with entire assurance.

Hume waved after them, offensively. "You've had it, Archibald!" he called.

*   *   *

They rode straight ahead, in front of the herd, on the shortest route to the Breamish, the man going harder than his body, as distinct from his mind, felt like doing. But his eyes were busy, and as the riders slanted down into a deep little valley and splashed across a burn, he reined up amongst the hazels of the waterside.

"Will you ride on, please? Straight up the hillside," he requested, carefully. "I'll catch up."

"All right," she nodded. Then, as he turned away from her quickly, she checked her steed, glancing down, a little diffidently for that young woman. "You're *sure* there's nothing wrong?"

"Of course not. I just . . ."

That was as far as he got. There and then he was violently

and comprehensively sick into the nearest hazel-clump, a painful process, physically and morally.

The girl sat her horse for a few difficult moments, uncertainly, biting her lip. Then she was out of the saddle to make, not for his heaving side but to the water's edge a few yards back. There she stooped, tugging an aluminium collapsible drinking-cup from her jacket-pocket, filled it a the stream, and returned. But she waited, behind the horses, until the man's paroxysms died away. Then stepping forward, she touched his hand, and gave the cup of water to him, silently. As, after a moment, he took it, almos grudgingly, she turned away, and went to busy herself a her mount's saddlery.

The man, resenting her presence, any presence, dreading fuss, and no better patient than any other man, had been prepared to unload some part of his spleen, at least metaphorically, on the young woman. But he knew an unwilling gratitude, for her silence as much as for the water. He grunted something, received no reply, and glancing round perceived that she was gone, some distance at least, and with her back to him. He was the better pleased.

Rinsing his mouth out once or twice, he sipped the res of the water. Then he moved down to the burnside, dran some more, washed and generally freshened himself up— and felt a deal more like Archie Scott in consequence. The pain in his groin still was there, but deadened considerably and the pit of his stomach no longer unnerved him.

Dabbing face and hair with his handkerchief, he returned to the horses. The young woman seemed to have finished adjusting her stirrup-leathers, and accepted her cup back gravely.

"Thanks," he said.

"Feeling better?" Though that was almost casually said her glance was searching.

"Much. Right as rain, now."

"Good. You know, I thought there was somethin wrong. What happened when you were thrown, bac there?"

114

"Nothing. Just gave myself a jolt, that's all. Upset my innards, I suppose. Damn' silly. Shall we move on again?"

"If you feel able."

"Of course."

"After you then . . . Archie!"

"That's better," he said, and hoisted himself up into the saddle without too much difficulty. He set no feverish pace, now, and it might have been noted that they rode side by side instead of in file as heretofore. So much for the triumph of the spirit over the flesh.

Over that next long slow ridge, and down a grassy brae beyond, they came to the River Breamish. But long before the deep murmur of its headlong waters reached their ears, they heard the lowing of cattle. It was a strangely exhilarating sound, for them, coming out of the dark womb of the hills. Involuntarily they urged on their horses to greater speed.

The going was improved for them now, too, for the bridle-path which they had been following from Alnham here joined the old drove-road that accompanied the river-bank, and overgrown, washed away in places, and generally sketchy as it was, it still represented a selected route for cattle. It smelt of cattle now, too, for the first time for many a generation, no doubt.

They made up on the source of sound and smell, quickly, to discover a sizeable herd strung out along the valley floor. At first, surprisingly, they discovered no men with them—though they had heard a shout or two previously—till, staring about them into the gloom, they sensed movement behind them and above, and Archie's subsequent hails brought answering calls from the scrub-grown valley-side. Horsemen came riding down to them. They had been taking the Callant's advice seriously, about not allowing themselves to be identified, and hearing hoof-beats behind them had taken to the scrub hurriedly.

There were two sections represented here, the parties that had dealt with the farms in the Alnham and Ingram areas,

115

with almost fifty cattle between them. They had joined up
over half an hour back, the Alnham lot having found a way
through the hills from the last farm raided, which had brought
them out just in front of the Ingram people coming straight
up Breamishside. In high spirits, they were all eight of
them clamorous with the gallant tale of their adventures—
the other two were on in front, picking out the route. It
had been easy, dead easy, money for old rope, apparently—
though of course less swack and tough characters than themselves might well have found it otherwise. Dammit—the job
had been to keep *all* the bluidy coos frae coming along!

Though there was a certain sameness about the enthusiastic
accounts, the new-comers were not allowed to forgo any of
them—and fortunately it was a long straight stretch of the
Breamish, under High Cantle Hill, and little droving other
than mere sustained forward movement was called for.
Archie was interested to discover incidentally, when he
turned off after an errant bullock that nobody else seemed
interested in, that it was not himself that was the principal
repository for these graphic recitals—for they continued
apparently without interruption, to his companion, meanwhile. Whether this was accounted for by Miss Hepburn's
sex, her good looks, or merely by her position as a channel
of newspaper publicity, was a matter for debate.

No intimations of disaster or bad news emerged from
these reports, at any rate. It was not thought that any of
the local people had been disturbed, no main roads had
been touched, and no damage done. Admittedly a drystone dyke beside a field-gate had collapsed under pressure
from one bunch of driven stirks—but that would be rectified
easily enough. And a drunk had been encountered sup-
porting the ironwork of the little bridge at Ingram—but he
had been left snoring contentedly in a more secure resting-
place, and was unlikely to trouble anyone with improbable
stories before breakfast-time at the earliest.

It was expected that the third section of Archie's original
party, that had departed with the Ingram lot to work the
farms from Hedgeley as far north as Ilderton, would be

coming along not far behind, They had had farther to go, but a straightforward task, and a fine disused road to follow all the way back from Ilderton.

Archie thought of turning back to meet them, but decided to see this present herd safely into the Lintlands Cleuch first, this being only a mile or so ahead.

The drove-road crossed the Breamish by a ford, and swung away westwards on its long climb towards high Windygate, just before the cleuch was reached. Fording the stream, now little more than a boisterous burn, presented no great difficulty, though a small landslide on the far bank complicated the crossing by preventing the beasts from finding a firm foothold for climbing out. However, just when the sight of some fifty steers stumbling about amongst the stony shallows, jostling each other and trying to turn back, began to look alarming, one enterprising bullock discovered a route out for itself, on the right side and some short distance upstream. Thankfully the drovers persuaded the rest to follow suit, and in loud-voiced complaint the entire steaming throng won out on to the base of Lintlands Hill. The cleuch yawned ahead of them, a pit of shadows, like a great quarry gouged out of the braeface. Into its shadowy depths the cattle were herded, with relief. A well-earned respite could now be enjoyed by man and beast, before the testing time of the great ascent to the Borderline. It was almost a quarter to three.

Archie left them all there— and this time Barbara Hepburn made no bones about accepting his advice that there was no point in her coming back with him. Alone he recrossed the ford and trotted down the drove-road again. His black, far from showing signs of fatigue, seemed to be glad to stretch its long legs again, after the constraint of keeping to the pace of stiff-legged cattle. At the great bend in the river, where he and the girl had come down to it previously, he paused. There was still no sight nor sound of Johnny Hume's party. Shrugging, he trotted away eastwards on the road towards Ingram. He was beginning to get a little bit worried about the time.

117

Fortunately he had not far to go down this farther stretch of Breamishside before a shadowy commotion ahead resolved itself into the Ilderton party under the Lauder Cornet coming up at an impressive turn of speed. They had been delayed, apparently, just west of Ingram, by some of their beasts escaping into rough pasture and there getting mixed up with local cattle. They had had the devil's own job disentangling them again—indeed, it seemed to be more than likely that they had left some of their carefully-collected beasts from the north there, and come away with an overdose of the Ingram brutes. A certain amount of disagreement was evident as to exactly whose fault this might be.

Archie assured everyone that it did not matter two hoots, and asserted stoutly that an excellent job had been done by all concerned—thereby much improving the atmosphere lowering between the rival herdsmen of Jedburgh and Lauder. But he made sure in no way to delay their rate of progress in the doing of it. He was becoming distinctly watch-conscious.

Back at the bend, there was still no sign of Johnny Hume. Urging the others to continue on up towards the cleuch, he remained behind, in two minds as to whether to wait there or to head back along the bridle-path over the ridge, to meet his former colleagues. Afraid that they might have strayed from the track, and he might well miss them in these jumbled night-bound hills, he stayed where he was, fretting.

As well that he did, for presently there sounded the beat of hooves behind him, and down the drove-road came a messenger from Lauder's Cornet, to inform him that Hume's lot were just ahead of them, up the valley.

Thankfully, Archie turned, and headed northwards once again.

The two parties joined up at the river-crossing below the cleuch. Showing them the way over, that had been pioneered by the earlier herd, Archie regretfully announced that there could be no respite for *them*. It was turned three-thirty now—there was no time to lose. Straight on up the drove-

118

road, westward, with them. He would get the others, corralled in the cleuch, after them right away.

And so the long and dreaded ascent was faced.

* * *

There was a total of 114 beef cattle—plus one slender heifer which had got included somehow, and for which no one would accept responsibility—and twenty-five drovers to herd them, counting in Barbara Hepburn. Her parallel situation to that of the unfortunate heifer did not go un-remarked. Weary now, and bewildered, they had to be driven, coaxed and cajoled from approximately the thousand-foot level to something above the seventeen-hundred, over a course of three rugged miles, and by a track that was considerably more evident as a dotted line on the map than it was on the ground. And Archie Scott, at least, was in a hurry.

At first, it seemed as though the task was going to be quite impossible. In loud-voiced milling confusion the brutes appeared to be prepared to do anything and go any-where save up the steeply-ascending narrow terrace of the Lintlands hillside that was their track. There was a wideish level area of reeds and marsh at the foot, which appeared to suit them much better—and a variety of other and evidently more enticing exits therefrom. Round and round, and in and out amongst the plunging, backing, snorting cattle, the drovers rode, loud-tongued as their charges. A stirring scene—for anyone sufficiently detached to appreciate it.

Perhaps the young woman's journalistic eye savoured it all adequately—for not unnaturally she refrained from any feverish participation in the circus. Nevertheless, that she was not entirely detached was made evident by her pointing out to the exasperated Callant, during one of his pauses for breath near-by, the figure of the shrinking and abashed white heifer standing, like herself, a little way apart from all this excitement, and not far from the start of the upward track.

"A pity they don't all take a leaf out of the lady's book, isn't it?" she mentioned. "She's the only one with any

119

sense." And, it may be with a certain smugness, she added, casually: "If, as in so many things, you could only get them to follow the female line, many of your troubles would be over—wouldn't they?"

If that was meant for mere facetious trick-scoring, the man took it otherwise. "Worth a trial, anyway," he jerked, nodding. "Come on."

He rode over towards the heifer, seeking to isolate it from the mass of the seething bullocks, the girl following.

He pointed. "Away up the track, will you," he cried. "Just walk it, quietly. By yourself, yes."

Barbara turned her horse's head, and walked it slowly away from all the commotion towards the shunned drove-road, passing quite close to the stationary heifer in the process. The young cow watched her, with mild-eyed interest.

Then Archie approached it, from the other side, gently, shooing it in placatory almost wooing fashion. And with a soft moo, the creature turned and walked quietly off up the track after Barbara Hepburn, entirely self-possessed and unflurried.

Archie swung off in a half-circle, curving round on the nearer stirks, not to alarm or drive them but to turn their square heads to face the track again. He did no more than that—and signed back a couple of herdsmen who were descending upon this bunch with typical sound and fury.

For a long moment the bullocks stood, heads swinging, steam jetting from their nostrils. Then two together started off after the pale form of the heifer, a third decided to outdo them, breaking into a trot, and thereafter every beast in the vicinity joined in the drift in that direction. Archie spurred back around the edge of the flat, calling off his riders. In a couple of minutes the entire herd was plodding upwards and westwards in the way that it had been so loath to go.

It made a lengthy, strung-out and astonishingly sedate procession, led by Barbara and the heifer, with the steers coming more or less in single file or two-by-two behind, constrained by the narrow nature of the route, and the squadron of rather sheepish horsemen away at the back. Archie, warning his companions not to hustle the creatures, rode away half-left, amongst the bog and rushes of the brae-foot, till he was well in front, and then put his black straight up the steep hillside, tacking this way and that, often with the horse practically sitting on its hind-quarters, until he reached the drove-road again, ahead of Barbara, and waited.

"I take off my hat to the ladies," he said, tipping finger to brow, as she came up. "The two of you certainly took that trick."

"Yes. There are more ways of threading a needle than trying to hurl the cotton through the eye!" she acceded, a trifle complacently. Presumably she had been thinking that one up, on the way. "Feeling better?"

"Physically—yes," he said, as he fell into place at her side.

Behind them, the little heifer mooed to herself in a sort of croon, pacing delicately.

And so, contrary to all anticipation, the whole extended column stalked quietly, deliberately, unhurried but without substantial pause or delay, like a crocodile of schoolgirls, up that long unbroken ascent. Taken in this placid fashion, the snags, the burnlets to be crossed, the earth-slides to be negotiated, the aprons of wet ground to be circumnavigated, seemed to lose their terrors and most of their difficulties. Calm prevailed—and consistent, almost uncanny progress. Archie Scott did not quite know whether to chuckle or to frown.

There were incidents, of course—as when one bullock lost its footing on a greasy patch, and thereafter slithered quite a distance down the steep hillside, before coming to rest shaken but unhurt against an outcrop of stone. Its companions passed on, unmoved. Again, there were two stirks which developed a sudden but serious disagreement as to priority at a difficult bit of the track, and decided to have it out there and then, head to head. The next-in-line did not even wait to observe the first round of this set-to, but promptly trod out a diversionary route around the contestants a few yards higher, which was automatically followed by the remainder of the procession—including presently the two gladiators themselves. But these were minor events, and held up the sober advance not at all.

It was only a few minutes past four when Archie and the girl breasted the summit of the ridge of Lintlands Hill, at sixteen hundred feet. Between them and the Border now was only the mile-wide moss of the Davidson's Burn watershed and the ultimate short climb thereafter.

Archie looked from the shadowy waste ahead back to their long tail, disappearing down into the pit of gloom behind, and shook his head. "This is astonishing," he said. "But can it possibly keep up? Across that open peat-bog? It was different on the hillside . . ."

"Why not?" Barbara asked. "The little cow's still there, perfectly happy apparently. They've got into the habit of just following on, now. No reason why they should stop it, just because they're not climbing, is there?"

"Maybe not. But it's a risk to take, just to lead on into this wet stuff and assume they'll follow in a string. If any of them took it into their heads to stray any distance off the route, they could be bogged here in no time."

"Wouldn't it be more of a risk to interfere with them now? The kind of to-do that you had down below there would be dangerous here, wouldn't it? And any sort of stampede would be fatal. . . ."

He nodded. "That's true, certainly. Come on, then. Let's hope this heifer doesn't weary in well-doing, in the middle!"

"She won't," the girl asserted, as in duty bound. "She's a sensible creature. I believe she likes going for a nice long walk in the dark, duly escorted of course. I think she's sweet."

They rode on, down into the shallow depression of the watershed.

Crossing that place of tussocks, peat-pools and moss-hags was no straightforward business, even though the dotted line on the map looked straight enough. It demanded a

122

zigzag progress, from point to point, avoiding the morasses, the black hollows, and the quaking flats. Archie was fairly conversant with the route by now, having crossed it twice already, but he was anxious to take no chances in the dark. It seemed quite crazy to be riding out in front into it, like mounted police in a royal procession, and expecting all that string of cattle to follow directly in their footsteps. If any of them started seeking paths for themselves . . .

But despite the fact that the man was almost afraid to turn round periodically to see what was happening, the beasts did indeed follow on, in a seemingly endless winding string, the tail lost in the gloom. And however it appeared from the front, that they did so was not so strange, either. Cattle are creatures of habit, and are apt to walk in file, head to tail, when left to themselves; the narrow tracks which they make across any habitual passage testify to the fact. Moreover, these beasts were tired, with their liveliness and initiative long walked out of them, and the stolid following in the steps of the brute in front had become next to automatic. Again, instinct may well have warned them that this was dangerous ground, and the path successfully negotiated by their predecessors the safest one.

Anyhow, be that as it may, the crossing was made, and in the most prosaic and humdrum manner possible, without event. Those bullocks had reached the stage of merely putting one foot before another, without question or break, and they kept on doing it right across the watershed, the little heifer leading—and apparently content to do so all night. The slope beyond quickly developed into short heather, which made safe and easy going, and before four-thirty the leaders were crossing the Borderline on the high ridge of Windygate. The chill night wind of the high places met them out of the west, out of Scotland. They had made it. Their appointed beef-tub lay only a short distance downhill to the left.

A group of half a dozen riders had been waiting for them on the ridge. This included Dod Wilson, the Kelso Laddie, and Sanny Elliot of Coldstream, who had been up here for

123

well over an hour, their Flodden-Wooler expedition being the shortest of the entire operation. They seemed to be in excellent form. Also present were two or three of Dand Fairgrieve's Teries, who had completed their efforts in Upper Redesdale under Jock Murray the Hawick Right-hand Man, and had been sent on here to see if they could be useful elsewhere. Jock himself was waiting at the Scrathy Holes.

Archie Scott, though he would have liked to see his own group's task to its conclusion, and his herd duly penned in Kelsocleuch below, reluctantly decided that he must forgo that satisfaction. He had too much on his mind—including the fact that it would be dawn in just over an hour.

Leaving Johnny Hume to see to the final disposal of their cattle in the beef-tub, and thereafter to dismiss his herdsmen homewards, he took his leave of them all.

"You've done a good job, boys," he called out. "Folk will talk about this night's work for a long time to come. It'll be the clash of every pub in the land. And, dammit— I bet you won't let the story lose a whole lot in the telling! But don't you forget the heifer, just the same!"

"Which yin?" somebody interpolated, and drew a cheer.

"Away home with you!" the Callant cried. "We'll have a get-together one of these days, and discuss the whole business. But meantime, don't hang about these hills. Cheerio, and good luck!"

"Up the Callant!"

"Jethart's here, all right!"

> "Well I never,
> Did you ever,
> Hear o' Erchie the Callant's
> Wee white heifer . . .?"

somebody yodelled—and a new Common Riding song was born, capable obviously of being elaborately, allusively, and indefinitely expanded.

In the laughter that followed, Archie turned to Dod and

124

Sanny. "With luck, you two should be in your beds by sunrise," he said.

"I'ph'mm. Aye," Dod Wilson acceded. "The pity o' it. It's an awfu' waste."

"What d'you mean?"

"A' that shut-eye goin' to waste, just." The other shook his head. "Och, an' I never thocht that much o' Hexham, anyway!"

"We're coming with you, Archie," Sanny Elliot declared.

The Callant looked from one to the other, and grinned whole-heartedly, boyishly. "More fools you!" he asserted, rudely.

"That makes four of us," Barbara Hepburn put in, at his back.

Wilson turned on her. "Dinna be daft, lassie—it's no' a ploy for a wumman. Are you no' tired . . .?"

"It's all right, Dod—she's not coming," Archie announced, with authority. "She can come as far as the Scrathy Holes, if she wants—but that's all. Shall we go?"

The girl said nothing, as they pulled their mounts' heads round, to face south-west.

125

10

They rode straight downhill, west by north, by the most direct route to Heatherhope Reservoir and the nearest road-head in Scotland.

On this three-mile trot, Archie elicited sufficient information to gain a fair overall impression of how at least this eastern end of the operation had fared. And it was an encouraging picture. The Wooler and Flodden district had yielded a rich crop of Hereford-Irish cross beasts, with some especially fine specimens from the well-known herd at Kilham. There had been no trouble worth recording—save in the case of a Hereford bull of outsize proportions that one inexperienced drover had attempted to include, at the farm of Howtell near Flodden field, and which had given its would-be captor a run for his money—fortunately with no more dire results than a certain chastening of spirit to the toreador. At Humbleton, or Homildon, near Wooler, the raiding party had been disturbed by the late homecoming of the farmer, who however apparently observed nothing suspicious in the sweep of his headlights—though one or two of the rustlers swore that they must have stood out a mile. At any rate, he had driven on into the farm-place, and they had seen no more of him. Of course, as Dod remarked, he wouldn't be the first farmer to cannily doubt the evidence of his own eyes late of a Saturday night. The droves, totalling 135 beasts altogether, had been herded up the College Burn valley, over the Border and up on to The Curr, without noteworthy incident. Three o'clock had seen them all safe in their improvised cleuch.

The tale from Upper Redesdale, evidently, had been

126

simple and almost disappointingly unvarnished. It had merely been a case of the opening of gates around Byrness and Blakehope, and driving bullocks out on to and along the deserted highway. Relying on the fact that there were practically no roadside houses for miles on this route, that it was seldom used by commercial transport, and that traffic of any sort was unlikely in the small hours of a Sunday morning, Jock Murray had merely herded right along the road for miles, past the lonely Catcleuch Reservoir right up to the Border at Redeswire itself. A straight road mounting steadily through a bare and empty valley, they could see car-lights miles away. Only three times in two hours' droving had they had to hide from cars, and since the flanking hillsides were open and unfenced, it presented no difficulty to drive the beasts a little way off the road until the cars were past. It had been an entirely straightforward, not to say dull, piece of herding for the Teries. At Carter Bar, where Jock Murray had left the highway to head along the Border-line towards the Scrathy Holes, he had decided that he did not need all of his ten men, and had detached three of them to ride east to Windygate in case their services would be useful elsewhere. Of Dand Fairgrieve's doings farther down Redesdale, there was no word.

The four riders came down from Windygate on to the head of the half-mile sheet of Heatherhope Reservoir, whence Kelso drew its water supply, by one of the myriad ancient tracks that veined these secretive green hills. At the lower end of the dark brooding water, a private road began, leading down to Hounam and the Kale Water. A few yards along it, in the shadow of some stunted trees, a car stood, dark and silent.

Inside, three men slept soundly. They got short shrift from the horsemen, receiving a quite undeserved barrage on the shame of slothfulness. Two of the yawning protesters were bundled out into the chill pre-dawn night, given the four horses, and told to beat it for home, and to consider themselves lucky. The riders piled into the warm car in their place, and ex-Callant Dan Grieve at the wheel was

127

ordered to see what speed he could wring out of his old crock in the direction of Deadwater and the North Tyne valley.

It was pleasant to sit back and be driven in comfort through the sleeping countryside—though in Archie's opinion there was no need for the three in the back so blatantly to express their satisfaction at being so tightly huddled together—the girl of course in the middle. Fortunately the fumes of malt liquor which had greeted the new-comers, indicative of the manner in which a long vigil had been supported, did not imply a wholly empty bottle. Sandwiches also were available and acceptable. Archie's hollow-feeling stomach was grateful. The pain had sunk to a dull throbbing.

The car had to make quite a journey of it, by Hounam, Morebattle and Oxnam, to cross the main Jedburgh highway, and then over the heights of Mervinslaw in the direction of Southdean to the Hawick-Tyne road. Along this, by the high pass of the Note o' the Gate they sped, down into upper Liddesdale, and left for the Border once more at Deadwater. It was grey dawn before they reached Liddelsdale.

They slowed down a mile short of the Border, where a drove-road led off eastwards to join the Roman Road called the Wheel Causeway. Archie had previously surveyed the spot, and was able to assure the driver that he could take the car some way along it. So, headlights switched off, they bumped and lurched over the grassy track on which cattle and horse droppings and the marks of heavy tyres were visible in the side-lights' glow, heading into the wan vacancy of the dawn.

But not for long. Perhaps half a mile along, a shadowy figure in riding-breeches materialised before them. It proved to be Galashiels' cheerful Braw Lad. Behind him, a large lorry loomed hugely, and nearby was a small group of men and horses.

This was all as it should be. The lorry, a cattle-truck, was of Archie's providing, a compromise in the vexed issue of those Hexham cattle. Two fresh horses had been brought in it, too. The Braw Lad had only recently arrived, with

128

the Tynedale herd, which was not far in front, and had waited behind here just in case he could be of some use on the Hexham ploy. Wat Hogarth, the Selkirk Standard-bearer, had plenty of drovers to get his hundred-odd cattle to the Scrathy Holes.

Archie consulted his watch. It was a quarter to six, and rapidly getting light. The sun would be up in half an hour. His thoughts were with Rab Pringle, his Right-hand Man, somewhere away down near Hexham, deep in the enemy country—that would soon be awaking. Much as he would have liked to hurry along this Wheel Causeway in the wake of the Tyne herd, to the Scrathy Holes, to view the greatest concourse of cattle that could have been seen in these hills in four hundred years penned therein, he just dare not spare the time. He was late already. It was galling, but he had too much on his plate.

The Braw Lad was recounting the saga of the Tynedale raid, and making a gallant tale of it, when Archie cut him short.

"Sorry, Tom," he said. "I'm late, as you know. Rab's relying on me. Afraid I can't take you along on this Hexham trip—we're limited by the fact that I don't want to put more than three horses in this cattle-truck. More would be risky. Dod and Sanny and I will manage—and it's time we were away. I want you to take Miss Hepburn, here, and let her see the show along at the Scrathy Holes. Dand Fairgrieve will look after her, after that . . ."

"But I want to come with you, to Hexham!" the girl cried. "That'll be the most exciting part of it all. Please, Archie . . .!"

He shook his head. "You heard what I said to Tom," he told her. "It just can't be done. I'm not risking more than three horses together in that truck."

"Can I not just travel in the truck, then, at least? Without a horse . . .?"

"There'll be three of us, besides the driver, packed into that cab, somehow, as it is. I'm sorry. There'll be much more to see at the beef-tub, anyway." He turned. "Will you blokes get three horses in there? Tom—tell Dand everything's fine at the east end. He's in charge of the operation, now. The main thing's to get everybody away from the scene and off home as quickly as possible. Okay?"

"You're a—a pig, Archibald Scott!" Barbara Hepburn exclaimed. "After all the help I've been to you . . .!"

"You tell that to the Braw Lad, my dear—he's a sympathetic man with the ladies. Ask the Braw Lass, some time! Give me a ring at the house, this evening, and I'll bring the story up to date for you. Coming, fellows?"

Rather more apologetically, the Coldstreamer and the Kelso Laddie took their leave of scorned and therefore dangerous womanhood, and crowded after Archie into the cab of the lorry, sitting on one another. The ramp was pushed in, the backboard secured behind the horses, and the driver cranked up. Any further exchange was mercifully precluded by the roar of the engine.

*   *   *

The truck, its number-plates obscured by carefully applied mud, swayed and rattled back to the main road, and turned southwards along it. By Deadwater and Kielder and Plashetts—names these on the map, rather than recognisable communities—they jolted and jounced down the long vale of North Tyne, beside the growing river and the slender railway. They passed no traffic, perceived no human activity. At six-twenty-five, nearing the little town o Bellingham, they glimpsed the first level rays of the new risen sun. They crossed the Tyne at Bellingham, heading east to cross the Rede also, at Reedsmouth, thankful for the low hills in front that helped to keep the yellow dazzle of the stripling sun out of their eyes. Reaching the main Redesdale-Corbridge road, they were about to turn southwards along its ruler-straight elongation—the Dere Street of the Romans—when Dod Wilson barked the warning:

"Traffic!"

His stare southwards, Archie's brows came down in

130

frown. "Yes. Better stop a minute." His frown darkened. "I don't like the look . . ." Swiftly he glanced round him. "Quick—back into that dip we've just come out of. Yes—reverse, man. This hedge'll help to hide us."

"You think . . .?"

"Two powerful low-set black cars, driving close together, at this time of the morning! The chances are they're police. Hurry, man. If they didn't spot us before, they'll probably not see us now."

It was only a small dip, where a stone bridge crossed a small burn, but it was enough to get their tall and kenspeckle cattle-truck hull-down as it were. The four men sat, staring. The road-end itself was not in view now, owing to the configuration of the ground, but all of the main road was, up to perhaps three hundred yards off. If the cars had seen this reversing process . . .! They were coming along at a great rate of speed, apparently undiminished, and there could be no doubt as to their character. Patrol-cars—and very much on duty.

The watchers hardly breathed as the cars swept out of sight behind the lift of the moorland. Give them twelve-fifteen seconds, and if they had not reappeared to the left along the main road northwards—then, they'd had it! Archie counted, below his breath. Five . . . six . . . seven . . . If they were caught thus, what could they do? Three horsemen who obviously hadn't been to bed, with three horses in the back . . . Glory be! The two cars came into sight again, still on the same course, travelling hard as ever.

As the young men watched them dwindle and disappear rapidly along that speed-challenging road, they tempered their relief with conjecture.

"It needn't be our show they're out on, of course," Sanny Elliot pointed out.

"*Two* patrol-cars, at this time of the morning, and going at that speed?" Archie said. "Too much of a coincidence, I'd say. They'll have come from the Divisional Office, at Hexham. I doubt some farmer's been an early riser!

131

Dammit—I'd reckoned on an hour or so yet, at least. This looks like complicating things, I'm afraid."

"Hoo far noo to whaur you'd to meet Rab Pringle?" Dod enquired.

"Only another three or four miles. There's a Roman Camp, called Pity Me Camp, a bit off the main road on this side, with a passable road up to it, and plenty of wood around. It's handy for the Chollerton and Swinburn areas, where they've been operating—that's as near Hexham as they would go. One of the Councillors farms at Chollerton. Unfortunately, Stannard's not a farmer. Well, better get on our way again . . . keeping our fingers crossed! There's precious little opportunity for getting off this road, once we're on it."

The truck moved on, turning into the main road. The driver accelerated till the vehicle was rattling and crashing southwards, going flat out—and nobody complained of too much speed. The sooner they were safely off that road, the better. Nevertheless, it seemed a long three miles before Archie, open map on knee, indicated a narrow side-road on the right soon after passing a large reservoir on the left. Thankfully they turned off, and immediately began to climb towards high woodland. No further traffic had materialised.

Half a mile of quickly rising ground brought them grinding up to the edge of the wood.

"I'm not just sure where they'll be," Archie admitted. "Somewhere about here, where the beasts can be hidden. We only picked the spot on the map. There are no houses nearby . . ."

But they did not have to search. Out from the first of the trees stepped Rab Pringle and one of his aides, looking as though they did not wish to look relieved to see them.

"Sorry we're late, Rab," Archie called. "It's all been a slightly bigger job than we'd reckoned. How did you manage?"

"No' so bad. But we were gettin' a wee thing tired o' hangin' aboot here. We've been here more'n two hours—an' it's a hell o' a long road back to Scotland!"

132

"I know. You got your beasts all right?"

"Och, aye. *They* were nae bother. We fetched eight, a'thegither—twa frae yon geyser on the Council's place at Chollerton, an' yin each frae six ither ferms. They're in a bit open space through the trees, yonder. Bring the truck roond this way—there's a way in, see."

With Rab leading, they drove off the narrow road, through a gate and into a green ride through the wood. In a hundred yards they were round a bend, and there were the eight bullocks, bunched together in bovine resignation, with the other two Jedburgh drovers and the four horses standing by.

There was no waste of time now, no delay. No one required to be told that minutes were precious. The truck was opened up, the ramp lowered, and the three extra horses led out. Getting the bullocks in, however, in their place, was not quite so simple an operation, occasioning considerable expenditure of time, energy, and eloquence, before the last stubbornly reluctant creature was whacked and chivvied up the ramp into the now tight-packed truck. The door was slammed on them, thankfully.

"Look," Archie said. "I'll go with the driver, meantime. Somebody lead my horse. We'll have to change our plans a bittie. With the police probably on the look-out, the main roads will be a trap for us. We can't risk driving this truck-load any distance on up Redesdale, as I'd intended. That's out. We've got to use the most unfrequented by-roads we can find—and yet not waste a lot of time on them— or the whole country will be roused round our ears. And we daren't go through any district that's been raided already. That doesn't leave us much choice, for we've covered the whole Borderline pretty well. But there *was* a gap, in one area—around Alwinton and the head of Coquetdale. That's between where we were working in the Rothbury-Alnham district, and Dand Fairgrieve's Otterburn-Redesdale country. That's due north of us, here. It's not been touched."

"You mean, up Hepple and Harbottle way, Archie?"

"Yes. Look—there we are, on the map. This line.

133

That should be reasonably safe—once we can get there. Fortunately, most of the way, we can go by side-roads. But there's this wretched long stretch of the main road, first. Afraid we can't avoid it. The truck, that is. To Woodburn. Then we can branch off to the right, cross the main Otterburn-Newcastle road, and then away north over Elsdon Common on this by-road, right up to Alwinton. Got it? You fellows on the horses will just have to travel cross-country all the way. It's twenty-five miles to Alwinton, from here, I reckon. Quite a ride. But it's not bad riding country, most of it. Can you do it in three hours, d'you think? It's just turned seven, now."

"Okay—we'll dae it," Dod Wilson declared. "You'll want us to meet you, somewhere?"

"Yes. We'll need to avoid the village of Alwinton itself. There's a bit road to the right, before you reach there. I want to drove the beasts up the Roman Road called Clennell Street, beyond. Meet you just where the side-road comes close to the River Alwin, there. Only one house between that and Windygate Hill. Right? At ten—or as near it as possible."

"Fair enough," Sanny Elliot acceded. "It's a big ride —but better for us on the horses than for you in that damn' kenspeckle truck!"

Archie shrugged. "It's a toss-up. You've got the longer ordeal, anyway." He grinned. "If you're challenged, put on English accents, and pretend you're angry Northumbrian farmers out looking for your stolen cattle!"

"Right, boys—let's go."

"Good luck!"

"Hell—you'll need it mair'n us! We'll come an' bail you oot o' Hexham jile, if you're no' at this Alwinton by ten-thirty!"

"Aye—the way the Teries did yon time . . ."

The horsemen mounted, and Archie and his driver climbed back into the cab of the lorry. It would be good to be moving northwards, homewards, at least.

*   *   *

Driving along that bare arrow-straight and seemingly endless main road in a high cattle-truck that sunny Sunday morning, Archie Scott felt more conspicuous than he could recollect ever having felt before—natural-born actor or none. The vehicle, which was the property of a Common Riding friend of his, who was prepared to take a risk in a good cause, seemed deadly slow, noisy, cumbrous, and generally shouting aloud to attract attention. There were not many houses hereabouts, fortunately. There was little traffic, either—but that tended to make their presence the more obvious, in a way. A private car passed them, going north also, loaded with luggage and apparently on a long journey. Later, a hackney carriage approached from the other direction, stuffed with people and with what looked like a Catholic priest sitting in front; what their errand was at that time of morning was anybody's guess—but they paid no attention to the cattle-truck.

"What happens if the cops stop us?" the driver asked, presently, out of an apparently parallel train of thought. "Do we ram them, jump oot an' gie them a run for't—or start arguin'?"

"I'm not quite sure," Archie admitted. "I'd never really bargained on the police getting involved—not at this stage, I mean . . ."

In a tight silence, human if not mechanical, they passed through the hamlet of Ridsdale, where one or two columns of blue smoke were rising from new-lit kitchen fires. Their anxious glances discovered no faces at cottage windows. They were thankful just beyond it, however, to negotiate the only major bend in fifteen miles of moorland road— but peered as earnestly along the next straight stretch beyond. It looked clear enough. Only another two miles, and they could turn off to the right, into the first of their succession of side-roads.

But they had not covered more than a quarter of a mile of it, before the driver nudged Archie's arm. "D'you see what I see?" he asked.

"Is . . . is it a car?"

135

"Uh-huh. Off the road. Parked—bonnet to the road. Waitin'. It's a black car tae!"

"M'mmm. Well—this looks like it, then." The Callant glanced behind them. "No use turning back—they'd soon catch us up. Nowhere to turn off between us and there . . ."

"We could still run for't. Cops canna run . . . wi' their feet . . ."

"And leave them Peter Anderson's truck! No. You run for it, if you like. I'd rather brazen it out."

"Okay by me . . ."

Tight-lipped they bore down on the dark car, half-hidden behind a bush. Suddenly both men's eyebrows rose. The other vehicle was moving slowly out into the road in front of them, still perhaps three hundred yards off.

"Baistards! They're blockin' the road."

"Well—makes no real difference, I suppose. It's all . . . No—they're not! They're turning along the road, away from us. And, look—that's *not* a police-car."

"So it's not, jings! But it's us they're waitin' on. See —they're stoppin' again. They're gettin' oot . . ."

Sure enough, the door of the now stationary car swung open, and a figure stepped out on to the road, to turn and face the oncoming truck. Another followed. And both wore riding-breeches.

"Well, I'm damned!" Archie swore. "Can you beat that! She's a, a . . ." Words failed him.

It was Dand Fairgrieve and Barbara Hepburn that stood there waiting—and the car, on closer inspection, was the same that they had ridden in earlier that morning; indeed ex-Callant Grieve stepped out as they drove up.

The truck came to a stop, with a screech of brakes. Archie's face thrust from the cab window, anything but wreathed in smiles of welcome.

"You great idiots!" he cried. "You just about had the pants scared off us! What d'you mean by coming away down here? It's crazy. Dressed as you are—and in a car with a Roxburgh registration . . ."

"Och, we just thought we'd come and see if we could

136

give you a hand, Archie," Dand declared. "The rest of the boys are all away home. So . . ."

"You mean that that female persuaded you to bring her down!"

The Cornet looked a little abashed. "Och, it wasn't just that, Archie . . ."

"He doesn't sound just wildly excited to see us, does he, Mr. Fairgrieve?" the young woman put in. "I wonder why? Our usefulness must be over, I suppose. A thoroughly objective character, our Archie. . . ."

"Look here—I'll deal with you later, young woman, in the way you richly deserve!" the Callant said grimly. "But meantime, you people had better get back across the Border and safely out of sight just as quickly as may be. The police are out. We thought *you* were a police-car, waiting for us. You didn't see any sign of them, yourselves— two patrol-cars, skelping up this road like nobody's business?"

"Whe-e-e-ew! The speed-cops . . .!" Dand looked suitably impressed. "That's pretty quick work, isn't it? No—we haven't seen any sign of them. We haven't been here long . . ."

"You're sure they were after *us*?" the girl enquired— and a less preoccupied man than Archie Scott might have noted that pronoun. "It seems a bit early, doesn't it?"

"What would two patrol-cars be doing belting up these lonely roads at this time of a Sunday?" the other demanded. "We can't be sure, of course—but the chances are that somebody's been on to them about us. The rest of the boys are riding cross-country, for Alwinton and Coquetdale. We're getting off this main road just as soon as we can—in about a mile. We daren't risk bringing them up Redesdale, now, as we intended . . ."

"You've got the brutes in there, then?"

"Of course. We don't know where those police were heading—but it's not likely to be the Upper Coquetdale area, which hasn't been touched. Once we can get off these main roads, we've a chance. . . . And, by the same token, Dand, I wouldn't go back the way you came—by Redesdale.

137

I'd carry on down this road for about five miles, turn off to the right, and head for home by Tynedale and the Note o' the Gate. The way we came."

"Damned, Archie—we're not going home and leaving you now!" the Cornet declared. "To hell with that. We're sticking by you."

"Don't be daft, man. What's the good of that?" Archie was glancing up and down the road as he spoke.

"Plenty good. If you think I'm going to scuttle off, tail between my legs . . ."

"Oh, skip it, Dand! Look—we can't argue the toss here. Something may come along any minute—and cattle-trucks and folk in riding-kit will stand out a mile. If the police are on to us, they may have alerted road-users. I'm getting on, off this road right away. We can work the thing out later."

"Right-ho. Suits me. Lead on, Macduff—we'll follow."

The lorry jerked forward again, and in a few seconds the car was tailing it. And although Archie muttered his disapprobation, he knew a certain warmth within him somewhere.

A signpost heralded a small cross-roads presently, and thankfully they swung off into a narrow side-turning, leading eastwards. Now they had five miles of quiet by-ways before them, till they had to cross the next main road. Over the brow of the first hill, Archie drew the truck up, and the car came level.

Dand got in the first blow. No doubt he had been well primed, in the brief interval. "See here, Archie," he said quickly. "You're going to need us. I know this district —this is the part we've been operating in. I can guide you. And what's going to happen when you get to Alwinton? You'll need a hand with these bullocks, till the others turn up. But you'll want to get the truck away out of it as quick's you can, won't you? You'll be glad of us."

There was truth in that, of course. "I'll manage fine," Archie contended nevertheless. "There's only eight beasts.

138

I've only to look after them till the rest of the boys come along. I don't have to herd them . . ."

"How d'you know? You can't tell what'll happen. You might have to move. And unless *your* bullocks are a sight better than the ones I've been handling . . . !"

"Oh, but he just walks on and they follow him—like Mary's little lamb!" Barbara's voice issued from within the car. "No trouble at all. . . ."

"Oh—come on, then!" Archie cried. "But if we're caught, you can talk your own way out of it!"

"That's what the Press here is for!" Dand announced. "We'll keep them talking, while you make a getaway. We'd better get in front, then, and lead the way. We'll keep a bittie ahead, in time to give you warning should there be any sign of bother. Okay?"

And so the journey was resumed. And even if he did not say so, Archie Scott found it a considerably more comfortable trip for the presence of that car in front.

Without incident they reached the Otterburn-Newcastle highway a quarter of an hour later, turned east along it for a mile, and then off on a side-road northwards once again. Some way on, the lorry found the car halted and waiting for it. Dand explained that two of the farms that he had raided were just ahead, on high ground to the right, with a single short road leading up to them. He suggested that the car went on and blocked that road-end, just in case there was any activity up at the farms. The truck could get past and on as quickly as possible. This was agreed.

Fortunately, barring some chimney-smoke from one or two of the farm cottages, there was no sign of activity as they passed. It was barely eight-fifteen, of course, and most farmers are content to leave their stirks uncounted at that hour of a Sunday morning. The car caught up with the truck again near the village of Elsdon, and Dand shouted in passing that all the land ahead was untouched, as far as cattle-reiving was concerned.

After that it was plain sailing. If the police-cars had come this way, they had left no alarm behind them. It

139

was practically unpopulated country till they reached the Coquet, and even then houses were few and far between. They had to pass through the little village of Harbottle, but apart from a small boy dilatorily driving two or three cows to be milked, there was nothing to be seen of its inhabitants. At about eight-forty, just short of Alwinton, in the very lap of the great hills again, they turned off along a lane that ran along the wooded banks of the River Alwin, stopped the truck in a leafy glade, and turned out the cattle. Only fisherman, poacher, or tinker would be likely to discover them here—Archie's map-reading was vindicated. The lorry was backed out, the driver shaken by the hand, and told to find his own way back to Scotland by whatever route he cared—but needless to say, as inconspicuously as possible. And good luck to him!

But just as his remaining companions were preparing to relax comfortably, and yawning in pleasant anticipation of a well-earned respite, the ever uncomfortable Archie Scott discovered a new source of disquiet. His fine map-reading, that time, had not gone quite far enough. Though their present situation was excellent, and they were fairly safe from observation, a brief survey of the actual surroundings revealed that they could not leave this spot in the direction in which they wanted to go without coming into clear view from the village for perhaps a quarter of a mile. The seriousness of this was evident—and the later in the morning that they left that unfortunate traverse, the more likely they would be to be seen. In fact, nothing would do but that they must move on right away, herding on foot, before the wretched village was likely to have rubbed the sleep from its eyes. Any resting and waiting would have to be done farther up into the hills. Thus Archie Scott—shrugging off the blatant, if at the same time slightly rueful, I-told-you-so smugness of Dand and Barbara.

So, with ex-Callant Grieve left in his car to re-direct the horsemen when they should arrive, the two other men and the girl armed themselves with sticks again, and without much enthusiasm started the urging and prodding and

140

whacking process once more. The gilt had worn off this form of activity, rather.

Keeping to the trees for as long as they could, they had to emerge into open ground presently—and if all three tended to try to keep the cattle between them and the distant scatter of houses, so that progress went in an erratic series of curves rather than in a good straight line, their modesty was understandable. These bullocks, fortunately, whether out of congenital dullness, weariness, or as a result of being bumped about in the truck, presented a chastened and spiritless demeanour to the world—which if it lacked dash and speed at least gave the drovers little trouble.

Following the bank of the Alwin, they went, barely daring to glance over in the direction of the village, for fear of what they might see. It seemed a long time before a green shoulder of hill intervened, and there was a general sighing with relief and straightening of necks and shoulders. If they had been seen—well, they had been seen, and repercussions might or might not eventuate; but at least they were out of sight now. The Alwin, ahead of them, in a long and twisting valley, came right out of the main spine of the Cheviots, and the Roman Road of Clennell Street could be picked out, climbing up above the valley to the left. Towards it they struck, to avoid passing the farm-place of Clennell down near the riverside, the cattle plodding stolidly and grumbling as they went, the herders themselves hardly filled with gaiety and zest, despite the sparkling morning and the Sabbath praise of the carolling larks.

Nearly a mile up, the track forked, the more prominent arm going on down into a curve of the Alwin valley again. But the other, less well-defined, was Clennell Street, and it would eventually take them almost all the way up to their Windygate Hill. A little way along it, and the ravine of a tributary of the Alwin opened invitingly to their left. Archie announced that they might go to ground in there—and there was no contrary motion. Dand Fairgrieve volunteered to go back to the wood where they had left the car, so that he could both keep an eye on the village and bring the horsemen to this hidden spot, which they might have difficulty in finding. He had another reason for going, too—though he did not state it.

Yawning cavernously, the other man nodded, sitting down on the grassy bank. Whatever he said . . .

That was the stage that Archie Scott had reached.

11

It was a pleasant place that little ravine, under the shapely pinnacle of Lord's Seat Hill, in the morning sun. Whins and yellowing bracken grew along its banks, small alders and hazels lined its burnside, where the dippers darted above amber pools and burbling chuckling runnels. The bees hummed already on their rapturous way towards the heather, the rabbits hopped amongst the ferns, and the cattle browsed thankfully, too well content to stray. It was a good place for tired bodies to lie and relax and rest themselves—if their owners would allow them.

The girl at least seemed to appreciate all this. She drew off her jacket and flung herself flat on her back amongst the bracken-fronds, breeched legs and somewhat rumpled silk-shirted arms thrown wide in a sufficiently abandoned attitude. Her ashen hair lay in rich disarray, she was spattered with peat-broth and mud, and there was a faint pencilling of dark shadow beneath eyes that seemed even a little larger than usual.

"You're not afraid of bury-bugs?" the man, sitting upright still, and chewing a grass-stem, observed.

"I'm not afraid of anything, this minute—bugs, bullocks, bogeymen . . . even bad-tempered Callants, for that matter! Nothing, except having to move another step, right now." She stretched herself comprehensively, like a cat. "Gosh —I'm tired!"

At the entire frankness and naturalness of her, Archie looked at her and smiled. "So am I," he admitted. "Hardly to be wondered at, I suppose. Seems a long time since my head touched a pillow."

"You're not feeling sick, any more?"

143

"No." The pain was still there—but that was not a matter to dilate on. He nibbled at his grass. "I imagine we've got an hour here, at least, before the others arrive."

"They can take as long as they like, as far as I'm concerned," the girl said. She gazed up at the pale blue infinity of the heaven, eyes narrowed, seeking to pin-point at least one of the larks that was shouting such carefree joy above them. "You still feel all this is worthwhile?" she asked presently, out of her searching.

"Of course. Why not? One doesn't change one's opinions on a major issue just because of feeling tired." He sounded a little short.

"No. No—of course. But . . . it seems a tremendous effort, taking big risks, and causing goodness knows how much upset—all for something extremely vague, all for a mere theory, an abstraction that may well not come off, in the end . . ."

"Practically every really worthwhile effort that mankind has ever made has been for a mere theory, something fairly vague," Archie asserted loftily. "It's the abstract cause that folk are willing to take the greatest risks for—where they'll take risks at all! Always has been. Why climb Everest? Or try to reach the Poles? Or cross oceans on rafts? It's the 'isms' and the 'ologies' that draw out the supreme effort. Aren't patriotism, liberty, Christianity itself—aren't these the supreme abstractions, vague to a degree? Yet there have always been men willing to die for them."

"Aren't you rating this little adventure on the exalted side?" Barbara hinted.

"Eh . . .? No, no—of course not." Hastily he assured her. "Nothing of the sort. I'm not making comparisons —only pointing out that there's nothing strange about going to some trouble over a mere theory, an abstraction. And as for the thing maybe not coming off, possible non-success —surely the important thing is to have made the attempt? Success is only a relative business, after all—the effort put forward is the real touchstone of any cause, isn't it, not the

144

actual result achieved. It's the spirit behind it all, that matters."

She raised herself on an elbow to look at him. "You are a strange man," she said. "An idealist, I suppose . . ."

"Good lord—no!" he disclaimed, shocked. "Nothing like that. You're talking nonsense. I've said nothing that isn't self-evident, basic. It's just . . ." He selected another grass-stem, with some care. "It's just that I believe the Common Riding spirit's a fine thing, a grand thing, and greatly needed today. Local patriotism—the whole country needs it to counter the standardisation of life, the mass-mind —or lack of it. It's a gospel worth spreading—and these north country English strike me as ripe for missionarising. Damn it—it's the least we can do!"

She had sunk back on the ground again. "Oh," she said. "Yes . . .?"

"You know as well as I do what's happening to folk today," the man declared warmly. "We're being constantly bludgeoned and dominated by mass-influence, by means of every medium of expression—radio, T.V., the film, the Press, the comic strip—regimenting folk to think alike, sound alike, act alike and even look alike. And you know the results—especially amongst the young people; the couldn't-care-less, okay-by-me, take-it-or-leave-it, sort of spirit. And that's dangerous—the soil out of which dictatorship and tyranny spring . . ."

He was well launched, now. The grass-stem jerked up and down, this way and that between his lips, as he dealt with the menace of the decay of initiative and self-reliance, both in the individual and in the community, and was working back to the tonic effect of the Common Riding tradition when he paused in mid-phrase to turn and stare at his companion. She was entitled to close her eyes against the glare of the sun. But . . .

The little pouting puff, regular and unhurried, was but a poor reaction to a stirring theme eloquently expounded—however fetching.

Archie's frown was involuntary, inevitable, and perhaps

N.R.—K

145

excusable—his masculine pride saw to that. But it was not of long continuance. Other fairly typical masculine attributes came to the fore. He looked down at the young woman and his brows cleared, and the hint of a smile began to dawn at the corners of his mouth. She lay, her face in half profile, one arm behind her head, the other outstretched with the fingers slightly cupped, with strangely appealing effect, a knee upraised. In sleep, her features had softened indefinably, the competent, sophisticated, slightly brittle mask had faded, and a milder, simpler, uncomplicated impression remained. Was this the real woman, the man wondered? The other only a pose adopted to screen an essentially gentle nature? Perhaps not—it was too facile a theory altogether probably. Anyhow, she was pretty good to look at, either way—though the man's preference was for her thus. Not, of course, that it mattered two hoots one way or the other. . . .

Nevertheless, Archie Scott did not turn his gaze deliberately elsewhere—though the scene in that green trough of the hills was a pleasing one, as has been indicated. Indeed, he turned over on his front, chin propped on one hand, the more comfortably to consider her. It was pleasant to lie thus, peaceably, after all the dashing hither and thither, the stress and the strain, with the bees and the birds and the burn all at their soothing refrain. He was prepared to lie like this more or less indefinitely. A woman's breathing was shorter than a man's, he decided, though productive of considerably more physical commotion. Nothing wrong with that, either . . .

With all this pleasantness and amenity, it was a great pity, a waste indeed, that Archie's head had to keep drooping, despite the propping hand. What he needed was something to keep his leaden eyelids propped up, likewise. Will-power was all very well . . .

Neither will-power, sleeping beauty, nor all the delights of nature *were* sufficient. Eyelids and head sank both, and stayed that way.

*   *   *

146

A fly walking on her face wakened the girl. For a moment or two, after brushing away the intruder, she gazed upwards blankly. Then she turned her head.

The man lay outstretched beside and just a little below her, head on arm and face towards her, eyes shut and lips just slightly parted. Blue-chinned and stubbly, drawn and weary-looking, with a smear of dirt on his cheek and a curling lock of his black hair drooping over his brow, he seemed a very different man from the dashing, handsomely-sardonic, fleering-eyed centaur who had all but ridden her down, spattered her with turf, and challenged everything—or most—that was in her, that day at the Redeswire ceremony. Though that had been a wrong impression, anyway, that she had gained that day. He was not that sort of man at all, she had come to realise. The daredevil, flamboyant, carelessly-confident cavalier, was nothing more than an act. Actually, she believed that he was a tense, sensitive, easily-hurt man, with a great driving-force and powers of leadership, but not very good at looking after himself, one way or another. He didn't give himself a chance, really . . .

Every now and then he twitched a little as he lay. She knew an urge to stop him doing that, to smooth away and ease that symptom of strain—but had no idea how it could be done. He looked absurdly young, like that, with the dirt on his face and the black curl fallen forward over his brow. On an impulse, Barbara leant over and gently pushed back that errant lock, with deft fingers reinserting it more tidily amongst its fellows. Her pink tongue tipped her upper lip as she did it. He did not stir.

For a little longer she sat there, her thoughts her own—but by her expression not altogether unpleasing. Then she glanced at her wrist-watch, saw that it was a quarter to ten, nodded briskly to herself, and got to her feet. Stretching arms luxuriously, she climbed the few yards to the crest of their bank, to look out over the route they had come. No sign of life showed on the sun-bathed slopes.

Satisfied, the girl turned and strode downhill, past the recumbent Archie, right to the burnside. Upstream she

147

went, a little way, till she found a sizeable pool, and there she knelt down.

Presently, the man up on the bank opened one eye, blinked it, opened the other, and raised his head. Quickly he found her. Her back half-turned to him, she was having a wash. Instead of dropping his head, as he ought to have done of course, he raised it a little higher—for it was a very thorough and whole-hearted sort of wash that she was giving herself, admirable in every respect. Archie was not lacking in his admiration. Himself, he would scarcely have gone the length of laying aside his shirt in the name of cleanliness—but then, of course, it might be the shirt that she was preserving from the splashes of burn-water? Or maybe, it was to act as a towel. . . .

This interesting problem was still unresolved when unfortunately the young woman turned her head to glance straight up towards him. He could move quickly, that man, on occasion—and instinct rather than any due consideration or nice judgment told him that this was an occasion. He flopped down on his face again, his own head turned the other way, quicker than thought, much quicker, like a rabbit into its burrow, and stayed that way. He shut his eyes again too—as well he might—in case that would help.

It was some time before he heard her coming up the slope towards him once more. She stood beside him for a while, too, during which interval he had considerable difficulty in keeping his eyelids from flickering.

Then she spoke. "You'd be a lot better down at the burn yourself, cleaning yourself up, instead of lying there pretending to be asleep!" she declared, in a superior tone. "You look far from beautiful, I can tell you!"

He stirred, opened those eyes again, yawned convincingly, and sat up. "Eh . . .? What's that?" he wondered.

"You heard!" Barbara asserted. "You're better at some acts than others! The least you can do now is to wash your face."

He was both dignified and specific—quite a feat in the

148

circumstances. "On an operation such as we are engaged upon, there are more important considerations than clean faces," he pronounced. But he got to his feet nevertheless, and after only a momentary pause for due effect, started off down to the stream. It was not only her strictures on his appearance that sent him thus promptly, but a laudable desire to avoid any possibly embarrassing exchange—a gentleman's simple duty, surely. Unfortunately, it all meant that he was forced to give himself a considerably more drastic and comprehensive washing in consequence, with no option but to strip to the waist. At least, it enabled him to take a long time about it. *He* did not turn his head upwards, once.

It was with some relief, undoubtedly, that, whilst meticulously and for the third time re-pinning his stock, he heard a commotion from above, and was able whole-heartedly to welcome his mounted friends and colleagues, dilatory as they had been.

*   *   *

Six mounted men and Archie's led horse had arrived, and Dand Fairgrieve was one of them. They seemed to be in excellent spirits, especially Dand. Listening to the epic account of horsemanship, fieldcraft, and cunning, whereby they had covered nearly thirty miles of deepest Northumbria in daylight without actual challenge, Archie considered them all, with somewhat divided attention.

"There's one of you missing," he inserted, into the panegyric. "Willie Dewar."

"Willie was feeling a bittie tired," Dod Wilson explained. "He's no' so young as some o' us, mind. So Dand jist took his place."

"Willie's better in the car," the Cornet agreed, sympathetically. "Och, yes—at his age."

"Willie's exactly a year older than myself!" Archie pointed out, coldly. "What you mean is, you bullied him into letting you have his horse, Dand Fairgrieve! I guessed that was why you were so keen to go back to meet these folk. Now, who's going to escort Miss Hepburn back to the car?"

"Nobody," that lady said, decidedly.

"Oh, yes—somebody is. Dand is. His is the responsibility. He brought you."

"But I'm not *going* back. I'm going with you. I'm seeing this thing through to the finish, now. In the admirable Common Riding spirit . . . !"

"No. I can't accept that responsibility. The last lap may well be difficult. The country will be roused, remember, even on the Scots side. We may have police to deal with. There could be complications—and you'd only add to them. Anyway, there's no horse for you."

"Seven husky men, and not one of them prepared to share his horse with a girl?" she cried. "I wonder!" Barbara ran her blue eye over the lot of them, and by her expression, appeared to be satisfied with what she saw. She turned back to the Callant. "I'm coming," she said, nodding portentously. "And look here, Archibald Scott—if you try to stop me, I'll tell these friends of yours just what you were up to a little while ago!"

"Whe-e-e-ew!"

"Say, boys—this is it!"

"Eh, Archie, Archie—what goes on?"

That sorely-wronged man swung on her. "Of all the little vixens . . . !" He swallowed. Hitherto he had managed to avoid looking directly at her. Now, faced not only with her smiling self-confidence but with the transformation that she had effected in her appearance during his own prolonged ablutions—hair combed, disciplined, and sleek, complexion powdered and immaculate, lips scarlet and provocative, clothing astonishingly spick, span and spruced up—he was most unfairly affected. The contrast with the others—and no doubt with his unshaven and unkempt self, wash or none—was telling out of all proportion to the basic values of the matter. "M'mmm," he said. "Er . . . i'ph'mmm." But he had reserves, the man, and was not done yet. He turned on the Hawick Cornet, forefinger jabbing. "Take

150

her away, Dand—back to the car!" he ordered. "This is all your fault. And don't believe the half she says. . . ."

Fairgrieve blinked, and coughed. "Afraid that's no good, Archie," he explained earnestly. "You see, the car's away. I . . . I knew you wouldn't want it to run any risks, by being unnecessarily delayed, so I just sent it away home."

"You did . . .?"

"That's right," Dod Wilson supported, stoutly if wary-eyed.

"Best thing to do," Sanny Elliot agreed.

"Och, aye—jist that," Rab Pringle added.

Archie looked from one to another, ferociously, opened his mouth to speak and shut it again, and then burst out. "Bah! A lot of gaping yokels swept off your feet by a girl's tricks! Let's get out of here! Where's that damned horse?"

151

12

There is neither necessity nor profit in recounting the passage of the next two hours and six uphill miles; it all will be almost as painfully familiar, by this time, to the reader as to the herdsmen. Suffice it to say that those cattle, proving neither better nor worse than the majority of their kind, were harried, prodded and impelled, somehow, upwards, approximately along the line of green Clennell Street and the Usway Burn to the eventual blessed ridge of Windygate. With almost one herder per bullock, the task was undoubtedly simplified, and daylight further assisted; moreover, by now the horsemen were all considerably wiser in the ways of cattle than when they started. Throughout this operation, Barbara Hepburn rode pillion to Dand Fairgrieve, of her own very express choice. If Dand was not always the most active of the drovers in consequence, he did not seem in the least downcast thereby—even as the recipient of occasional highly-critical glances from Jethart's Callant.

By noon, when they were nearing the final ridge, Archie's eyes were increasingly on the wider vistas. How soon they might expect to glimpse angry Northumbrian farmers on the trail of their filched property, was anybody's guess, but obviously it was possible for certain of the nearer-at-hand to be up here by now. Some quick decisions would fall to be made, if such materialised.

They reached the summit, however, without sight of other humanity, trotted over the Borderline at last with something of a flourish, all things considered, and loosed off a ragged but spontaneous cheer in celebration. Not halting on any skyline, they nevertheless with one accord turned in their saddles and looked backwards. It was a far cry from Hexham.

But it was a far-ish cry to Jedburgh, Hawick and the rest, too—a thought which was by no means lost on weary travellers. Before them now the land dropped away mightily, sweeping down through all the northern foothills to the far-flung verdant dales of the Scottish Borderland, rimmed by the blue scalloping of a further thousand hills. Sheer distance spread itself in front of them—and in their present state, none went unaffected thereby.

Archie pointed out the more immediate objective, the cleuch just down below them. Only another half-mile, he assured. Indeed, when he held up his hand for quiet, and they listened, they could hear a deep rumbling sound that rose and fell like the swelling tide, and was the lowing of many cattle.

Fearful that any of their little herd should rush down towards their vociferous fellows and tumble over the lip of the cleuch, Archie led two or three of his riders forward to form a protective screen between the bullocks and the top of the bank. And there, looking down at last into that deep gouge in the face of the hill, even he who had visualised it all was impressed, forcibly struck, by the sight. Despite himself, he beckoned forward Dand Fairgrieve and his tightly-clinging passenger, pointing downwards.

The term beef-tub scarcely could have been more apt. The narrow floor of the hollow was entirely hidden under the variegated mass of beasts, reddish-brown predominating, that seethed and milled and heaved, never for a moment still. Steers mounted on each other's backs, momentarily, and subsided, like bubbles bursting. Steam rose up from the pack of them in drifts and eddies. The sound of their complaint was like a solid wall. So steep were the sides of the place and so high, that, facing due north, little or no sunlight reached the bottom of it even at midday. The sense of helpless, hopeless incarceration, entombment, produced, further conjured up dire and inescapable impressions of the Pit itself.

"Mercy—the poor brutes!" the girl cried. "What a horrible place! It's a shame . . .!"

"They're all right, there," Archie said. "Come to no harm."

"Maybe not. All the same, I don't see their owners thanking you when they find them down there!"

"Better all penned neatly there than roaming loose about the hills," the other was asserting, when a shout from Sanny Elliot stopped him.

"Archie! Do you see what I see?" The Coldstreamer was pointing down, west by north.

They turned to stare. Down there, clearly to be seen about three miles away was the same Heatherhope Reservoir where they had rendezvoused with the car seven hours before. And moving up the thread of roadway to it was a string of five vehicles, a small one leading. Something about the relative size of those moving specks brought Archie's brows down hard. He reached for his binoculars.

"Dammit—that's quick work, if you like!" he cried. "Cattle-trucks—four of them, with a car in front." He lowered the glasses, handing them to Dand. "Now how in the name of all that's wonderful did they get on to us so quickly? This spot, I mean. Confound it, it's hardly possible . . .!"

"Aye—they're cattle-trucks all right," Dand agreed. "Somebody's been out of bed mighty early this morning."

"The same folk that got in touch with the police, perhaps?" Sanny suggested.

"But how *could* they?" the Callant demanded. "To reach there, those trucks will have to have come all the way round by Hounam and Morebattle and the Jedburgh road. Even if they came up Redesdale from Bellingham, the nearest place in England likely to produce four cattle-trucks, they'd have had to be on the road for an hour-and-a-half at the very least. More, probably. Now could anyone have managed to trace the cattle up here, and then got down again, even to the nearest house with a phone, in time to

154

have had those trucks started by ten-thirty or so? Short of a helicopter, I just don't see it. . . ."

"Maybe they don't know the brutes *are* up here," Dand suggested. "Maybe they're just bringing the trucks up to the nearest point a road comes, to this part of the Cheviots, on the off chance? They could fan out from down there, looking for their cattle . . .?"

"But even that would mean they had a pretty shrewd idea what had happened and where we'd brought the critturs," Archie objected. "I don't see how they'd tumble to Heatherhope right away, like this. . . ."

"Whether you do or not—there they are!" Barbara pointed out with feminine practicality. "They could hardly be any of your own people, could they?"

"No, no. What would anyone do that for? They've stopped, at the foot of the reservoir. Give me those glasses, Dand . . . Yes—there's a whole bunch of men. A dozen or more. They're started walking up the track that edges the water, this side. They've left three or four at the trucks. Looks as though they're going to follow the same path that we went down last night . . . this morning. And that'll bring them right up here." He lowered the binoculars, and turned. "Look—we can't stay here, for all to see. They might have seen us already." Swiftly he scanned the hillsides around. "If we carry on down the side of the cleuch, and in, they're bound to see us. There's dead ground behind that sort of knoll over there, on the right—out of sight from down there, anyway. Better get the cattle and horses behind that, meantime. Quickly."

A small spur of the hill face a few hundred yards over gave them cover from view, but from below only. There they dismounted, and leaving three of their number to ensure that the cattle did not stray, the others crept back to a spot where they could overlook both the cleuch and all its long approaches.

The bunch of men were still working along the shore of the reservoir. There was a footpath there. "They'll see our hoof-marks on that path," Archie said. "Bring them

155

right up. A little elementary tracking and they'll walk straight into Kelsocleuch."

Not that the oncoming party seemed in any way concerned about tracking. They came on steadily, without any hesitation or casting about, a tight group of twelve or fourteen men. Once past the end of the reservoir, they struck up over the rising ground, directly in line for the cleuch.

"Something mighty queer about this," Archie declared. "Looks as though this lot has been tipped off, doesn't it?"

"It does that," Dod Wilson nodded. "These boys ken where they're goin'."

"I don't see why you should be so concerned," Barbara put in. "What does it matter, now? You've achieved all you wanted, haven't you? You *want* these cattle to be recovered, don't you? It seems to me, it doesn't matter how they get them back to their farms, or how soon—so long as you people get safely away. Why not just leave these eight bullocks where they are, and make tracks right away, while the going's good? Even if they see you riding off, they can't do anything about stopping you, unmounted as they are."

"That's right enough, of course," Archie conceded. "But . . . well, I'd just like to stay and see what goes on here. This is rather interesting. Maybe most of the rest of you ought to get cracking? These folk will be out of sight behind that shoulder, in a minute or two. Then will be your chance to scram. Cut over to your right, down the Kelsocleuch Burn and into the valley of the Bowmont Water. That'll take you right down to Yetholm, and you've a choice of roads from there."

"No' me," Wilson said briefly. "I'm bidin' here a wee."

"Same here," Dand agreed.

"Suits me," the girl declared. "The more I see, the better for my story. I just thought that the idea was to disperse and get away from the vicinity as quickly as possible, without getting involved in anything?"

"So it is," Archie asserted. "We'll still be able to do that, even if we let these characters come right up to the

156

cleuch. They won't see us up above, here, and anyway, with the horses we can leave them standing."

And so they waited, all of them, while the other party came on, now plainly visible, now hidden behind some feature of the ground, but making steady progress. Something over half-an-hour of this, and they halted for a breather about a mile below the cleuch. The watchers, lying on the warm hillside, did not blame them.

"That's no' a polisman wi' them, is it, Archie?" Rab Pringle asked.

"No. It's a bloke in a dark jacket. I can see them fairly well, now. A fairly tough-looking lot. Cattlemen and farm-hands rather than actual farmers, I'd say. There's fifteen of them, and they've all got sticks I think. . . ."

Presently the new-comers resumed their determined progress, and in a little while they were covering the last stretch of hillside below the beef-tub. It was possible with the naked eye to perceive something of the style of them, now, and the general impression given was, somehow, of formidability. Mention was being made of this, when the sharp-eyed Sanny Elliot once more interjected.

"Ah-ah—the plot thickens! Look yonder."

Away over on the summit-ridge of Crookedsike Head, a hill between them and Cheviot itself, two horsemen had appeared. They would be between two and three miles off, and had obviously come over from the south side. They were moving downhill, slanting northwards, as the watchers gazed.

"Look—there's another two! No, three," Dand cried, pointing. "Over to their left, on the next hill. One with a white horse. Looks like the first two are working over to meet them . . ."

"It's okay—they're no' comin' this way, anyhow."

"Guid for us, boys—we've got the English ower the Border, at last!"

"They'll likely be popping up all round, now . . ."

"Will they see us, Archie? Or these guys doon below?"

157

"I don't think so. They might just catch a glimpse of these few cattle up here, though." He was assessing the lie of the land, and frowning. "Probably not. But it's not that that's worrying me. It's that they're right at the head of Bowmont Water, there. All round about there they look straight down its valley. If we've got to make a quick getaway from here, they're going to be rather close to our line."

"Maybe they'll work over the other way, towards The Curr . . ."

"Maybe. If not, we'll just have to beat it westwards, instead of east. Try and get down the Kale Water. It's longer, but . . ." He shrugged.

They turned their attention to the climbing party again, now approaching the entrance to the cattle-filled cleuch. The watchers, crouched above, had a grandstand view of the proceedings. They speculated on what the new-comers would do, in whispers—an unnecessary precaution, with all the noise from the cattle.

The men from the trucks gave the impression of knowing just what they were about. They made straight for the narrow entrance wedge to the cleuch, climbed the small grassy bank that blocked it, and stood looking in at the cattle-packed arena. But they did not spend more than a few seconds thus. Without any delay some of them jumped down and began to remove the roughly-heaped barricade of stones that had been erected to fill the gap. Others were pointing with their sticks, apparently indicating some method of procedure or selection. As soon as a way was cleared through the gap, men climbed down on either side, and commenced to lay about them with their sticks, whacking and urging the suspicious beasts between towards the opening. The indication was that time was valuable, and all this a routine business to be got through as efficiently and expeditiously as possible.

"They're right go-getters, them," Dod Wilson declared. "Hell—they're no' wastin' any time!"

"They knew just what they were going to do, that's

158

certain," Archie agreed. "I can't help feeling that there's something behind all this that needs explaining. . . ."

"Perhaps it's just that our level-headed English friends can think of better ways of passing their Sunday, and want to get it over as soon as may be," the young woman suggested.

The doubts of the first bullocks having been overcome, the beasts now were streaming towards and through the narrow exit. Slender enough in the first place, as the previous drovers had discovered, the new-comers had removed only sufficient of the piled stones to allow one beast through at a time—a point that did not go un-noted.

"For folk in a hurry, they'd be a sight quicker widening that gap," somebody said.

"They can count them, this way. Maybe they're looking for the brand-marks, too?"

"Maybe," Archie nodded. "But they're taking all comers. They're not trying to select any special beasts."

"There's seventeen out, now," Barbara counted. "Eighteen . . ."

There was a general drift of cattle towards the exiguous exit, now, with consequent crushing and crowding in the narrow neck of the cleuch, where three or four men laboured heroically with their sticks to keep the weight of beef back from blocking the passage.

"Twenty-nine . . . thirty . . . thirty-one . . ." the girl chanted. "Look—isn't that the little white cow, over there to the left?"

When exactly forty bullocks had passed through, there was a sudden change in the activity below. The men within the arena began to beat back all the forward-pressing beasts, with much waving of arms and hallooing, whilst their colleagues beyond the barrier commenced to refill the gap with the stones.

"So that's all they're taking!" Archie cried. "Forty, just."

"Four truck-loads," Wilson pointed out. "Ten to a truck. They'll no' get more'n that in, full-grown beasts."

159

"They'll likely be doin' a ferry-service," Rab Pringle suggested. "Comin' back for more."

"Yes—but in that case, why not take the lot down to the road in one go? Then they wouldn't have to come all the way up here each time for further loads. Seems queer to me that they should be penning the rest of the brutes up again, like this."

Whether out of disappointment or bewilderment, there followed a sudden drop in the cattle's lowing, almost a momentary silence as the creatures presumably assimilated the fact that they were not gaining their freedom after all. And into the comparative quiet shouted voices rose up clearly.

"Get your skates on, yous yins! We havena a' the bluidy day, look."

"Och, gie's a haun' wi' this yuckie, then . . ."

"Nivver heed. Yon's okay. Come oan!"

The listeners turned to look at each other, astonished.

"D'you hear that?" Archie exclaimed. "They're as Scots as we are! More so."

"Glasgow!" Sanny Elliot declared. "You'd know that singsong anywhere."

"Well, I'm damned!"

"What goes on, here . . .?"

"I *said* it might be some of your own people, didn't I?"

"These are no people of ours. What would they be doing this for, anyway?"

"Goodness knows. But . . ."

"They could still be from England, Archie," Dand pointed out. "I dare say there's plenty of Scots employed one way or another in Northumberland. I know one Scots farmer, near Alnwick, myself. Hang it, they could even have hired a Scots firm's trucks for the job."

"Early on a Sunday morning! Is that likely? Is it possible, in fact?"

"Well . . . what *is* the answer, then?"

Archie Scott looked grim, and sounded it. "It'll tell

160

you what *I* think the answer is—that those forty bullocks are being *stolen* from under our noses!" he said.

"You mean . . . really stolen? Pinched? Not just shifted, like we've done . . .?"

"Hell, Archie—you're not serious? I mean, genuine theft . . .?"

"I am so. That's the way it looks to me."

"Oh, nonsense!" the young woman broke in. "That's just too much. I'll swallow so much—but not that. Cattle-stealing, in this day and age!"

"Why not? It would be a heaven-sent opportunity."

"But people don't *do* that sort of thing, any more."

"Do they not? I'd have thought the *News* would have known better! Sheep-stealing's going on nowadays on a bigger scale than ever before. There's been questions in Parliament about it. And cattle too, on occasion. It's an organised racket, with gangs and lorries."

"But to go to all this trouble . . ."

"Dammit—it's us that's gone to the trouble for them! And forty prime bullocks are worth going to some trouble. D'you know that even on the legitimate market, these brutes are fetching £7 a hundredweight as beef on the hoof—and they average from ten to twelve hundredweight apiece. They're worth £70 to £80 each, those bullocks—more on the black market. These folk are away with £3,000 worth right now!"

"My goodness—I'd no idea!"

"Goad, Archie—an' it's us'll get the blame o' this!" Rab gasped. "Damned—we could be sued for the money!"

"D'you think the fact's escaped me?"

"By Hokey, then what are we jawin' here for? Lettin' them away wi't. Come on, boys—we'll need to get those stirks back!"

"Jings, you're right, Rab!"

"Just a minute! Just a minute!" Archie cried. "Look—we can't be *certain* these people aren't on the level. We can't just rush down and accuse them of stealing the brutes. Especially as they're not our cattle, to start with!"

"I agree," Sanny Elliot put in. "All this is sheer conjecture. We could make pretty fine fools of ourselves if we went down bald-headed at them . . . besides running into a load of trouble. They looked a pretty tough crew, I'd say."

"But we've got to do something."

"Yes—but what?"

They looked at each other, and then below them to where the precious bunch of cattle were being herded downhill at a trot. Something like a groan arose.

Archie was biting his lower lip. "See here," he said. "If we could get down and have a look at those trucks, we might learn something. They only left three or four men there. If we question *them* first, we might get a line on those others—especially if we came up from the other side, as though we hadn't seen this piece of work . . .?"

"Pretend we're from the English side, ourselves? Looking for our cattle?"

"Sure—that's the idea."

"Good enough. Let's get cracking."

"Come on."

Whether it was the best course to pursue; whether it was even a good plan, everybody was for it, there and then. It represented action, at least, and was infinitely to be preferred to sitting there and watching £3,000 worth of beef steadily receding and possibly turning itself into a personal liability. And no one else had a better proposal. There was a general move back towards the horses.

"These boys'll maybe see us," Dand pointed out. "Does it matter?"

"Better if they don't," Archie said. "If we keep well over to the right, to start with, we'll probably be hidden by the lie of the ground for quite a bit. Then we can belt right down the far side of this spine of hill, and over the ridge just below the reservoir."

"Just the job. What about these eight bullocks up here?"

"Leave them. No—they might fall over into the cleuch,

162

here. We'll drive them before us a wee bit, and then leave them."

There was a hurried mounting. Dand took the girl up with him again—though it might have been noted that she did not automatically look towards him as cavalier. But Archie Scott's attention was fully occupied otherwise.

Nobody troubled their heads over the whereabouts of English horsemen.

13

After driving their eight stirks a short distance over the open hillside, the riders gladly left them to their own devices, and set spurs to their horses' flanks. At first they were shielded, by the configuration of the ground, from sight of the herding party below, but presently they came into view. However, as the two groups were now the best part of a mile apart, the horsemen well behind and above the others as well as proceeding at right angles, the probability was that they would not be observed.

The mounted party made an exhilarating dash of it, thankful to be doing something, free from the restraint of slow-moving cattle, and anxious to get down to those trucks as quickly as possible. Pounding down over the sward and tussocks, turf flying, they leapt the Calroust Burn in its upper reaches and thundered on along the east side of the sinking hog's-back that separated that stream's valley from that of the Heatherhope Burn. They were out of sight of the mysterious herdsmen now, and would remain so.

In fine style they streamed down over fairly firm ground, where sheep plunged off in alarm, Archie well to the fore. That is, until, glancing round, where a burnlet scored a deep dip in the ridge, he descried Dand Fairgrieve's horse, with its double burden, left well behind away uphill. Signing the others on, he reined up to await the stragglers.

As they came down to him, the Callant called, "Sorry—I rather forgot your situation. You all right?"

"Not so bad," Dand told him. "The nag could go faster, maybe—but my passenger's having enough difficulty to hang on as it is, I imagine!"

164

The girl certainly looked a little flushed and breathless—and none the worse for that, if the enquirer had been in an objective frame of mind. She was sharing the saddle with the Cornet, and necessarily clinging close as any limpet; but lacking stirrups to support her feet, inevitably she was being jolted about unmercifully.

"Maybe . . . I'd better . . . just walk . . . the rest," she panted.

"Nonsense," Archie declared. "You'd be better in front, though, I think. Look—I'll take over for a bit."

"Och. I'll manage fine," Dand asserted. "Just give us time . . ."

"Not at all. Your beast is bound to be tired. Anyway, this young woman's really my responsibility."

"Since when?" Barbara demanded, with spirit. "You've changed . . . your tune a bit . . . haven't you? Since morning. Anyway, I'm . . . nobody's responsibility but my own—now or any time!"

"You can spare us the tantrums," Archie directed sternly. "We're in a hurry, I'd remind you. Come on."

Whether or not Barbara would have protested further, Dand edged his mount alongside Archie's, and that man reached out an authoritative arm for the passenger. The girl bowed to circumstances with such dignity as her position allowed—and made the transfer with considerable agility, even if a certain amount of clutching and clinging was inevitable. Archie, sitting as far back on his saddle as possible, got her firmly established in front of him, his arms enclosing her.

"I suggest we take a stirrup each," he said, kicking his left foot free. "Are you reasonably comfortable?"

"Physically, yes," she said, her chin lifting to emphasise the qualification.

"Then see if you can keep your hair out of my mouth, will you!" he gave back, swiftly—and saw her head jerk forward again. He heeled his mount's ribs with an obscure satisfaction.

Some satisfaction was maintained, for undoubtedly they

165

made better progress this way, and soon they were obviously lessening the distance between themselves and the other horsemen. Also, it might be that even in his preoccupied and weary state of mind, the man was aware of something basically satisfactory in holding a shapely young woman thus, in synchronising their every movement, in sharing a mutual reaction to the continuous challenge of a heaving horse's back with rough country beneath. At any rate, he made no more complaints about her hair, or anything else —any more than she did about the firmness of his grip about her middle. In fact, after a particularly jerky landing or an involved sideways balancing feat, they even synchronised involuntary laughter between them.

Where the ridge they followed rose to a minor summit, called Mow Law, they pulled away left-handed, westwards to surmount the spine and slant down into the Heatherhope glen beyond. They were just below the reservoir. Beneath, they could see the car and trucks plainly. Down to them they rode, at a less headlong, desperate-seeming pace.

They reached the road a few hundred yards below the vehicles, and turned to trot straight for them, without dissembling or hesitation. Four men stood bunched together, watching them with no noticeable kindliness.

Seen at close quarters, the cattle-trucks were old ex-Army vehicles, roughly converted, with high wooden sides non-professionally painted. Archie noted that no names were inscribed thereon—and each bore a Glasgow or West of Scotland registration number. The car, however, was both powerful and modern, though distinctly battered-looking and dirty.

"D'you want me out of the way? While you talk to these people?" Barbara asked, over her shoulder.

"No. You're fine where you are. You make us look more respectable." Archie's glance darted away southwards, uphill, beyond the blue mirror of the reservoir. The herd could be seen moving down, still more than a mile off. He reined up, a few yards from the silent watchful men, his companions close at his back, and nodded pleasantly.

166

"A fine day," he said. "Warm in these hills."

"Aye." A small sandy-haired man, dressed in a shiny navy-blue suit, off-white muffler, sagging cloth-cap and pointed thin shoes, nodded, and spat. His colleagues held their peace.

"I suppose you're out after these stolen cattle, too? A shocking affair, altogether. We've ridden over from Coquetdale in Northumberland." Archie hoped he was making his voice sound as non-Scottish as possible.

"That a fact?"

"Yes. Have you lost some beasts, too?"

The quartet exchanged glances. "Aye," their spokesman said cautiously.

"Which part are you people from?" Archie went on, with comradely interest.

"Och—a' pairts, jist." The speaker turned round deliberately, and moved away, over to one of the trucks. His three companions were following suit, and Archie spoke quickly.

"I see your vehicles are from Glasgow. Have you Scotch been losing your cattle, too?"

There was a moment's silence, and then the sandy man spoke again, from over at the cab of a truck, without turning his head. "I dinna ken. We're jist drivers, see. You'd need tae see the boss."

"I see." The Callant's glance flickered over his friends' faces. "All right. Good day to you." And he touched up his horse.

In close formation the riders moved on, up to the foot of the reservoir. As soon as they were out of earshot of the vehicle-minders, a subdued clamour broke out. None had the least doubt that those characters were crooks. All were convinced that Archie's fears were well founded—even Barbara Hepburn. If they didn't want to find themselves up to the neck in financial trouble, they would have to do something, quickly.

Strangely enough, it was Archie Scott who now pointed out that the matter was not yet proved—though admittedly

167

he feared the worst. These folk *could* have been enlisted by the Northumbrian interests, in certain circumstances. The drivers, who obviously were no countrymen, *could* be pretty ignorant of what it was all about—or told not to talk to suspicious customers who might have done the reiving . . . and a more hollow-eyed, unwashed and unshaven bunch of desperadoes than themselves at the moment, would be hard to find of a Sunday afternoon, Miss Hepburn excluded. Himself, he saw as their only course, to carry on and interview these herders up bye—and be prepared for action.

"What sort of action?" Sanny Elliot put to him.

"Any sort!" he was told, grimly.

"Hell—aye! Wade intae them . . .!"

"Gloves off, boys!"

"There's fifteen of them, remember. Two-to-one."

"Mounted men have always an advantage," Archie pointed out. "And the cattle could hamper them a bit. In fact, we might make the cattle fight for us. . . ."

"What aboot *her*?" Dod Wilson enquired, jerking his head at the young woman.

"Yes. This is where the *News* takes a seat in the stand! See that hummock up there? You can watch events from there—I'll give you my glasses."

"Oh, no . . ."

"Oh, yes! This time, there's going to be no argument about it. If there's going to be any sort of trouble, you'd be a grave handicap to us—you must see that. You'll be out of the way, up there, and at the same time able to see what's going on."

Barbara Hepburn may have been feeling the effects of her sleepless night, for she voiced no further objection. Indeed, when up at the head of the reservoir, Archie, pointing to the hillock, reined up and assisted her to alight, she turned to him, simply, earnestly, a hand on his knee.

"I don't like this," she said. "Really I don't. You'll be careful . . .?"

"Of course. Never fear—we'll be all right."

168

"It's not worth risking real trouble for. Not danger, Archie!"

"It's worth £3,000-worth of risk—for those who might find themselves called on to pay for it!" he said, handing her his binoculars. "But don't worry your head—we'll look after ourselves. Chins up, the Hepburns! Coming, boys?"

The approaching herd was now less than half a mile off. At a trot the horsemen closed with it, while the girl climbed up her knoll, chin over her shoulder.

* * *

The people driving the cattle did not halt as the mounted party came up, though a number of them moved together into a tight group at the rear. At close quarters they looked a formidable lot. In the centre was a fat bald-headed man, short-legs in Wellington boots, red face perspiring freely. He it had been who had given most of the orders, up above. Circling round the cattle, Archie brought his little band to a walk alongside this group. Lowering glances met them, save from the fat man, who chuckled at them and waved a ham-like and be-ringed hand.

"Warrm, warrm, gen'lemen," he wheezed, in a squeaky high-pitched voice. "Fine for them's on cuddies, heh?"

Archie nodded curtly. "May we ask where you're taking those cattle, sir?" he demanded, at his sternest this time.

"Och, aye—fine that. We're jist ta'en them back whaur they cam frae."

"M'mmm. You mean, to *England*?"

"Jist that. Whaur you frae yoursel's, gen'lemen?"

"We have just ridden over the hills from Alwinton and Coquetdale."

"Ooh, aye. Fine country, yon. We're frae a bittie farther south, oorsels."

"Indeed? You don't sound it, I must say. I'd have thought you came from farther *north*, myself—considerably farther north!"

The other chuckled again. "Och, aye—but there's guid

fowk frae a' pairts. Come to think on it, laddie—you've a guid Scots-soundin' tongue in your ain heid, at that!"

"You compliment me! I . . . look, I've been in touch with others about this cattle-stealing business. It would be a help to know who *you're* acting for? It's going to be a big job sorting these beasts out."

"You're tellin' me! We're actin' for a bunch o' fairmers . . . roond Redesdale an' Bell'n'm way."

"Is that so? Then you've got hold of the wrong cattle, I'm afraid," Archie pointed. "If I mistake not, those two last beasts there carry Councillor Dr. White's mark, from Snitter, up near Rothbury!"

The fat man shrugged. "I shouldna wonder. We jist tak whatever comes. We'll sort 'em oot at Bell'n'm."

"Since when has Bellin*jam* been pronounced Bellnum?" Sanny Elliot asked nobody in particular.

Archie nodded briefly. "I would like to know, too, how you *found* these bullocks? How you knew where to look?"

"Easy that. We seen them frae the road."

"That's a lie, at any rate!" Rab Pringle pointed out.

There rose a growl from the walking herdsmen. They had been muttering amongst themselves for a little while.

Archie frowned. "No—I'm afraid that is hardly possible. . . ."

"Hoo do *you* ken, mister?" The fat man was not smiling any more. His red face was thrust forward. "Eh? Hoo *d'you* ken sae much aboot it? You've jist cam up frae the roadie, there. Hoo d'you ken whaur the bluidy brutes were—an' whether we seen them or no'?"

"Never mind how we know. We know a few things, my friend—for instance, that you're not what you pretend to be, by a long chalk. Your trucks are from Glasgow, and you all speak with Glasgow voices. You're not from the Bellingham area, or you'd know the right way to pronounce the place. That road down there's a dead-end, and leads nowhere; you weren't just passing—you came there because you knew where these cattle were. I suggest that you're

170

not thinking of taking these bullocks back to their owners —you're going to take them to Glasgow, and sell them for beef!"

"Shut your bluidy trap, you . . .!" somebody snarled.

"Hell, mister—you ken ower much, a'thegither! Seems like you ken mair'n you should, aboot these brutes. Aye —an' damned if you havena the look o' bein' oot a' nicht, tae, the lot o' yous! I bluidy-well reckon it was yous that *stole* them, see!"

"That's enough of that sort of talk!" Archie barked, at his most authoritative. "I'm concerned to see that those cattle get back to Northumberland. They're certainly not going to be stolen under our noses. Your game's up, my friend. You'd better turn round, and drive the beasts back where you got them, right away."

"Like bluidy hell, we will! Look, you damned . . ." The fat man's angry falsetto was drowned in the roar of threat, abuse and challenge from his supporters. There was a general movement towards the horsemen, leaving the cattle to go their own way.

"That sort of line won't do you any good!" the Callant called loudly. "You can't get away with the cattle, now."

"An' whae's stoppin' us?" a big hulking fellow demanded, advancing towards Archie's horse.

"We are." The Callant dug in his spurs, and at the same time pulled hard on his reins, and his mount reared up pawing the air and sidling, so that the big man drew back hurriedly. "Look—we don't particularly want a lot of trouble. To save a fuss, we're willing to let you people scram off, and say no more about it. Just leave the cattle where they are. . . ."

"Damn that!" the fat man cried. "Bluidy true you're no' wantin' ony trouble. You stole the brutes in the first place. You canna dae a thing tae us. An' keep your damned cuddy awa' frae me! You'll no' go to the polis or anybody else, blast you. You'll no' stop us, any . . ."

"That's where you're wrong," Archie cried. "You've asked for this, confound you!" And jerking his horse's

171

head round, right-handed, he waved his friends on in a wide sweeping movement. "Round the front!" he shouted.

Nothing loath, the horsemen kicked their steeds into action and wheeled round whence they had come. Past the cattle they cantered, close on Archie's heels, following his example as his hand rose and fell, beating his mount into a gallop. On he pounded for a good three or four hundred yards; it might have been assumed by the watchers that he was heading back to their trucks. Then, raising his arm high, he swung it in a circular motion, at the same time pulling his steed round in a great arc, without any slackening of pace.

"Let them have it!" he bawled, to the six riders circling at his back. "Spread out. Hell for leather! Yell blue murder! Stampede those cattle back through them. Come on—Jethart's here!"

"To hell with Jethart! Teri-bus y Teri Odin!" Dand roared, at the pitch of his lungs, swinging out into line. "Ha'ick for ever!"

"Kelsa! Kelsa!"

"Jethart's here! Jethart's here!" There were four Jedburgh men to three others, and that slogan prevailed. Weariness forgotten, voices and arms upraised, they thundered on, straight at the advancing cattle.

Alarmed, the foremost bullocks slowed, tried to halt, and were pressed on by beasts and urgent men behind. Snorting, stumbling, slewing this way and that, they faced the vociferous line of galloping horsemen. At their backs the herdsmen saw, cursed, and apparently chose defiance rather than safety. Raising their own voices in turn, they sought to stem the tide. The bewildered steers, caught between two fires, bunched and crowded, irresolute.

But not for long. Whites of eyes gleaming, rearing and stamping in their agitation, the forty bullocks, while still the riders were a hundred yards off, turned and set off in stiff-legged panic back on their tracks, tails in the air.

Desperately some of the herders at the rear fled for life and limb. Those at the sides were lucky, and could make

172

good their escape; but the group in the centre had neither time nor opportunity to bolt—and that fat man would be no runner. But they did not panic. Hurling themselves together in a tight mass, they did all that they could—shouted, waved arms, and swung their heavy sticks like windmills— as the tide of beeves swept upon them.

As well for them that the cattle were so close as not to have worked up any great speed or impetus. Otherwise they might well have been overwhelmed and trampled in that surge. But their firm stand, the hullabaloo, and those thrashing clubs, with the fact that there were only the forty bullocks and therefore no massive weight behind the first brutes, served to save them. The cattle divided and swept round and past them, a brown torrent flooding past a tiny island.

Behind came the horsemen, headlong, in line. As the last of the steers charged past, Archie, centrally placed, found himself almost on top of the hedgehog of shaken but unharmed men. Still shouting his slogan, he slewed his mount's head round, to clear them, ignoring the fist-shaking, stick-brandishing roar which greeted him, to continue on after the cattle. They were what mattered.

But it was not to be so simple as all that. One of the men, the same big fellow who had interposed previously, leapt forward, arm raised, and hurled his heavy cudgel, viciously. Whether it was aimed at Archie, or his mount, was not to be known, but, spinning, it struck the horse full on the nose. The beast threw up its head with a squeal of pain, reared, and went on rearing, side-stepping on its hind-legs.

With a hoarse yell the big man flung himself after his stick, hands outstretched, reaching for the rider. Archie, fully occupied in keeping his seat and seeking to soothe his mount, nevertheless saw him coming, kicked his right foot free of its stirrup, and met the man's rush with a boot planted plumb on his chest. The attacker reeled backwards, clawing at Archie's leg.

But there were other men behind him, and equally angry.

173

the hill, the cattle were being driven at a spanking pace by the remaining two Jedburgh youths.

Archie might have said something appropriate to the occasion, was not all the breath being jolted out of him by the wretched saddle-pommel in his middle.

They did not head straight after the climbing cattle, but over half-left to where Archie's horse stood nervously waiting. There they pulled up, for its master thankfully to transfer to his own saddle. Glancing back, they saw that the opposition was huddled together in a gesticulating bunch about a quarter of a mile away, and showing no signs of what could only be fruitless pursuit, either of the cattle or of the horsemen.

"Say—we gave that lot a bellyful!" Dod cried. "Yon was great, was it no'?"

"Lots of fun," Sanny agreed. "Are you all right, Archie?"

"Not so bad—had it not been for Dod's damned saddle!" that ingrate asserted. "If anybody got a bellyful, it was me! You've got an awful shoogly horse, man, and a cast-iron pommel!"

"At least, I manage to stay on my perishin' horse!" the Kelso Laddie gave back. "You think those boys've had enough?"

"Looks like it." The Glasgow contingent had started to straggle off downhill towards the reservoir and their trucks.

"What else can they do?" Dand said. "They can't make up on horses."

"They could awa' back to the cleuch for anither dose o' stirks."

"And have the same thing happen again? No—horsemen can always stampede cattle, and men on foot can do little to stop them, I reckon."

"Then they've had it, the baistards! We've won oor bit battle . . ."

"We've won this round, anyway." That was Archie Scott speaking, and sounding unsuitably grave.

176

"Eh? What d'you mean? This round . . .?"

"Just this. Whoever gave those folk the tip that there were prime cattle for the taking, up here at Kelsocleuch, isn't likely to have failed to mention the Curr and the Scrathy Holes!"

"My Goad—I nivver thocht on that!"

"Losh—d'you think, Archie . . .?"

"I don't *know*. We may have just happened to stumble on their only effort. But I wouldn't like to bank on it! Those two other beef-tubs have got nobody guarding them. And look—even supposing this *was* their only attempt so far; those characters don't look like the type that would give up easily. What's to prevent them getting back into their trucks and away along to either of these other lots of cattle?"

They stared at each other, appalled. Triumph forgotten, their weariness surged back on them like a flood.

"What's to do now, then?" Dand asked, flat-voiced.

Archie was gingerly nibbling a bruised lip. "Dand— you ran the Scrathy Holes show. How near could they get trucks to there? From either side—the Redesdale or Tyndale roads?"

The Cornet brightened, even as he answered. "They couldn't get them within five miles, on the Tyne side, and gey rough going at that. More on the Rede side. There's no roads."

The other nodded. "Just what I was thinking. The chances are, then, that they'd leave that one alone. Too big a job. At first, anyway—though now they've been foiled here, they might have a go at it. *We've* driven the beasts a lot more than five miles, mind, and they're bound to know it. But it would take them a long time, especially without horses. The Curr's much more likely. We all know that you can get cars up from the Yetholm road to within a mile or two of it. It's easier than this is."

"Up the Atton Burn, frae Blackdean—it's no more'n a mile-an'-a-half," Dod declared. "An' a track near a' the way."

"Yes. Afraid so. How far's that from here? Five

miles? Uh-huh." Archie sighed. "Well, looks like there's nothing for it, boys. We can't go home yet!"

In silence they eyed him.

In his turn, the Callant considered each of his friends. "I know you fellows are tired. What's worse, the horses are tired. But they're not done—and we've always got that extra notch in our belts!"

"Sure, Archie," Dand said briefly. "Spill the beans."

"Anither hundred miles'll fair kill me," Dod mentioned heavily.

"That's the spirit. Here's the way I see it. Obviously, the Curr is the most likely bet, and we daren't miss it. But I feel we can't afford to leave the Scrathy Holes out of it, either—especially since this lot have been repulsed here. I'm afraid we'll have to divide up, some going east, some west."

"It's a long way, Archie, to the Scrathy Holes."

"I know it is. The best part of twenty miles, I'd say. But it would take these types a long time to get there too, mind. Fifty miles by road, round about, and then a five-mile walk. You'd be there first, I reckon, Dand."

"Me . . .?"

"Och, it's on your way home to Hawick, sort of!"

The other swallowed. "Oh, sure. Sure. By Carlisle, Dumfries, Langholm and points west!"

"Never mind—Rab'll keep you company. Eh, Rab? You had a fine sleep back at yon Pity Me place—or you should have done!"

"Okay," his taciturn Right-hand nodded. "I'm no' speaking to my wife the noo, onyway! I'll go."

"Good man. Whoever gets down to a phone first, can ring Hawick to send out cars and horse-boxes to meet you along the Carter Bar road. . . ."

"But say, Archie—if we split up, what good are two or three of us going to be against a big gang?" Sanny Elliot demanded. "It was a near enough thing back there, with the seven of us."

"I realise that." The Callant sighed. "And there's

178

only one answer. Since all our own boys are away home hours ago, there's unlikely to be anybody else in these hills we can appeal to for reinforcements . . . except English farmers out looking for their stock!"

"Well, cooper me . . .!"

"Good Lord!"

"Save us a'—you're no' serious, Archie?"

"I am, yes. I don't see what else we can do. It's our responsibility to see that those cattle are not stolen, at all costs. And swallowing a mouthful of our pride seems to be one of the costs. The main thing now, is not to lose any of the beasts. And it might be worse, you know. We've made our gesture. We've got these Englishmen out, over the Border. We've achieved our main object . . ."

"An' noo we'll achieve the jail, jist!"

"It's a risk we've got to take. I'd rather risk jail for what we've done than be presented with a bill for thousands of pounds for stolen cattle."

"He's right, there," Sanny agreed soberly.

"It maybe won't come to that, of course," Archie consoled them. "It could be that some of these farmers will have discovered their cattle for themselves, by now. We know some of them rode over to the east, there—they were not all that far from the Curr. The hills may be littered with them, by this time. In which case they'll be evacuating the brutes themselves, and these Glasgow folk presumably will sheer off."

"Maybe. But we'll no' ken till we get there."

"No. But it just means we'd be wise to be careful how much we tell the Englishmen beforehand. No need to incriminate ourselves more deeply than we must."

"You've said it!"

"By Hokey—you're right there!"

"Yes. Well—the sooner we're on our way, the better . . ."

"What about the two boys up there with the cattle?"

"Yes. I think one should stay near the beasts meantime— keep an eye on them just in case of further trouble here. The other had better go west with you, Dand. Even things up."

179

"Right. Good luck, you blokes. See you in jail!"

"So long as it's a Scots jail . . ."

"So long, you lucky people!"

Archie pulled his mount's head round. "Now for the Curr," he said. "And no dawdling."

"Say—what aboot your lady-friend, man? You're no' goin' to leave her sittin' on her bit hill?"

"Damn it, Dod—I clean forgot all about her!"

"Yon one wouldn't like to hear you say that, I'm thinkin'. Anythin' but that!"

"You mean, she doesn't like to be overlooked?"

"Och, aye—I could mean that, too!" Dod conceded, mildly.

"For a creature from Kelso, you talk too much!" Archie said, with conviction.

14

"Are you hurt, Archie? Are you all right?" Half-way down her hill, the girl came to them, running.

"Of course I'm all right. Apart from being treated like a sack of potatoes by this man Wilson . . . !"

"Oh, thank goodness! I was afraid . . . It looked awful. Through the glasses. You seemed to be having a terrible time, being battered to death almost. Those horrible brutes . . . !" Her agitation was frank, and visible as well as audible.

The man was flattered, of course—though how much of it all might be due to her race downhill was a moot point. "A little horse-play, that was all," he said lightly. "Are you coming up? Put your foot in this stirrup. . . ." And stooping, he hoisted her up before him again.

"It was ghastly being stuck up there on that hill," Barbara told him. "Seeing you going down, with all those cowardly thugs on top of you, and not being able to do a thing to help. And after that fall you had, that made you sick . . ."

"Aren't you rather forgetting to be the calm detached and objective journalist?" Archie suggested. "Shouldn't the *Daily News* really take a less partisan view?"

"What nonsense!" she cried. "I'm a human being, am I not? A flesh-and-blood woman, with more than printer's ink in my veins!"

"H'rr'mm . . . quite. That, ah, is the impression one gets, yes. At least, latterly . . . !" He gripped her round the middle the more comprehensively, as though to emphasise his point. "Oh, definitely."

181

Her essential feminity was promptly demonstrated in further degree by her twisting round to face him. "Am I expected to stand unmoved, watching a brutal assault by a horde of ruffians on one man—even an ill-mannered insufferably-conceited small-town paladin like yourself, Archibald Scott?"

"Oh." The Callant blinked, licked swollen lips, cleared his throat, and was silent.

"My goodness—it's a right warm afternoon for September!" Dod Wilson observed earnestly.

The girl turned face to the front again, head high. But only for a half-minute perhaps. Then, glancing this way and that, she became aware of the topographical situation. "I say—where are we going? What's happened to the others?" she demanded.

Picking his words with care and with all the dignity available on a trotting horse, Archie told her, as they headed eastwards.

There were two ridges and the valleys of the Calroust Burn and Bowmont Water to cross before the tall peak of The Curr rose before them like a flying buttress of great Cheviot. They had topped the second ridge, and were dropping down towards Bowmont, when they saw the two groups of horsemen below them—one riding up the road by the waterside, the other slanting downhill to meet them. Judging by the white horse, the latter seemed to be the trio that they had observed earlier.

"Well, there they are—the Auld Enemy," Sanny called. "What do we do now? Keep out of their way, or go and spill the beans?"

Archie's brows were furrowed. "It's a bit of a problem, isn't it? We don't want to commit ourselves, if it's unnecessary—if there's no assault on The Curr cattle. That would be tragic. On the other hand, we may well need these folk—and if we do, it might be in a hurry. If only we didn't have to take a decision till we'd seen over that next ridge. . . ."

"Perhaps they won't leave all the decision to you!" the

182

girl suggested. "When they see us, *they* may do the approaching."

"That's true."

Before they were far down into the valley, they saw the two parties of horsemen join up, and only a little later it was clear that the combined company was coming back, downstream, towards them. There was no hiding themselves on the open bracken slopes. Quite evidently the Scots party had been seen, and a meeting was contemplated.

Archie was measuring distances with his eye, a dulled and heavy-lidded eye screwed up against the glare of the early afternoon sun. "At the angle they're coming, they're bound to come close to us," he said. "It'll look damn' queer if we sheer off, deliberately avoiding them. Look, Dod. If you were to barge ahead on your own, up to the top of that ridge opposite, you'd see down into the valley of the Atton Burn you were talking about, from there. Wouldn't you? Take my glasses. We'll move over and have a chat with these Englishmen—keep them occupied, if we can. Then you signal down to us if there's any sign of trouble in the next valley. We'll keep an eye on you. That do?"

"Uh-huh. Fair enough. An' if there's nothin' there, I'll jist come back. What signal will I gie you, that you can see?"

"Take your jacket off and wave it back and forwards. We'd see that. That is, if there's any sign of a gang or vehicles down there."

"Right. S'long. An' watch what you say to yon English, mind."

Dod slanted away at a canter to cross the Bowmont some way downstream. The others turned to face directly towards the horsemen farther up the valley.

As they drew near, the approaching party could be seen to consist of nine or ten men, in the main middle-aged, well dressed and well mounted. There was something distinctly substantial and solid, not to say stolid, about them—the well-doing, well-nourished salt-of-the-earth,

183

obviously. What they thought of what they saw, was anybody's guess.

Archie sketched a salute, seeking to appear entirely at ease behind his passenger. "Good hunting?" he called. "You people had any luck, yet?"

An iron-grey, square-faced, heavy-shouldered man on a roan horse answered him. "We followed tracks right up the College Water back there, but lost them up on the heather on top." He spoke with a rich north country voice. "This is a damn'-fool business, if ever I heard of one!"

"Isn't it!" Archie agreed. "What d'you think's behind it all?"

"Lord knows! I hear it's been going on right down to Cumberland. Some of these Scotch Nationalists gone hay-wire, by the looks of it. Can't see what else it can be."

"I got it on good authority," a younger man, with a handsome fair moustache said. "It's something to do with Scotch beef going to London. They object, for some reason or other. This is a sort of propaganda move to draw attention to it all. That's the police view."

"Ah." The Callant nodded. "I see. I hadn't thought of that."

"What else could it be? This must have been organised on a big scale. It's not ordinary cattle-stealing, that's clear."

"You think not . . .?"

"Of course not. They only took four of my beasts, at Howtel, out of a herd of forty-odd. The same thing at Downham and Kilham and the rest. Why go to all that trouble?"

"To hell with *their* trouble!" a bull-like man on a huge grey hunter roared. "What about *our* trouble? By God—when I get my hands on these blasted Jocks . . .!"

"Oh, quite," Archie said briefly. "Quite. You're from the Flodden area, I take it then, gentlemen?"

"Flodden, Branxton, and Wooler," the grey-haired first speaker told him. "And you? You sound as though

184

you might be Scotch yourself?" That went with upraised bushy eyebrows.

"We are, yes. We heard about this astonishing business, and came to see what went on. Quite a sensation it's causing . . ."

"What d'*you* think's behind it all—being Scotch yourselves?"

"Well, now. I wouldn't like to commit myself, just off-hand as it were," Archie said carefully. "But it certainly looks as though it has been done for some special reason. I mean, it's not commercial, in any way. . . ."

"There's a hell of a lot of money in prime beef, young feller—commercial or not!" That was the bull-necked individual, in a voice to match.

"Oh, yes—I realise that. But surely this isn't the way it would have been done—for money? As our friend says. That seems self-evident."

"I agree," Sanny Elliot observed gravely.

"Isn't that what I told you, Dusty?" the young man with the moustache said querulously. "It's politics. The police ought to know, surely."

"The police must have got on to all this pretty quickly?" Archie suggested.

"Oh, yes. To give them credit where due. They were phoning farms along the foothills roads before nine this morning, asking if they'd bullocks missing."

"You must have got on to it pretty quick, yourselves—eh?" An elderly thin man who had not spoken hitherto said that—and there was no disguising the challenge in his tone. "You look as though you might have been out pretty early—all night, even. Or do you Jocks never shave on a Sunday?"

Archie felt his chin, and mustered a rueful smile. "A bit shaggy," he acceded. "But the lady hasn't complained! We've been out a few hours, now, admittedly." He cleared his throat, and took a chance. "The Scots police were informed, of course. Some of us, who knew these hills, decided to have a look round. . . ."

185

"And have you seen anything? Any sign of cattle?" the grey man on the roan asked.

"Yes. We saw eight bullocks, up on the side of Windygate Hill, back there. About half an hour ago. One of our fellows is up keeping an eye on them."

"Eight, only? Confound it, there's hundreds missing!"

"At least we have found *some*, which seems to be more than you have done, gentlemen!"

Somebody laughed. "He could have something there, Major."

"We'll find them, never fear," the other declared. "We'll have half the North Northumberland Hunt up here in an hour or so. Not to mention the Percy and the Morpeth."

"Oh."

"What about the lady? Does she always ride half a horse?" That elderly man was suspicious by nature, very evidently.

"This is a—a temporary measure . . ." Archie began, when Barbara interrupted him.

"My mare and I parted company," she explained, with a winning smile. "And . . . I really think my escort prefers me this way!"

This produced the looked-for, indeed inevitable, guffaw of male laughter, of course. There were one or two comments of an appropriate nature. But the sour-visaged questioner was apparently past the age of being vulnerable to women's wiles—if ever he had been.

"Did your mare break its neck, or something?" he demanded.

"No. Oh, no. *My* neck was in the more danger, I assure you." She sounded entirely at ease. "One of the others took her in tow, for me. The suggestion is, I think, that I'm more use assisting my friend here to manage *his* mettlesome beast!" She waxed confidential. "Though, to be quite honest, probably what I need is a couple more riding-lessons!"

"I'd give you them free, with pleasure, miss," the moustachioed gallant declared.

186

"And damn it, I'd shave first, too!" Bull-neck bellowed. "Say—*you* won't teach these Jocks anything, Dusty!"

When the girl could make herself heard, she spoke demurely. "You are all most kind, I'm sure."

Archie Scott squeezed her a little, in acknowledgment of services rendered. At the same time, however, his glance strayed away sidelong and uphill to where Dod Wilson could be picked out, a small lonely figure nearing the summit of the long grassy slope.

Perhaps the elderly farmer intercepted that glance. "And where's your friend off to, in such a hurry, I wonder?" he grated.

"Oh, he's just away up to the ridge, there, to see if there's anything over in the valley beyond—the Atton Burn valley," Archie explained, readily enough. "It struck us as a likely place. There's a road of sorts up it, and the deserted farm-place of Blackdean."

"He could have saved himself the trouble." The man on the white horse, youngish and black-browed, made his first contribution to the discussion. "I've not long come from that ridge. That valley's being looked after, all right."

"Good. No cattle there?"

"None that I could see. There's one or two denes farther up, that I couldn't see into—but they'll be looked after. A party of searchers arrived by road, while I was up there."

"By . . . by road? With horses . . .?"

"No. In cars. At least, in lorries—cattle-floats. Quite a good idea. Save a lot of time."

Archie swallowed, audibly enough for at least the girl to hear him. "You're . . . you're sure they were cattle-trucks?"

"Of course. Not a thing you're likely to mistake, even at that distance. Anyway, it's the obvious thing, isn't it? Take the beasts home by road?"

"You hadn't arranged it? Any of your friends, I mean?"

"*We* hadn't, no." The speaker glanced about him, to a shaking of heads. "But some of the other farmers presumably have done it—the farther-out people."

"Why should they choose the Atton Burn valley, specially? There's a hundred similar valleys in these hills. Have they been tipped off . . .?"

His informant shrugged. "Search me. But why not try there? You yourself said it was a likely spot. And you've sent this bloke up to see. . . ."

"Look here—I don't get all this." The middle-aged man on the roan, who appeared to be the leader of the party, put in. "What's it all about? I don't see anything queer about stock-owners sending up cattle-trucks."

The Callant took a long breath, and looked at the Coldstreamer. That man sighed slightly, opened an expressive hand, and shook his head. The game was up, obviously. The girl, watching, twisted round suddenly to face the man behind her.

"Oh, I'm sorry, Archie!" she breathed.

Stiffly he nodded, and then looked past her. "Gentlemen," he said firmly, "I'm afraid I've got serious information for you. I believe that you're in danger, in immediate danger, of losing a lot of your prime cattle—for good. I don't think those cattle-trucks have come from Northumberland, at all. I believe they belong to a gang of Glasgow crooks who see an ideal opportunity to make an easy haul, with other folk getting the blame."

"What d'you mean, man . . .?"

"Good Lord—what sort of tale's this?"

"It could be a long story. But I suggest, gentlemen, that we haven't time for details—not if we're going to stop what I fear is going on. . . ."

"But, damn and confound it, man—you don't expect us to swallow a yarn like this, out of the blue?"

"Your cattle have been taken, haven't they—out of the blue? That's no yarn. Well, you can take it from me, what I'm saying now's not, either."

"But how d'you know? How do *you* know all this . . .?"

188

"Anyway, there may be no cattle in that valley, at all. Fenwick here didn't see any."

"I'm afraid these people with the trucks know better!" Archie said. "They knew all about it, back where we've just come from, you see. We've just had a set-to with some of them. They had forty bullocks that they'd taken from a big concentration of beasts in a cleuch up on the side of Windygate Hill. We got them back, but it was a near thing."

"You're trying to tell us that you've just had a fight with cattle-thieves, and rescued forty beasts?" Incredulity could hardly have been less disguised.

"Yes."

"Where are they now, then? The bullocks?"

"Back up in the cleuch, with the others. We sent them back."

"Hey, you—I thought you said you'd seen only eight beasts?"

"And how do you know where these forty came from?"

"What d'you mean by the others? In this cleuch . . .?"

Archie confronted this barrage grim-faced. "There are about one hundred and twenty cattle in Kelsocleuch, on Windygate," he said evenly. "From the Alnham-Ingram-Rothbury area. But what's more important, at the moment—there's as many penned up at the head of the Curr Burn, behind that hill there. It's them . . ."

"How d'you know?"

"Because I put them there," he said, quietly.

"*We* did," Sanny amended.

"Well, I'm damned!"

"I knew it! I knew it!" That was the original doubter. "I could see these people were no good, from the start. Crooks, that's what they are! I wouldn't believe a word this feller says—not a damned word!"

"If I'm a crook, why should I be telling you all this?" Archie demanded. "I didn't need to tell you a thing. We could leave you to lose your own stock, lose it for good, and to hell with you—couldn't we?" The Callant looked

189

at the others, not at his elderly accuser, challengingly now.

"Maybe. Maybe you could. Look, man—you admit it was you who stole the beasts from us, from our farms, in the first place?" the grizzled man on the road put to him.

"Yes. Took—not stole, though. We had no intention that you wouldn't get them back."

"But why, in the name of all that's wonderful? What on earth possessed you? Are you Nationalists, then . . .?"

"No. At least, not with a capital N. We did it to make you do just what you have done—to come storming over the Border, like your forefathers used to do. To try and arouse some spirit amongst you, the Common Riding spirit. Put crudely, like that, I know it sounds damn' silly—but maybe you'll be thanking us in a year or two's time."

"Well, of all the utter nonsense . . . !"

"Are you completely crazy, man?"

"You don't really expect us to accept that, do you?"

Archie had to shout to make himself heard. "Look— you can call me any names you like. You can take what steps you think fit . . . afterwards. But right now your cattle are in danger of being filched, properly stolen, from under your noses. Every minute may count. This is no time for explanations. I'm telling you, once those bullocks reach those cattle-trucks, you'll never see them again. You can chew the rag afterwards—now's the time for a bit of action."

"He's right enough there, Major."

"Yes—let's *do* something. We can puzzle it out, later. . . ."

"How long is it since you saw those trucks arriving?" Archie called to the fellow on the white horse. "Roughly?"

"Well . . . it's a little while. I didn't come straight back. I went round by that hill—what's it called? The Schel, isn't it? Let's see—it will be an hour at least. Oh, more probably."

190

"Then, confound it—it's time we weren't here! By the time we can get over to those trucks, they'll have had ninety minutes at least. Long enough to . . ."

"Archie—look!" Elliot pointed.

Away up on the skyline the mounted figure of Dod Wilson could be distinguished waving his jacket. He might well have been at it for some time.

"Wave back to him, Sanny. Move a bit apart from the rest of us, so's he can see you," the Callant directed. To the others he spoke crisply. "That's the signal that there's trouble over here. *We're* going to try to save those cattle—whether you come or not. And right away. How about it?"

The big man on the roan, referred to as the Major, nodded. "I agree. We're not doing any good here, anyway. We'll talk afterwards. You chaps coming?"

There was a chorus, in the main clearly of assent.

"Thank heaven for that!" Archie exclaimed, and dragged his horse's head round once more.

*   *   *

Down along the waterside for half a mile, and then up the long green ascent they rode—and the gentlemen of the North Northumberland Hunt proved themselves to be no laggards. Indeed, the boot was rather on the other foot, with the Scots' horses weary and one double-burdened. They made a somewhat strung-out cavalcade—but then, fox-hunters would find that normal.

In ones and twos, eventually, they reached the summit of the ridge, that was an outrider of White Law, where Dod Wilson awaited them, almost dancing with impatience. He did not have to speak, as, near the tail of the party, Archie and the girl came up. All eyes were trained on the floor of the new valley opening beneath them perhaps a mile off.

It was a short narrow steep glen, this of the Atton Burn, more of a corrie than a true valley, quickly rising, and fading eventually into the broad south-western flank of

191

The Curr. A thread of narrow roadway ran up it from the Lower Bowmont to the deserted house of Blackdean within its few gnarled and stunted guardian trees. Drawn up on the greensward around the house were at least five trucks. And only two or three hundred yards above, a tight herd of cattle were approaching it at a smart trot, drovers on foot running at sides and rear.

"Blast it!" Archie cried. "They're as far as that? They've not been long. . . ."

"They've been goin' like stour, a' the time you've been climbin' that damned hill!" the exasperated Dod shouted. "They saw me, up here, likely, whenever I came ower the skyline. You've been the hell o' a time!"

"Looks as though there was something in your story," the Major-man said at Archie's side.

The Callant did not answer either of them. He was assessing distances, judging ground, calculating times. He shook his head. "We'll not do it," he decided. "Not to the trucks in time. There's more than a mile of broken wet ground in between. And we've got to cross the burn. They'll have some of the brutes trucked before we get there, at least. They'd see us coming, and get away with those. Look—there's nothing for it but to cut down left-handed, to half-way down the valley, and block that road. It's narrow, with the stream close beside it. I reckon we can get there before them."

"Yes. Yes—probably you're right. . . ."

"What'll we block the road with?" somebody wondered.

"Damn it—ourselves, if nothing else! Come on."

So once more it was plunging steeds, creaking saddlery, and busy spurs. Archie shouted to the girl to hang on to him, and that she did tightly, frankly, convulsively—for he by no means held in his mount. He led a jolting, slithering chase slantwise downhill over a long slow water-logged slope, terraced above and steep below—and though many, perhaps all, might have passed him thereon, none did.

He did not devote all his attention to picking his way. Intermittently he scanned all the valley and roadway below

192

them, and frequently his glance darted upstream to the once-again busy Blackdean. Their charge could not be expected to go unobserved.

They were two-thirds of the way down, with only a tussocky shelf, a steepish bank, and then the stream before them, when Dod, at the Callant's right hand, cried out:

"One o' the trucks movin' off, Archie. Tak us a' oor time."

"Yes. They'll probably all come, now—loaded or not." He shot a quick look behind him. Some of the older men were a fair distance back. "This is going to be tricky."

"Don't mind me. I'll jump off . . . if you like. If it will help . . .?" Barbara panted.

Archie shook his head. Across the tussocks they plunged, hooves scattering divots and mud, straight now for the steep drop to the waterside. "Hold tight," he warned.

With only a slight diminution of speed, the three young men put their horses to the bank. Slipping and sliding, the creatures went down, practically sitting on their haunches, shoes scoring great red weals in the earth. The Major, the man Fenwick, and one or two others were close at their heels, but others of the farmers preferred a less headlong descent. Up the valley, all five trucks could be seen, lurching and bucketing down towards them, unevenly spaced out, the first only a quarter of a mile off.

"We won't do it . . .!" Sanny exclaimed.

"We've got to! Make for that bend. Best place . . ."

Archie's gallant mount glissaded down the final earth-shute almost on its belly, and into the water amidst a cataract of turf and gravel and stones. But it did not topple over. Recovering itself, it splashed across the dozen feet of the burn to the much less formidable bank beyond. As it scrabbled to find a foothold and a way up thereon, Barbara Hepburn swung her leg over its arching neck and slid to the ground, landing on all fours.

"Leave you free," she gasped. "Don't be . . . rasher than . . . you must!" She was learning, that young woman.

N.R.—N

Clambering, the horse heaved itself up the bank, scattering drops of burn water in a shower. On the grass-grown and rutted road above, it stood for a moment, trembling, before being urged on the score of paces to the bend where a bluff of the hillside turned both road and stream almost at right angles.

Rounding this corner, Archie Scott reined up his foaming, sweating, mount. Directly in front, not two hundred yards away, the first truck bore down on him, its towering sides swaying.

15

For two or three moments the man sat his horse there, alone in the middle of the roadway, facing the oncoming vehicle. Then Dod Wilson was on one side of him, Sanny on the other, and the Major and the man Fenwick close behind. Quite obviously there was neither time nor material to block the road with anything other than their own persons.

They could see four men crowded into the cab of the approaching truck, the driver hunched forward tensely over his wheel. Behind, another truck now came into view.

Archie had his hand upraised, in the halt sign. The vehicle slowed, lurched on again, and then, brakes squealing, came to a halt about thirty yards from them.

The driver's head thrust out from his window. He did not speak, but merely glowered at the horsemen.

"Might we ask where you're taking those cattle?" the Callant called.

"Eh . . .?"

Archie repeated his question, authoritatively.

It was another man, whose head jerked out from the other window, who answered him. "Back where they came frae," he said curtly. "Ony objections?"

"We might have. We'd like to know on whose authority you're taking them?"

"That's oor business." The spokesman was a dour craggy-faced individual, very different from the fat leader of the previous gang—though he sounded no less of a Glaswegian. "Oot the way!"

"Just a minute. Some of the owners of these bullocks are here. We'd like to have a look at them. . . ."

"Look, mister—we're no argy-bargyin'. We're hired to tak these bluidy stirks back tae Rothbury, see. If yous yins wants tae see them, you can see them there."

"But these beasts don't come from Rothbury . . . !"

"I canna help that. That's my orders, jist. Noo—oot the road!"

The head was pulled back inside the cab, the engine roared, and the truck jerked forward again. Urgently Archie glanced behind him. Two or three more of the farmers had come up at his back now. Seven or eight horsemen effectively blocked the narrow track. "Hold hard!" he yelled to them. "We'll stop them."

But the heavy lumbering truck showed no sign that it was making any more threat or gesture. It came on, changing up from bottom to second gear, and gaining speed.

"Damn it—he'll ram us!" the Major shouted.

"No' him," Dod cried. "He'll no' risk that . . ."

But there was a lack of conviction in the Kelso Laddie's voice. The driver was still accelerating, and with less than twenty yards to cover, he had barely time to draw up now, even if he wanted to.

Sundry warning shouts from the riders were drowned in the sudden furious blaring of the lorry's klaxon. The imperative raucous noise maintained. That truck was coming on, indubitably.

Desperately the horsemen reacted, in a chaos of rearing, backing, jostling animals. There was little room for manœuvre. On the one side there was only a yard or so of grass verge before the drop to the stream. On the other, there was a reed-filled ditch and then the bluff rose sharply. The road was little wider than the truck itself.

Most of the mounted men spurred and kicked their beasts towards the burnside, the verge, the bank, even down to the water. Archie pulled the other way, to the left, forcing his horse to the edge of the ditch—and perforce Sanny Elliot, who was on that side of him, was pushed floundering

196

into the ditch itself. There his steed lost its footing in the constricted space and soft bottom, rolled over, and flung its rider headlong. Fortunately he fell on the left or hill side, and not on the right on to the road in front of the truck's wheels.

But Archie Scott had no eyes for his friend's plight, to which he had materially contributed. His eyes were on the vehicle as it roared up alongside him, with only a foot or so to spare. And judging his time and distance to a second, he dug in his spurs and at the same time wrenched his beast's head hard round to the right. Forced back on its haunches, forelegs beating the air, even striking the truck's planking sides, the horse came round facing the same way as the vehicle. Constrained by the sharp corner to brake a little, the driver swung his lorry to the bend at the same moment as Archie's horse touched down, and, vehemently urged by spur and beating hand, bounded forward. For a second or two horse and truck were moving side by side, with Archie staring down through the open window on to the driver crouched over his wheel.

All this activity had occupied infinitely less time than it takes to tell. And equally swift was what followed. Archie kicked his feet free of his stirrups, tensed in the saddle, and then hurled himself bodily from his horse, arms outstretched, fingers clutching. Down he crashed against the side of the lurching cab, head and both arms through the open window, bearing down on the driver's hunched shoulders. One hand beat at the man's head, the other grabbed the driving-wheel, and wrenched it round towards him, to the right, his falling weight adding to the force of the drag. The lorry swung round, bucking, its front wheels left the road, one dropped straight down into the ditch, and with a jarring crash the vehicle came to an abrupt halt, canted at an alarming angle and completely blocking the narrow roadway. Archie Scott, still clinging to the driving-wheel, received a vicious buffet on the head from the fist of the man sitting next to the driver, and slid dazed to the ground, half on the road, half in the ditch.

197

After that, no coherent account is possible of what transpired. The second truck skidded to a stop within a few yards of the first. Men spilled out of both cabs—and as of one accord hurled themselves upon the author of their troubles. For the second time that afternoon, Archie Scott found himself on the ground being assaulted by balked and infuriated gangsters. But on this occasion he had no one to lie upon, and, being face down, failed to pull anyone down on top of him. All that he could do was to curl up, grasp somebody's ankles within one arm, and try to cover his head with the other—and take his punishment.

Help was closer at hand, of course. Sanny Elliot, picking himself up groggily, was the first to fling himself to his colleague's aid. Dod Wilson, kicking his mount round the bulk of the ditched truck and shouting up the farmers to the fight, rode into the mêlée, effective as before. The Major was next on the scene, lashing out with his riding-whip. Others followed, with varying degrees of pugnacity and enthusiasm. In that narrow space, between the two vehicles the stream and the hillside, utter confusion reigned, while from the closed trucks the bellowing of frightened cattle resounded.

Archie, at the centre of it all, knew only a rain of blows, multiple and comprehensive pains, and the fury of his inability to do anything much about it. In his own private hell he squirmed and rolled and cringed, debarred by the weight and press of men about and above him from adding anything more valuable to the struggle than his dogged clinging to the heavy-booted feet of one contestant.

Undoubtedly, however, that same cramping press of his assailants saved him from the direst punishment; the thing worked both ways, and no really vital blows could be aimed and delivered owing to the press. This was proved only too clearly when presently, after an interval that was not to be assessed by any normal computation of time, the rescuers had managed to disperse some considerable weight of the attack, and only two or three determined characters were left to concentrate on the fallen Callant. Three times more punishing fell the blows, and to save neck and head, Archie was forced to relax his grip on those hard-held ankles. And there and then his fate was sealed. The man thus released, drew back his booted foot and kicked with all his strength, once, twice, thrice, before Dod, driving in desperately right above his recumbent friend, felled the fellow with one furious swinging pile-driver of his clenched fist. Archie knew a sudden searing pulverising torture in his right side, jerked over on his back, knees up, gasping with the excruciating pain—and saw through red-filmed eyes Dod's horse's hoof descending upon him. His head seemed to explode, in shattering disintegration, and mercifully he knew no more at all.

*   *   *

It was slowly, painfully, out of a swirling heaving pit of black waters that the man dragged himself to the surface of consciousness eventually, out of vague and formless horror into real and most certain agony. His head was opening and shutting, opening and shutting, and only by keeping his eyes screwed tight shut could he keep the two pieces from falling wholly apart, he felt. For long he struggled with this difficult task, groping mind questioning blind instinct. He heard sounds about him, voices, the lowing of cattle, and from some corner his fugitive brain told him that struggle and strife were ceased—that is, except in his splitting head. By a quite enormous effort of will, he opened his eyes.

He had difficulty in focusing, the sun was blinding, and the world was unsteady. All that his eyes saw did not register. But certain basic facts about the situation did, and he took them in slowly, almost grudgingly, for ultimate consideration. Over some, he knew a sense of satisfaction; others vaguely irritated. But all were accepted only through the billowing curtain of pain, which precluded any very definite reaction.

Barbara Hepburn's face came and went just above his

199

own, now near, now far away. Her hand, stroking up and down, seemed to be helping to keep his bandaged head together—and he was obscurely grateful for that. There were other faces, too, but they were much farther away, and not all the right way up. Voices too, jumbled and mixed up with the cattle's mooing. But the girl's voice was continuous, rising and falling like the sigh of a summer sea, soothing, reassuring. He liked hearing it, without any particular urge to know what it was she said. But to be able to distinguish it, above those other noises, he had to listen. And listening, not just hearing, involuntarily, reluctantly, his mind found itself coping with actual words and meanings.

". . . all right . . . all right, Archie. Everything's fine . . . everything's all right, my dear," she was saying. "Don't worry, Archie . . . they've all gone. Gone—they've all gone. Shut your eyes again, Archie . . . it's all right. All right. Shut your eyes . . ."

He was very glad to do as he was told. But in a moment his eyes were open again, and he was peering up, biting his lip with the pain. "Gone . . .?" he croaked. "They've . . . gone?"

"Yes. All gone. Don't worry. . . ."

From a distance Dod Wilson's distinctive voice reached him. ". . . cut their stick, Archie. Left their trucks . . . couldna get them past . . . you fair coopered them. Game up. They bolted. Take it easy, Archie boy . . ."

"Sanny!" Archie said suddenly. "Sanny fell. I . . . I . . . Sanny fell." Abruptly he raised his head, and struggled to sit up. He did not hear Sanny's reassuring word. Like a red-hot sword plunged into his right side, the agony struck at him again, and under an overwhelming flood of torment he sank back into oblivion on the girl's lap, there in the middle of the road up the little glen of the Atton Burn.

200

16

"Three ribs broken, a gash on the scalp requiring seven stitches, slight concussion, multiple abrasions, and your entire body black-and-blue!" the doctor said, nodding cheerfully. "My goodness, Scott—why didn't you get your neck broken while you were at it, and save yourself a hanging?"

Peering out owlishly from under white bandages and over white sheets, Archie looked from the doctor to the nurse, and swallowed. "Oh," he said.

"You might as well have finished the job. You'd have saved *us* a pack of trouble, too. Then we'd only have had an undertaker to deal with, instead of policemen, reporters, photographers, farmers, Cornets, Provosts, film-magnates, and importunate young women! Eh, nurse?"

The young lady did not commit herself beyond a smile.

The patient licked his dry lips with an exploratory tongue-tip. "Oh," he said again. "Just where . . . am I?"

"Kelso Cottage Hospital," he was informed. "At least, it used to be. Since you descended upon us, it's been more like the Southern Counties Criminal Lunatic Asylum!"

"Since I . . .?" Archie glanced over to the window, but slowly, circumspectly, for to turn his head, even to move his eyes, produced dizziness. The sun seemed to be almost directly overhead. That could only mean that it was tomorrow . . . or at least, Monday. "I've been here . . . some time, then?"

"It *seems* a long time," the doctor agreed. "At least, for us!"

The little nurse found boldness enough to chide, albeit with a giggle to her frown. "You'll excite the patient, doctor!"

"Excite this one! Lassie—d'you think a man who steals anything up to a thousand cattle, all but touches off a war, wrecks trucks single-handed, and challenges rival gangsters to mortal combat, could get excited over anything I could say to him? Or even you, nurse! Remember that blonde?" The doctor leaned over, and felt the patient's pulse. "Steady as a rock," he lied. "How's the head?"

"A bittie sore," Archie admitted. "I feel sort of light-headed . . ."

"I dare say you do. You're lucky if that's all you feel! What about your side? The ribs?"

"Just a dull burning feeling. Did you say I'd broken them?"

"Three of them, yes. As well that somebody had their head screwed on in this damn' ridiculous business, and looked after you fairly efficiently. If you hadn't been brought here with a minimum of disturbance, and straight away, you'd have had your lungs well punctured. The X-ray showed that it was touch and go. But you're all strapped up now. You've just got to lie still, and do what you're told . . . and we'll have you ready for the jail in a month!"

Archie digested that. He found that he had to consider tems very much one at a time. There was an awful lot that he didn't know—but the lack of knowledge did not seem vastly important, somehow. There was something that *was* vital, though . . . if he could only just remember what it was. Something on his mind, on his conscience . . . "Sanny!" he said, suddenly. "Sanny Elliot. How is he? I knocked him . . . into the ditch."

"And him not the only one, by all accounts! If it's the Coldstreamer you're meaning—he's fine. He was here twice yesterday, morning and evening, asking for you."

202

"Yesterday? Morning . . .?" In an effort at concentration, the Callant wrinkled his brows—and very promptly desisted.

"Yes. This is Tuesday. Yesterday was the busiest day this hospital's ever had."

"Tuesday! I've been out all that time?"

"Well, we gave you an injection or two to keep you quiet. You were tossing and turning—most unco-operative. Bad for the ribs. Do you think you could eat something, now?"

"I don't know. Perhaps." He was rather out of touch with food, that young man.

"Try," the doctor said. "If you're good, and eat something suitable, like a fine dish of bread-saps or even a cup of arrowroot, we might let you have a visitor this afternoon—eh, nurse? A nice fat policeman, maybe—or would you prefer a bereaved English cattle-breeder?"

Archie mustered the flicker of a smile. "You wouldn't hit a man when he's down, doc?"

"It's the only chance some of us get," the medico confided. "Now, if you'd let me in on all this earlier, and provided me with a nice quiet horse and a lasso, I might have been more sympathetic—you hero, you!" He straightened up, sternly. "Nurse, the patient must be rigorously disciplined. No fun and games. The authorities want him in good order to face the music as soon as possible. He can have two visitors this afternoon—five minutes each. And, understand—no journalists, of any sort . . . or sex!" And his left eyelid drooped significantly, as he made briskly for the door.

"He's an awful man, is Dr. McQuarrie," the little nurse revealed, patting pillows and tucking-in bedclothes. "But he thinks you've done a wonderful thing, really." She flushed. "So do we all, Mr. Scott—if you don't mind me saying so. Now, everything's just here, if you need it. You can reach out? There'll be a bite to eat in about half an hour, a wee sleep after that, and then we'll see who

203

we can let in to visit you. Perhaps you'd like just to glance at the papers . . .?"

*   *   *

The newspapers deserved more than a glance, deserved indeed a closer perusal than Archie Scott was in a state to bring to bear upon them there and then, however interested. Their accounts and interpretations of the week-end's events upon the Border were varied, highly imaginative, and individual in treatment, slant, comment, and certainly in accuracy—but all were in unison as to prodigality in space, headlines, and printer's ink generally. Needless to say, the Glasgow *Daily News* was most authoritative and factual, if not the most sympathetic in its editorial comment. Its Monday issue carried headlines an inch high: "MOSS-TROOPERS RIDE AGAIN. *Inside Story by* News *Staff Correspondent*. Only the bare bones of the business followed, for the *News* was not the *Scotsman* and made its impact by shock tactics rather than by patient exposition. But Archie, even bemused, was journalist enough to recognise that it was skilfully done, and in implication favourable to their attempt. It was a saga, a tale of heroes, one gathered. Tired though she must have been, Barbara Hepburn had not been idle on Sunday night. The full story was to follow in more intriguing detail throughout the week.

But the *News* leader-writer played a different tune. In laconic concern he tersely deplored irresponsibility, violence, and the deliberate disinterment of practices long dead and safely buried. Youthful high spirits were all very well, but the upholding of law and order, the sanctity of property, and peace and goodwill amongst men, held priority. Attempts to create trouble on the Border could not be condoned. The perpetrators of this somewhat juvenile exploit must be shown that the community was not to be subjected to such outbreaks of lawlessness and licence. While it was to be assumed that judgment would be tempered with a degree of mercy in view of the apparently disinterested motives of those involved, should it be shown that there

204

was any more sordid or commercial objective behind the demonstration, the authorities undoubtedly would be justified in imposing severe penalties.

Archie lay back on his pillows, eyes closed. Just what did they mean by that last bit? More sordid or commercial objectives . . .? He didn't know—he just couldn't be sure. But like the, the—what was it? The scorpion. Like the scorpion, the sting was in the tail, for sure. That matter of the film, now . . .?

The other papers he did not take so seriously. They were very largely headline, and lacking real meat. There was a great deal of conjecture, following up of side-issues, slants, and angles, and solicited comment, but little authentic information other than what could be filched or inferred from the *News*. Archie's own Common Riding colleagues and accomplices, it appeared, had kept their mouths shut, as had the police.

Under trumpeting captions such as: "RUSTLERS ON THE CHEVIOT TRAIL," "SENSATION ON THE BORDER—HUNDREDS OF CATTLE STOLEN," "20TH CENTURY REIVERS' RAID," and "WILD WEST COMES TO THE BORDERLAND," a lot of steam was let off, exhilarating resounding stuff, if lacking substance. Great fun, cried the *Mail*. Youthful revolt against the cloying embrace of the Welfare State, declared the *Express*. Uncommon Riding, indeed, said the *Record*. Extraordinary situation that may be indicative of deeper politico-social issues than have yet appeared, observed the *Scotsman*. Beef, biffs, and balefires, barked the *Bulletin*. A disgraceful display that can only harm our vital interests in the South, frowned the *Glasgow Herald*. It was all most confusing for a man with a sore head.

Solicited comment ranged from "Good show. Wish I'd been there," by General Sir Aylmer Campbell; "As Chief Magistrate, I must deplore any wilful infringement of the law, but am prepared to suspend judgment until further details are available," by the Provost of Jedburgh; "Extraordinary!" by the Provost of Hawick; to "I am

205

shocked. These Nationalists again. Nothing is safe; nothing is sacred, by a prominent member of the Scottish Council on Civil Aviation; and "Tally-ho! The Jocks had better watch out, in future," by Dr. Josiah White, of the Rothbury District Council. "No comment," said the Mayor of Hexham.

The patient skimmed these outpourings and averments in a distinctly lackadaisical, not to say sceptical, fashion. The doctor's course of injections might have had something to do with that. Deplorable to relate, he was sound asleep again when the nurse arrived with his tray, newspapers or none.

* * *

Archie had to be wakened up a second time, to receive his first visitor that afternoon—the Chief Constable of the County. Despite the pleasant appearance of the tall youngish-seeming man in informal tweeds, it was something of an off-putting visitation to wake up to, in the circumstances, and the patient was forced to swallow both tonsils before he could emit a suitable welcome.

"H'mmm," he said. "How d'you do?"

Perhaps the Chief Constable found himself not entirely at ease, either. "Well, Mr. Scott," he said. "I . . . ah . . . and how are you, today?"

"I might be worse. A lot worse. Can you find the Chief Constable a seat, nurse?"

"I shan't stay long. Just a minute or two. Thank you, nurse. M'mmm. Ah . . . quite."

As the door closed behind the young woman, they eyed each other for a moment or two, warily.

"Go on then, Chief. Let fly," Archie told him, sighing. "The stage is yours."

"I don't know just where to begin," the visitor admitted. "I'm a police officer, with my duty to perform. It's all very difficult."

"Sure. Sure—I know. You can skip all that, Chief.

206

I went into this with my eyes open. Do you slip on the handcuffs now, or as you go out?"

"Archie Scott," the other said, leaning forward suddenly. "Do you realise that you have caused me more trouble than anyone I can remember in twenty years? That I've hardly had a wink of sleep since Saturday night, over you? That you've set the police forces of two countries and half a dozen counties by the ears, set the law at naught, caused untold disturbance and worry to the lieges? That questions are to be asked in Parliament? That newspapers are asking —what was the police doing over the week-end? In fact, that you're the biggest damned headache to legitimate authority and all right-minded sane and respectable folk? Do you realise it, I say?"

"Go on, Chief—spare yourself," Archie urged. "Get it over with. This is as bad for you as for me, apparently. Give me the charges, one, two, and three. It's quicker."

"Confound you, man—if I hadn't been told that I was on no account to excite you, I'd shake you! Excite *you*, by Gemini! There you lie, hollow-eyed, croaking like a cavern, a sawdust hero with one foot in the grave—and grinning all over such of your wretched face as is safely hidden behind all that bandage, beard, and ballyhoo!"

"I'm not grinning," Archie protested wearily. "What have I got to grin about?"

"Plenty, unfortunately. Through Machiavellian cunning, the devil's own luck, the utter folly of all Englishmen, and loopholes in the law that you could drive a—a herd of cattle through, you've got every reason to grin. And I can't stop you!"

"Eh . . .? What do you mean?"

"I mean that, despite the fact that you've committed a series of offences that in any properly-run country would land you in clink for half a lifetime, you can sit there and twiddle your thumbs at me. It's a disgrace, that's what it is."

The patient sat forward, thought better of it, and sank back, involuntarily screwing up his features with the pain.

207

"Take it easy, take it easy—or I'll be getting into trouble with that little nurse!" the Chief Constable said, a hand on the other's arm.

"But, look—I don't get this," Archie panted. "What's it all about? What are you trying to tell me?"

"Nothing to get worked up over—nothing for *you* to get worked up over, anyway! Merely that in defiance of all that's right, just, and proper, you're likely to leave this establishment not merely a pampered hero but a free man—however much it hurts me to tell you so!"

"You're not just being funny, Chief—pulling my leg . . .?"

"Do I look funny, man? Can you not see that this is breaking my heart?" The visitor shook his head. "Either you've got some pretty good and active friends, Archie Scott—or the north country English are the most incurably romantic easy-going folk in these islands, though they don't look it. Both, I suspect."

"Go on."

"Well, it boils down to this. Though you have obviously and outrageously broken the law, no single individual has so far come forward to charge you. Moving cattle from one place to another is not in itself an offence—though any of the owners could charge you with theft or injury to their interests. But none have done so, nor seem likely to do so. The fact is, your final ridiculous display of strong-arm stuff against these Glasgow toughs, and you going and getting yourself conveniently crocked up, wounded-hero style, and in a pretty girl's arms into the bargain, has completely bowled over these great soft-hearted Northumbrian farmers. That's the worst of them all being fox-hunters. They've decided that this was a sporting event, a good run on a hot scent, with a satisfactory kill, and all the rest of it. They've got their beasts back, it's given them a day out in the off-season, there's no hard feelings—and you're the little white-headed boy. Bah!"

"That's . . . that's . . . pretty decent."

"Decent! I could call it something else."

"And is that the only thing? I mean, is there nothing

208

else the police could get me on?" Archie wondered unbelieving.

"Well, I suppose we *could* have tried out a charge of acting in a manner liable to provoke a breach of the peace. But the penalty for that would be so small as just to look foolish. Moreover, we could hardly have singled you out on that one—we'd have had to pull in the whole lot of you. Up to a hundred of you young idiots, by all accounts. And that might not have been very practical politics, might it? One thing we're not so very keen on, is making penny martyrs!"

"I see. Then—you've decided to pin nothing on me at all?"

"Oh, well—that doesn't lie with me, you know. That's the Fiscal's business. But, of course, technically you've committed no offence in *Scotland*. And so far, as I say, we've had no charges from England."

The Callant's breath came out on a long sigh of frank relief. "Well, I can only say thank you, Chief . . ."

The other held up his hand. "Don't thank *me*. I told you—it shakes me to the core to have to admit all this, as a good policeman. You've nobody to thank but your own lucky stars, these fox-hunting sports, and perhaps one or two busy friends, who certainly should be nameless. Oh, yes—and maybe you should spare one word of thanks to Glasgow C.I.D., and certain higher but necessarily vague authorities who balanced up your contra-account for you."

"Ah! Now we're getting somewhere."

"Are we? I was just going to suggest that perhaps the breaking up of a notorious and highly-organised gang of deer-poachers that has been troubling the West of Scotland police for years, may possibly have added just a little to your credit. Just possibly, I say."

"Deer-poachers! So that was it. I never thought of that."

"Yes. Tubby Noonan's gang were old friends—though they'd never functioned in these parts before. They've been running a good-going racket in the large-scale stolen venison trade ever since the war. Armed with automatic rifles, they've been decimating the Highland deer-forests and bringing back the carcasses by the score in their cattle-trucks to Glasgow, to supply hotels and sundry other meat-hungry folk who found shortages trying. With the end of meat-rationing their clients have got a bit more choosey, of course. They've been turning their attention to mutton, of late, and the odd side of beef. You can imagine how your little adventure appealed to them. Hundreds of prime steers all ready gathered and waiting for them —and somebody else to carry the can! And they very nearly got away with it. That they did not, seems to be largely due to unforeseen circumstances, for which you may or may not take some slight credit."

"It was due to the fact that we had a bone to pick with Mayor Stannard, and decided that Hexham mustn't get off, er, scot-free," Archie corrected. "That's why the eight of us were late, why we were thereabouts at midday, at all. Otherwise, they'd have had a free run in, and out. Stannard's the man to thank."

"I'll inform the Chief Constable of Northumberland to that effect," the other said gravely.

"But how did they find out—I mean, these Glasgow types? How did they get to know exactly where the cattle were being penned?"

"I'd remind you that a secret that's known by up to a hundred folk is not likely to remain a secret for long."

"But they didn't know. Not all of them. Not until the actual event. Not more than a dozen knew the precise spots selected, beforehand—and I'd trust every one of *them*."

"Well, it's no part of my duty to put you wise to leakages in your own nefarious organisation . . . but I wouldn't like you to suspect any of your Border colleagues, misguided as they may be. Our enquiries lead us to believe that the information came from two newspaper offices."

"You mean, the Glasgow *News*? They knew that something was to take place, I admit. They knew about the cattle. But not the locations. Not where they were to be penned."

"Maybe not. But somebody seemed to have talked in a pub in Glasgow—somebody from the *News*. And Tubby Noonan's boys got to hear of it. They went right to the source for further information—right to your own office, in fact. That's where the details of your rascally scheme came from, my lad—papers in your own desk. Someone came and had a quiet look one night—and that was that. Let it be a lesson to you. Either never commit plans to paper—or buy a padlock! Better still, don't *make* any more plans—much better!"

Crestfallen, the invalid stared at him. "Dammit—was I as easy meat as that! It never crossed my mind . . ."

"Never heed. You may not have proved a match for the criminal mind in one respect, but you did in another. In fact, I shouldn't wonder if we don't have to provide you with police protection when these boys come out!"

"You caught them, then?"

"Your farmer friends collected two of them, on the spot —including the gent who kicked in your ribs, I understand. Somebody had been rather unkind to him in the meantime, I gather! The rest took to the hills, when they saw that they couldn't extricate their trucks. However, our two friends talked, eventually, after a little persuasion, and now we have most of the rest of them where we want them. And we picked up the vehicles, of course."

"But the other lot? Did they try the Scrathy Holes . . .?"

"Look here, my sham invalid—I'm the policeman, not you!" the Chief Constable said sternly. He got to his feet. "I didn't come here to answer your questions—I came to impress upon you that crime does not pay! I hope I've done so, in the limited time at my disposal? I hope you realise it? If anybody asks you, you'll tell them I said so, won't you?"

Archie produced his first grin for quite some time. "Yes, Chief. And thanks for coming."

"My duty, nothing else. Policemen are always very

211

dutiful," the other said. "And don't you ever get the idea otherwise. Now I'll be off. I wouldn't like to get myself thrown out. Besides, there are others waiting. I hope they'll be as dutiful as I have been—though I doubt it!" He held out his hand. "Good luck, Archie—where you weren't breaking the law, you put up a pretty good show. But don't do it again—not ever! And next year, let's hope Jedburgh chooses a nice quiet level-headed Callant . . . or this county's going to need a new Chief Constable!"

* * *

The nurse came in when the policeman had left. "Are you quite all right, Mr. Scott? Tired? It hasn't been too much for you?"

"Too much? That man was a tonic. Done me a power of good . . ."

"I wonder? You sound excited. Dr. McQuarrie wouldn't like that. Maybe I oughtn't to allow anybody else in?"

"Hang Dr. McQuarrie! Look, nurse—you don't want to take doctors too seriously. They don't themselves, you know—so why should anybody else?"

"My, you are coming on! I think a sedative is what's required, really. If I allow anybody else to see you, it'll just be for five minutes . . . and it'll have to be somebody who won't excite you!"

"M'mmm," Archie licked his lips. "See here, nurse— who have you got out there? I mean, if there's to be any selection of visitors . . ."

"*We'll* make the selection, Mr. Scott! It'll be somebody quiet and soothing." She turned, opened the door, and beckoned.

Barbara Hepburn and Dand Fairgrieve stood there, waiting, side by side. A sister was talking to them, who now raised her voice.

"The patient mustn't be excited, remember. And you can only stay for a few minutes." And the door closed behind the two nurses. The thing looked like a conspiracy.

"Hiyah, Jethart!"

212

"Archie! How are you?" the girl cried. In four swift steps she was at his bedside.

"I'm feeling fine," the patient assured. "Just fine. And the better for seeing you both." He screwed up his face. "Though you're a bit hard on the eyes. Dazzling, you know!" The young woman certainly looked very different from his last sight of her.

"He's all right," Dand declared, with conviction. "Obviously."

"He doesn't look it, to me, I must say," Barbara exclaimed. "So thin, and wan, and—and woebegone!"

"My goodness—the last one said I was grinning all over my face!" the patient objected.

"Your poor head! And your side. Are they terribly sore? Are they treating you well, here?"

"No complaints. The wee nurse holds my hand . . ."

"You watch out, Archie," Dand advised. "While you're weak and helpless—that's when they get their claws in. *She* must think you're going to live, anyway!" The Cornet's voice changed. "What did that big polisman have to say, man?"

"Plenty. But nothing that hurt. He seems to think that I've got a lot of luck and some pretty good and active friends!" And the speaker glanced from one to the other of them.

"It doesn't hurt you when you breathe, does it?" the girl asked, earnestly. "Broken ribs can be dangerous, you know."

"What else did he say, the man?" Dand persisted.

"Just that, thanks to this and that, but particularly the way the English farmers have taken it all, I'm to get off. No charges. All washed up. But I'm not to do it again!"

"Jove—that's great! Grand. Splendid, Archie. The boys are going to be bucked about this."

"It's horribly easy to puncture the lung, you see. You've got to be very careful, Archie."

It occurred to the victim that his news did not seem greatly to surprise the young woman. But he kept the

213

thought to himself, meantime. "I'm trussed up like a boiling-fowl, and couldn't be anything but careful even if I tried," he assured. "But let's skip this morbid brooding about ribs and things. I want to hear what happened. Did you get to the Scrathy Holes, Dand?"

"Oh, yes. We picked up some Englishmen on the way, too. Told them we'd been tipped off that the cattle were there, and that there might be a raid on them. They came along nicely, and didn't ask too many questions. But there was no raid. No sign of trouble. Whether the corner-boys had had enough, whether they did not know about the Scrathy Holes, or whether they just reckoned that they couldn't get their trucks up near enough, I don't know. They didn't try it, anyway."

"Possibly they thought it was too risky, too late in the day, with the country getting roused?" Barbara put in. "I gather that they were much later than they'd intended. It seems they got lost a bit—went up some wrong side-roads into the hills, by mistake. . . ."

"Indeed," Archie said, sounding much less of an invalid than he looked. "And how did you find that out, may I ask?"

"Oh, well . . . you know how it is with the Press."

"Only the police could know that—or the gang themselves."

"I believe it *was* some policeman or other that told me, now you mention it."

"Uh-huh." He eyed her with something of his old fleering look, before he turned away. "What happened then, Dand—about the cattle? Did they get them home all right?"

"Apparently. We left them making plans to drive the beasts to the Tyne road, at Deadwater. We hadn't any trouble getting away—said we were going to look for more bullocks. They hadn't much reason to suspect us, when we'd led them to the beasts. And they took it all pretty well, considering—I'll say that for them. They all seemed quite sure that the whole thing was political. They moaned

214

a bit, of course—not unnaturally. But they didn't seem to have any sort of hate on."

"The English are not good haters," Barbara said. "They take things easier than we do."

"I seem to have heard that before, somewhere!" Archie mentioned. "It almost seems as though it might be true, too."

"It is true," she insisted. "I . . . I . . . well, it is."

"Uh-huh," the Callant commented, once again.

"After we left them, we directed one or two more farmers we found riding about, and then beat it for home," Dand went on. "And, damn it—we had to ride all the way back to Hawick, nearly! Nobody made that phone call for us!"

"H'rr'mmm. A pity. Afraid we must have been rather preoccupied . . . So you think they all got their cattle back safely?"

"I believe so. I haven't heard of any trouble, anyway. A lot would be taken back by trucks, of course."

"One bullock was gored by another's horn, in our lot—the Kelsocleuch lot," the girl informed. "But a vet patched it up. Another fell, getting out of the truck at its home farm, near Flodden, and broke its leg. It had to be killed. But I don't think the farmer's going to make any claim. He'll get full price for the beef, anyway."

"You don't think he'll claim, you say?"

"I'm practically sure of it."

"Uh-huh," the man said to her significantly, for the third time.

"I think we could raise a fund, easy enough, if there are any claims," Dand said. "There's plenty of folk just tickled to death about all this, you know, Archie. I've had offers, already. From some unlikely sources, too."

"Don't tell me the Provosts are tickled to death—or the Common Riding Committees?"

"Well, maybe not the Provosts. Not on the surface, anyway. They couldn't be, of course. But I haven't heard of any Common Riding Committee that's found it

215

necessary to meet and make any official pronouncement on the subject!"

"And what did your own man say? The Provost of Hawick?"

"Oh, he said plenty. Plenty. We had quite an interview. He said it was a scandalous business. But he didn't make it very clear as to which business he was referring—the cattle-rustling idea, your getting knocked about, or the Glasgow gangsters' piece! Most of his time, he spent pointing out that he had no reason to suspect that I, as Hawick Cornet, had been mixed up in the affair, for which he was very thankful. He rather stressed that. Oh, and he sent you a message, Archie. He said, 'If you happen to see that unprincipled scoundrel Scott, you can tell him from me that he deserves all he's likely to get—deserves it richly!' That was all."

"A pretty nasty crack, that?" the recipient suggested.

"I think it was a very nice thing to say," Barbara contended. "It's all in the interpretation. I think he's sweet, personally. He was very sweet to me, anyway."

The men exchanged glances.

"Oh, aye," Dand observed. He cleared his throat. "Well, I'll be on my way, Archie. Just looked in, you know. Glad you *sound* so fit, at any rate. I'll be over again, in a day or so."

"But you're just in . . .!"

"In *here*, maybe. But the hours we've been waiting outside! I've got work to do, mind—we're not all newspaper folk! Oh, Dod and Sanny and all the boys send their salaams. They'll all be in to see you, as soon as they're allowed. And say, by the way—what's this song about a wee white heifer? They're all singing it. I heard it in a pub in Hawick, last night . . ."

"You'd better ask Miss Hepburn about that," the Callant told him. "It was her heifer."

"Oh, I wouldn't like to do that, maybe. It's not always just awful respectable . . ."

"Neither is Miss Hepburn—always!"

216

"And just what do you mean by that, Archibald Scott, I'd like to know? Don't think that just because you're lying there all tied up in bandages, you can get away with everything! If . . ."

"My, oh my—time I was out of here!" Dand declared hurriedly. "Cheerio, then. Will I send in some nurses to your rescue, Archie?"

"Give me two minutes with this, this young person, and then the nurse can come for what remains!" the patient said grimly.

"Whose remains?" Dand Fairgrieve wondered, and got out while the going was good.

17

"Well, Barbara Hepburn—I want an explanation!" Archie Scott said, frowning fiercely—for his focusing was not yet perfect.

"Me? What have I to explain?" she wondered, wide-eyed.

"Plenty," the man asserted. "It's going to take you quite a while, too, so you'd better get started, or that nurse will be back."

"You know," she said, gravely, "maybe I ought to go now? You sound tired, and as though you might be getting a little worked up about something—and that mightn't be good for you. Perhaps . . ."

"Perhaps you'll stop stalling, and tell me just what you've been up to these last two days? While I've been lying here unconscious. I want to know how it was that you knew that I wasn't going to be charged. And how you knew that the Glasgow boys had been late and lost their way? I imagine you've been talking to the Chief Constable? I want to know how you came to be so certain that these Englishmen are so well-disposed, how you knew about the bullock that gored itself, and the one that broke its leg—at Flodden somewhere, wasn't it? And how you're so sure that the owner isn't going to make a claim?" The effort of concentration was telling on him. He was keeping his eyebrows forcibly upraised. "And, and lastly, what you've been seeing the Provost of Hawick about?"

She shook her ashen-fair head. "I don't know why you're bothering yourself with all this just now, Archie. It's not important. And you're in no state to trouble with details."

218

"Better details than suspicions, I'd say."

"Suspicions? I don't know what you mean . . ."

"Yes, you do. It strikes me you've been getting around a bit."

"I am a journalist, you know, with a story to write up."

"That's what I'm afraid of. I don't trust your *Daily News*."

"The *News*? Good gracious—d'you think I've been doing all this for the sake of the *News*?"

"Ah! So you admit you've been up to your tricks . . .?"

"If you call it tricks to try to make sure that all our efforts —all *your* efforts, anyway—weren't wasted, didn't go for nothing! Somebody had to do something, hadn't they, if the whole thing wasn't going to fizzle out ingloriously? And it wouldn't be you, lying here!" Suddenly, she was aroused, almost passionate.

Warily he eyed her. "M'mmm. So you, er, did something?"

"I did. And I'd have thought you might have thanked me for it, instead of grouching away there like a bear with a sore head." She took a quick breath, and leaned forward. "Oh, I'm sorry, Archie—you *have* a sore head, of course. Forgive me. But . . . but you *are* a bit of a bear, sometimes. In fact, you can be utterly infuriating!" Her lightning changes of front could be almost as breathtaking as was her appearance, to a man whose defences were far from impregnable.

He gulped something down. "Yes," he said. "What did you do?"

"I'll tell you what I did. I spent yesterday driving around Northumberland interviewing farmers whose cattle had been taken, explaining, putting your point of view, singing your praises, convincing them that your motives were good, playing up the Englishman's love of sport and his weakness for the man that's down. And not only the farmers. I've been at Wooler and Rothbury and Morpeth and Hexham, seeing the Mayors and Councillors and Magistrates, pleading your case—or at least, the Common

219

Riding case. I worked more than any eight-hour day yesterday, on your behalf, Archie Scott."

The man moistened his lips. "Go on."

"That's why I can be so sure that there's not likely to be any charges and claims and things. Admittedly, I've had a talk or two with the Chief Constable. As well that somebody did. I've had a word with the Provost of Hawick, too—and not only him. The telephones have been pretty busy around here, I can tell you. And if you haven't the grace to thank me for it just now, maybe you will next July!"

"July . . .?" he repeated, huskily.

"Yes. Next July. Next Redeswire Day. For I've got a pretty safe undertaking from not only the municipal people of those English towns, but many of the farmers and hunting folk too, that they'll be represented at Redeswire next year—if only to unhorse the Callant!"

The patient made an indeterminate noise, in marked contrast to the vehement spate of eloquence from his visitor. "You . . . you . . . we've brought it off, then? After all . . .?"

"Except at Hexham." Her voice took on a more abstracted quality. "I'm afraid Mayor Stannard is not very . . . impressionable! I can't vouch for it that Hexham will be there. But one never knows."

"No. One never knows. About quite a lot of things!" He seemed to have been smitten with her reflective mood, now. His head back on his pillow, he considered the ceiling. "You have been very busy. Very effective Most, er, helpful. You are to be congratulated, undoubtedly. . . ."

The girl looked at him keenly, a shade anxiously. "Is anything wrong? Are you not glad, Archie? Is there something I shouldn't have done?"

"No. No—of course not." He could hardly tell her that sheer sinful masculine pride was his trouble, that deplorably, his make-up was such that he could not swallow, without a struggle, success that was snatched from the jaws

220

of failure almost solely by the frail hands of a woman. He was struggling and swallowing, now. "Not at all."

Barbara transferred her gaze from his face to the slender fingers of her own hand. Perhaps it was her trump card that she was selecting therefrom. "I didn't only drive south, either, you know," she went on slowly. "I drove north, too—to Glasgow. This morning. I'm only just back. I went to see Mr. John W. Corson in his suite at the Central Hotel. He's sailing for the States next week. But before that, he wants to come down and see you, here."

"He does?" Archie was not interested in the ceiling any more.

"Yes. We had quite a talk. He's rather changed his mind about the film idea, in the light of events."

"You mean—he's thinking of making it, after all?"

"No. Not exactly. Not 'it', at least—not the documentary about the Common Riding tradition. We . . . he's got a much bigger and better idea. He's almost decided to make a full-length picture based on last week-end's cantrips—a hundred per cent star-spangled romantic adventure epic in the full-blooded Western tradition! Galloping hooves, stampeding steers, rustlers, bad men, and all! To be entitled 'The Ride Out', or something like that. A major film, anyway—the whole cheese. That is," she added, demurely, ". . . if we—if *you* let him have the exclusive rights to the story."

"I . . . if I . . . if he . . .? My godfather!" Archie Scott said. "He actually means all that? On the level?"

"Oh, yes. Our Mr. Corson is much impressed with the whole business, with what's already appeared in the Press . . . and still more so with what I might conceivably write for him, exclusively!"

"But this is wonderful. Priceless! This'll put the Border spirit on the map, all right. Though, mind you, we'll have to see that he doesn't turn the thing into something false, phoney, just for the sake of popular appeal. The Common Riding spirit is not to be prostituted for any . . ." The abruptly revived invalid paused, as a new thought

221

struck him. "But—what about you? I mean—the *News*? They're not going to like this!"

"I must admit," she observed airily, "I'm not greatly concerned whether they like it or not."

"But won't there be repercussions? On you? After all, they may take this hard. Look at that leader they printed yesterday . . ."

"I looked," the girl admitted. "I did more than look, in fact. I wrote to them, there and then—to the editor. And not copy, this time. No more copy for the *News*, from B. Hepburn. I terminated my connection with the wretched paper as from first post this morning. I am a free woman . . . or an unemployed one—whichever you prefer!"

"Well . . . I'm . . . damned!"

"No—that's me," she amended. "*You're* on top of the world, Master Scott. I don't think I ever knew such a lucky man!"

The lucky man could only stare at her, his Adam's-apple working up and down ridiculously, a picture of punch-drunk inadequacy.

"Well?" she asked, after a moment or two, her voice just a little tremulous for that young woman. "Do you think you owe me a brief word of commendation, after all— or do you not?"

"Owe you . . .?" he answered slowly. "I think I owe you something, at least. I owe you a job!"

"Oh."

"Look." He leaned towards her a little. "Jedburgh's not Glasgow, I know, and the *Jedburgh Journal*'s not a very big paper. But, if you'd come . . .?"

She reached a hand to lay impulsively on his. "Thank you, Archie—that's kind. It's nice of you. But, heavens —what would I do on the *Jedburgh Journal*?"

"Goodness knows," he admitted. "But we'd find something . . ."

"Wouldn't I do better, perhaps, as the script-writer, on this film?"

"Oh, financially, maybe. But money's not everything,

222

my girl. You should have learned that. You'd be much better on the *Journal*. You could do the other in your spare time."

"Ah. I was wondering what I'd find to do in my spare time . . . in Jedburgh!"

"I'd see to that, too, maybe," he suggested.

"Oh? You think of everything. But wouldn't it all look rather, rather compromising? Rather a difficult situation for me? One of the papers has linked our names together, already, you know, in a foolishly suggestive fashion . . ."

"So I read," the man mentioned, briefly. "The only sensible deduction in anything I *did* read!"

"Oh," she said, again.

"Yes," he nodded authoritatively. It seemed that he had gained the initiative now, somehow, and to prove it, his hand it was now that gripped hers. "I'm all for a compromising situation, Barbara Hepburn. This job on the *Journal* I have in mind for you is only a temporary one, you see—a sort of trial run for a much more important job together. Just so as I can keep you under my eye for a little while—get you used to me being the boss."

"I see," she said, small-voiced. "And this important job. Do you think I'd like it? Be suitable for it, even?"

"Oh, yes. Definitely. No doubts about that, at all."

"You seem awfully sure. But you've not known me so very long, have you? I mean, to be recommending me . . .?"

"Hang it all, woman—if I've not actually known you all my life, at least I've known you all the really important part of it, the part that matters!" he asserted stoutly. Then he wavered. "I . . . look, Barbara—I'm not making an awfully good job of this, am I?"

"For a man with even mild concussion, I think you're doing not too badly!" she told him, gravely. Then she smiled, a warm smile. "But I think you've done enough for one day—quite enough, Archie. I'm going, now. Yes, I am. I promised only to stay a few minutes, and not to allow you to get excited. I don't know whether I've kept my promise very well. I seem to have worked

223

you up to making some fairly extravagant proposals. Or suggestions might be the more suitable word . . .!"

"Let proposals stand!" he declared, deep-voiced. "And I mean what I say. I am not concussed, at all. There's nothing wrong with my head. Only my heart, girl . . ."

Barbara rose, and reaching over laid a finger on his lips. "Hush," she said, but gently. "I'm not worried about your heart. Something tells me it's in good order . . . and safe keeping. I'm only worried about your poor head. We'll talk about your heart . . . later. Shall we?"

"But . . . you do understand? You will think about what I've been trying to say? Think about those jobs . . . both of them?"

"Oh, my dear foolish ridiculous Archie—I shall think of nothing else! Now—let me out of here . . . before I burst into tears!" And stooping, she brushed his lips with her own, and fled.

THE END